THE JULIETTE SOCIETY, BOOK II:
THE JANUS CHAMBER

T0105322

THE JULIETTE SOCIETY, BOOK II:
THE JANUS CHAMBER

SASHA GREY

CLEiS
PRESS

Published in the United States by Cleis Press, an imprint of Start Midnight, LLC, 101 Hudson Street, Thirty-Seventh Floor, Suite 3705, Jersey City, NJ 07302.

Printed in the United States.
Cover design: Scott Idleman/Blink
Cover photograph: iStock Photos
Text design: Frank Wiedemann

First Edition.
10 9 8 7 6 5 4 3 2 1

Trade paper ISBN: 978-1-62778-180-0
E-book ISBN: 978-1-62778-181-7

PROLOGUE

ASK YOURSELF THIS.

If you had a key that promised to unlock the secrets of the world, wouldn't you want to use it?

If you could catch the rich and powerful stripped naked, *in flagrante delicto,* exposing all their closeted kinks and perversions, wouldn't you be tempted?

If that's what you want, come with me.

But I have to warn you: Once you cross that threshold, nothing will ever be the same.

You will never be the same.

I'm not.

Nearly four years ago, a statue of Pan looked on while the core of my life was cracked open on a platform as one of the most powerful men in the world marked me as his equal. No, not his equal—as one of his own, like attracting like though we're not quite the same. I could protest all I wanted, but my moral compass had somehow led me to the same dark room as DeVille, and I can't deny that a part of me belonged there. A part of me liked squeezing his throat.

A part of me remains there, floating in a sky the color of his oxygen-deprived lips.

A part of me that knows I'm not like other people, not like Jack.

Too much like DeVille and others in The Juliette Society.

But the larger part of me locked that experience deep down inside. It's easier to pretend it never happened—especially since I never saw Anna again.

I haven't thought of my friend in ages.

At first, Anna's empty chair behind me in Marcus's class had gravity to it, filled with the weight of my expectations and hopes and my frustration that she never returned. At least not before I started to resent the hell out of her.

I chose frustration over her absence rather than believe someone as vibrant as Anna could be extinguished by someone who appreciated neither her inner flame nor the curves containing it. She was more than a reaction to pleasure or pain. Locked in a cage and used for someone else's pleasure, she was an atomic detonation.

But seeing the way she simmered with the rest of us was like watching the already lit fuse. You couldn't look away, and if you did, it was to see the looks on the faces of everyone around her. Gauge their reactions to decide what yours should be. What was safe to share.

People like her don't exist in your life for long.

There's a reason she stopped answering my calls. There had to have been.

Because why would she disappear after connecting me to a lifestyle that she embraced on a more fundamental level than I ever did?

Was that it? Could she sense, underneath it all, that I would turn from it, put all memories of it away to have a normal life with my Jack?

Was it disappointment that turned her from me? Her absence was a rejection that stung worse than any breakup I'd experienced.

I had to will myself to move on from the easy friendship we'd enjoyed together. I thought I'd meant more to her than I had. I imagine she kept in touch with others in her life; it was me who wasn't important enough for her to bother with calling, so I chose to forget about her, too. Even a few months later, the brash, wild things we'd done together felt more like dreams than memories.

Maybe because the things we'd shared had been so fantastical, it was easier to pretend they'd been imagined and to put them firmly behind me. I graduated, found a job as a beat reporter at a newspaper. Settled deeper into my life with Jack, but both of us too busy, too consumed with work, to lock down a date to actually say our forever vows. At this point it's pure ceremony; I'm already committed to him. Normalcy and comfort cover my memories of Anna and The Juliette Society like a warm blanket until it felt like they had happened to someone else.

Life goes on. We move on from the people we knew and the people we were, especially at that age.

Especially from the things that moan in the night.

Does this happen to everyone who embarks on a journey of the senses? Do they all eventually disappear, having felt too much?

I don't think of Anna often. The disappointment is embarrassing. And yet...

It's an uncomfortable truth when you get a good look in the mirror and what you see makes you want to cringe—but you can't, because you wouldn't take it back. It felt too good. Still, the knowledge crawls across your skin like a dried film of soap you didn't quite rinse away in the shower, always there embracing you, reminding you every time you have to restrict your movements so you can ignore the fact that your skin feels too tight. Like you're stuffed full of *more* and sooner or later it's going to split you in two and break free.

Four years is a long time to change, and shift, and grow. Four years is a long time to bury memories deep down until they're etched upon your bones and you can almost forget that you were the person who once ached to have those experiences.

Almost…

Is character subservient to desire?

Are we driven by our desires, or do they drive us completely?

ONE

AS A GENERAL RULE, PEOPLE who work in hotels know better than to ever stay in one. This is not unique in the service industry. People who work in airports have their own version. They will tell you they always take a packed lunch to work and never eat at the concession stands. That's because they know something you don't: All that uneaten airline food that gets dumped out of every arriving flight is a magnet for vermin and cockroaches.

Same deal with hotel employees. If they really have to, they will only stay in large hotels. The bigger the better—preferably the super-sized resorts with a thousand rooms or more. Why?

They know it's the only way to beat the odds.

Let me explain.

At some point in its history, every hotel in the world has hosted at least one guest who checked in but never checked out. Or rather, they checked out, but never settled the bill.

If you've ever stayed in a hotel, you'll know that scenario is highly unlikely unless you've been comped, and in this case, I'll tell you right up front, that didn't happen. What we're left with is a paradox, one that can only be resolved if the person occupying the room fulfilled one condition, and one condition only:

They expired.

Scientists have done statistical studies on this—the number of people who have died in hotels, the number of hotels that have had dead people in them. That means it's a fact. Not just a freak occurrence, and actually far more common than you'd think. It happens almost every day.

Say a group of retirees on a package tour arrives at their hotel. The eventuality that at least one of them is going to get off the bus, and not back on, is pretty damn high. He or she might not even get the opportunity to play a full round of mini-golf.

According to the world wide web, at last count, globally, there were estimated to be something like 17.3 million hotel rooms in 187,000 hotels. That means wherever you travel in the world, whichever class of hotel you stay in, during high season or low, there's a one in ninety-three chance you'll be sleeping with the dead.

You might think that's an acceptable risk, something you could easily live with.

Wait.

You don't even know how the person died.

There are several options. I'll warn you now, they get progressively worse.

First, there are the natural deaths. This could include any number of sudden fatal illnesses, viruses or superbugs, heart attacks, aneurysms, embolisms, a massive hemorrhage, or—are you ready for this?—spontaneous combustion.

Don't laugh—it's been known to happen. And there's nothing funny about it if you're the one who has to clean up the mess afterwards. But we'll get to that in a bit.

Then there's death by misadventure. One clumsy fumble with an electrical gadget in the bathroom could lead to a nasty shock that might prove terminal. An unexpected trip or fall after a long night at the hotel bar may result in severe head trauma, or a laceration or amputation and, from there, catastrophic blood loss. That one last drink to wash down a cocktail of prescription meds before bed might mean that tomorrow morning's wake-up call goes unanswered.

With suicides, there are a few things that are, if you'll excuse the unfortunate turn of phrase, a dead cert. One, you know the deaths definitely occur inside the room, because you sure as hell can't open the window to jump out. Two, with not a lot at hand in the way of props, the chosen method of exit has to be both creative and effective. And, three, the body won't be found for a while. Because if you have decided to kill yourself in a hotel room, the very first thing you're going to do is hang the "Do Not Disturb" sign on the door-knob.

Finally, there's murder. The number of homicides in hotel rooms is second only to those that happen at home. But let's just skip the gory details and leave the rest up to your imagination. One thing that's a given, though: murder most foul is never pretty.

At this point, let's take a second to spare a thought for the person who has to clean up after all this—the hotel maid. As jobs go, being a hotel maid is an utterly thankless task. It really, really sucks.

People who clean up crime scenes are considered specialists in their field. They will launder the carpet, rugs, linen, and soft furnishings to remove any unsightly stains and completely sterilize and deodorize the environment. By the time they're finished, you'd never believe anything happened there at all. That's why the really good ones often make six-figure salaries. Even the poor schlub who has the task of cleaning up after a porn shoot—he's called the "jizz mopper," but never, ever to his face—can expect to make a decent salary.

A maid has to do the same job in less time, fifteen to thirty times a day, every day, and all for minimum wage and whatever's been left for her under the pillow—with no guarantee that it will be money.

But if she's done her job properly, when you enter your room for the first time, there are two things that will never cross your mind. The first is: *Who died here?* And the second is: *Who last fucked in this bed?*

Which reminds me, there's one last category I forgot to mention. One that's definitely worthy of discussion on its own merits: the final fuck.

If you have an interest in this stuff—and you can probably tell I do—there's a story that almost every hotel employee is dying to tell you, and will, with just a little prodding. Really, it's been told so many times that it's become something of an urban myth. So forgive me if I embellish a little here and there.

This story, it begins with a man and a woman checking into a hotel. They're booked into the best room in the place: the penthouse suite. What he does exactly, that's not important. He could be a venture capitalist, a corporate litigator, a tech entrepreneur, maybe even a black marketeer. All you need to know is that he's Loaded— with a capital L—and so the world is his oyster. Which is good for him, because he was never going to get by on looks or presence alone.

If you wanted to visualize the word *unattractive*, this guy would be it: tall but grotesquely overweight, with ruddy skin, small piggy eyes, a thin hollow smile. And he has, shall we say, a hydration issue: He sweats. A lot. Consequently, he's enveloped in a permanent fetid funk. He smells like a men's bathroom that hasn't been cleaned in a while.

The girl he's with, she's his girlfriend—but only for the night, if you get my drift—and almost his exact opposite. She's tiny, around a third of his size, and sex personified. Blonde hair that falls to her shoulders in cute Shirley Temple curls, framing a heart-shaped face and full, plump lips like soft pillows. A body that's a work of art—the perfect *S*-curve, just like the Venus de Milo: small, perky tits, slim waist, and a big curvy ass, the kind you want to bury your entire face in.

And right at this moment, the point at which we enter this story, that's exactly what he's doing. She's naked on all fours on a double-wide bed and he's positioned behind her, stuffing his face (which, as you might imagine, is second nature to him), nosing the crack of her ass like a pig hunting for truffles to snuffle up all her scent. The smell of that ass mingled with her sex is like honeysuckle, sweet and tart at the same time, and it's driving him wild.

This guy, he's in heaven. He's really getting in there, has his fingers in lots of pies, so to speak. And he just can't believe his luck, making it with this super-hot chick who under normal circumstances wouldn't even give him a first look, let alone a second. Even better, she's digging it, responding to his every thrust and stroke. At least, that's how it seems to him.

Pretty soon, she's riding him. She's moaning and groaning and grinding, putting on a real performance, giving it her all, trying to get him off. Because, despite appearances to the contrary, he's actually really grossing her out and all she wants to do is jump in the shower and wash him off. But this guy, he just doesn't want to come.

She has this one trick up her sleeve that she only uses in very special circumstances, as a last resort, when everything else fails. This time, she really wants this to be over, like *now*, so she's decided to skip ahead and pull out her secret weapon. And this thing, it only ever works with the element of surprise.

She's maneuvered herself into exactly the right position now, reverse cowgirl, so that all he can see of her is that ass pumping up and down in perfect, fluid motion like an oil derrick in full swing. She leans all the way forward to give him a better view and waits for her cue, that pained little moan that guys sometimes let out when they're starting to lose control. When she hears that, she jams her middle finger right up his ass. And twists.

If it's not timed right, this kind of thing can be a real passion-killer. Because guys get pretty weird very quickly if you go anywhere near their ass. But catch them by surprise, and they'll come before they've realized what's going on. Afterward, they won't mention it, they'll pretend like it never even happened. That's because, like hotel employees and people who work at airports, she knows something they don't:

These guys liked it and they just can't bring themselves to admit it.

This time, she shoves her middle finger in right up to the knuckle, just to make sure, and it works better than she expected, better than it ever has before. Because all of a sudden, he ejaculates, and *BANG*—his heart explodes. Right at the same time.

Brings a whole new understanding to the phrase *simultaneous orgasm*, doesn't it.

There's another version of this story. The same basic scenario, apart from one minor detail: The position has changed. He's on top of her, pounding away, when she reaches around to stick it to him. His fuse blows—*PIFF*, just like that—and he falls like a giant monolith, right on top of her, and…well, you can probably guess the rest.

Who these people were, it doesn't really matter. Their names will be scrubbed from the register, like they never even existed. Some vaguely plausible story will be concocted to preserve their dignity and absolve them of shame. It will all be covered up. Nobody will be any the wiser.

You want to know why?

Because hotels are like embassies. Hotbeds of covert activity that takes place beyond the reach of the law. Repositories for secrets and transgressions. A place where all the bodies are buried.

Right about now, you're probably asking yourself, *Where all this is leading?* Good question. I was just getting to that.

You see, Inana was one of these people who had access to all things exclusive. Like the blonde, she was an expert in her field, a pro—and unlike the blonde, not *that* kind of pro. She did it purely because she enjoyed it, because she wanted to understand the limits of female desire—to better know herself. She acquired a reputation, became wanted and desired by some of the most powerful people in the world. Through that reputation, she learned things, the same secrets and transgressions that hotels try so hard to hide.

Maybe Inana kept her work life and private life separate, and like Einstein at the patent office, this was a way for her to get outside her own head and be immersed in something completely different as a means of inspiration.

Or maybe there's something secret in this hotel, based on the way it doesn't show up in any fucking browser or map I've searched online.

I just know she's not around to speak for herself. And I need to find out more, because I feel like her experience resonates with mine and she might have all the answers I've been seeking about myself.

This hotel, the last place she was known to have worked, is so exclusive that it doesn't appear in any guidebook or on any map. You couldn't book a room here even if you wanted to. That's not as unusual as it may sound.

That's another thing the hotel industry doesn't want you to know. There are hotels built in secret locations all around the world that are anything but what they seem. If you were to look out the window of your room in one of these hotels, you'd swear you were in Paris, Rome, New York, Tokyo—any of the world's most glamorous cities. In actual fact, it is a room without a view at all, like an old movie set with pictures or paintings on the windows, located in some desolate backwater of China or the UAE, away from prying eyes. The room is an exact mock-up, a prototype, for a hotel that has not yet been built, so that its architects can test out new designs, tailored precisely to the demands of their clientele.

In the same way, there are Middle Eastern villages located in the ass-end of Louisiana and North Dakota populated by actors dressed as natives, selling cans of cheap knock-off Coca-Cola. Everything there is recreated down to the smallest detail, just so it can be blown sky-high by the latest technology; a means to test and refine new military strategies, minimizing the risk of casualties, before they are used in the field of war.

These hotels work on the same principle. Minus the guns, ammo, and fake blood. They provide a means to make mistakes so they don't get made in the real world.

TWO

~o))))ω~

HIS HANDS WHISPER UP MY thighs, easing me awake like a secret he tells my body with his own, and I lie still, feigning sleep so he'll continue his gentle violation. If I wake up his touch will turn demanding, but not quite demanding enough, and right now all I want are Jack's unhurried hands.

With his schedule, lately we communicate in gropes, hungry hands that devour in a utilitarian way instead of giving. We use each other to get off, our connection frenzied like we're always saying goodbye before we both slip into unconsciousness. For once, I want this tender, tentative hello.

He teases my hair back over my shoulder, kissing me on the soft skin where my neck meets my jaw. Through my eyelashes, the angry red numbers of the alarm clock stare back at me. 2:37 a.m. It's the middle of the night when Jack steals into our bed, stealing kisses like he's someone else—or I am.

The thief of pleasure is mine for the taking. My hands itch with the sudden need to cup his balls and see if he's already hard, or if he's only flirting with the idea of making love to me before giving up completely and passing out.

Then I feel it sliding up my thigh, warm from sleep. Jack's hard cock. Men's cocks are hard but so damn smooth. Maybe the friction of masturbation helps exfoliate them.

I sigh and tip my ass back to invite him to come a little closer and enjoy the burn of my skin and the wet heat between my thighs.

His touch meanders up the back of my leg, grazing, teasing, almost burning me with its lightness. Just once, I'd love for him to fuck me awake. No gentle fingers waiting for permission, waiting for me to be ready. I want him to take me hard and fast and deep so I wake up already speared by his cock, surprised by what's happening before knowing it's him.

But Jack's too nice, too good not to be shocked by that fantasy, so I locked it down when he asked, "What if I hurt you?"

Sometimes I want it to hurt, I hadn't said, not wanting to see the shock on his face. He thinks I got all "that" out of my system years ago.

"Cath," he sighs now against my earlobe before taking it in his mouth.

I moan.

"Are you awake?"

Fantasy already ruined, I nod and press closer to him as he spoons me from behind, pinching a nipple between his fingers.

I'd wanted gentle Jack, but as soon as I had him I wanted more. I always want more of Jack. Suddenly filled with an acute awareness of how much I love him, I turn and pull his lips to mine, kissing him deeply as he eases himself down onto me, stiff dress shirt lightly abrading my nipples. I like it but want to feel the warmth of his skin against mine.

He kneels and shrugs out of his shirt, then moves down my belly, leaving kisses all the way to my Velcro, nudging at my thighs.

I spread for him, eager to feel his hot tongue lap at my clit, and he slings my legs over his shoulders and gives me a long, slow lick that makes my heels dig into his back, wanting him to do the same and go harder.

He surprises me by shoving a finger inside my wet sweet spot, curling the tip and pressing into my G-spot. I twine my fingers through his hair, gripping him tighter, trying to lock him in place as I grind my hips like a dance-hall queen.

He enters me with his tongue, working my clit with his fingers now. I moan and groan with pleasure because I want him to know how good it feels, how glad I am he woke me up this way. That all I want is more and more of him, of us, of this.

"Fuck me, Jack. Fuck me hard."

He licks a long line from my pussy all the way up to my mouth, sucking my tongue into his, blending my desire with his kiss, and thrusts home in one hard, deep motion.

My head falls back, and I feel myself spread open like a flower— *the better to pluck you with*—and I wrap my legs around his back and squeeze.

I want him to take me over, wear me as a costume, make me do things he'd want if he were able to be me for a night and I were a disguise made of flesh designed for his amusement.

What would I do if I were Jack for a day?

Everything. I'd fuck me to see what I felt like on the inside.

I'd piss standing up.

I'd jerk off, milking my cock for every last drop of come to see who has better orgasms—men or women.

I'd eat the insanely spicy wings he gets from time to time that sizzle a layer of tissue from my tongue, to see how it is to enjoy something I normally hate.

I'd walk around feeling powerful and masculine, broad-shouldered and tight-assed, and no one would fuck with me.

I'd grow the stubble on my jaw as long as I could, then shave it to see if it made my face feel different.

Would Jack do things equally random if we switched bodies?

I grind against his cock, frantically turned on at the idea of Jack using my body to explore the impossible.

What would he do with me?

If we made love in each other's bodies, what would that reveal, or even change? What if being him was so much better during sex than being me that I could never forget it? Would I come to resent him, or him me, if the reverse was true?

I want to ask him what he'd do if he were inside my body for a day, to hear the things he'd do and see if they match mine. My lips part to ask, but he takes my mouth, deeply in sync with his cock, and it no longer matters.

Regardless of the bodies we were in, Jack would make my body sing.

He twists his fingers through mine and pins my hands above my head, pulling back to watch my tits bounce as he pounds at me like John Bonham hit the snare drum. No one hit it harder than he did.

His balls get coated with my come and slap my ass with every thrust, and I want Jack in my ass, too, but he does a funny little sideways hitch with his hips that takes me by surprise, and it feels like my head spins around from the way an orgasm sneaks up on me and makes my pussy clamp down on his cock, slowing his thrusts.

It's sharp and sweet and almost fucking hurts, cramping my belly, but damn if he doesn't draw it out and make it last longer than it should, forever, and while I'm still shaking beneath him he fills me with a giant load of come so hot and thick it's almost heavy, shooting into my body like a Super Soaker.

I want him to use it as lube to fuck my ass next.

My favorite kind of recycling.

Like so many others, I've gone green in my mid-twenties.

Afterward, I take my deliciously sore ass into the living room to watch a movie without disturbing Jack's sleep. Sex is strange like that, as though humans are batteries with give and take. Sometimes you can throw your body into it more than with a workout, but still come out of it with more energy than when you started, feeling like you could run a marathon. Other times, you can slip into some afternoon delight with all the energy in the world, and crash afterward like it's been days since you slept. Maybe we do transfer energy to each other through our touch, through pleasure given and received.

Either way, I know I won't be sleeping for a while, so I peruse the shelf of movies, our eclectic tastes pressed together into a strange collection. I like to think my foreign film collection is slumming it with his action movies, but I like the things Jack watches, too— testosterone-filled adventures that feature bromances and aging heroes.

Besides, I pollute the shelf with a few romantic comedies as well, though mostly classics from the nineties. Junk food for the mind.

Right now I don't feel like something light. I'm craving something meaty and substantial, something new that I can savor, but nothing jumps out at me until I see *L'Amore in Città*—Love in the City, a collection from the fifties where seven Italian directors each contribute a segment. I haven't seen this film before—Jack bought it for me for Christmas, but I've been saving it for a rainy day. Maybe I'm a little sadomasochistic at night when it comes to my film predilections, but I have to believe that some of the filmmakers I love best are—or were, as well.

But patience only goes so far, and I've waited long enough.

I tear through the cellophane and pop it in, settling on the couch with a glass of water.

The music is a little jarring, the opening credits set on what looks like concrete—a nod to the title.

I skip ahead to Antonioni's entry, *Tentato Suicidio*—Attempted Suicide. I can't not watch it first—if I wait, I'd only be speculating about Antonioni's upcoming episode and how it would relate to the others, and I wouldn't be able to focus on the rest. So it's best to savor his first, then go back and watch the whole thing again.

I don't know what it is about his work that grips me so intensely as of late, but something I love about black-and-white movies is that there's not as much to distract the eye.

We've all got predilections when it comes to shades, clothes, walls. Carpets matching drapes.

The right shade of blue can feel like the sky on a clear day, make us breathe deeper in delight and imagine puffy clouds. We've all got that favorite outfit that brings out our eyes and puts some swagger in our step.

The wrong shade of green can bring to mind hospital walls where we spent a hellish twenty-four hours when we were a kid, our parents worrying that the fever wouldn't go down.

In black and white, there are only shades upon shades upon shades. Textures become more important, patterns. It's harder to be distracted by garish or gorgeous colors in the background.

But it can also be harder to catch the eye. The props directors had to work harder back then—but they didn't have to make sure the colors were harmonious.

They didn't have to find a pillow the exact shade of the leading lady's lipstick to give a subtle background echo.

The characters walk along a huge, curved, white wall, and for a few seconds their numbers grow as actors and shadows become nearly indistinct. You can't tell which is which, and I know Antonioni didn't do that accidentally.

Every choice he made was deliberate. We can't have control in life, yet somehow, he controlled his canvas so fluidly. I admire that.

The story is about bringing people who have tried to commit suicide together to talk about their motivations. The narrator says that no matter how different they are, all of the people seem to really have a need to talk about their experience that seems contrary to the way suicide was handled back then, so taboo and unspoken.

Maybe that's why they had a great need to talk to others about it. Express their feelings to others who wouldn't look at them as histrionic or crazy. Unstable. They think maybe this gathering could help themselves, but also others, to deal with things.

They're so somber, dressed well in suits and jackets, put together in a way only the Italians are. The musical lilt of the narrator's voice makes me again wish I spoke more Italian, but that's something I always idly regret. It's surprising how much I've picked up just by watching foreign films.

The narrator says that suicide is the only truly irreparable act in life.

Everyone gathered for *Tentato Suicidio* has their reasons for wanting to escape. Some of them gaze at each other with such passionate sympathy, move to almost hug one another, then stop themselves, as though a kind touch would blow them apart.

Maybe it would.

I can understand wanting pain to end, but he's right—it's irreparable. Whether there's a God and pearly gates, or nothing at all after we blink out of existence, why take a shortcut to the end of what might be the only life we get? Don't we owe it to ourselves to feel as much, cram as much experience as humanly possible into the time we have?

I think it is truly selfish, as escapes go. Everyone has someone who loves them. But maybe that's the only point of view we can have, if we've never attempted the "irreparable act."

I've researched suicide for stories before, an unpleasant task because of the amount of pain and raw emotion it's steeped in. I can't help but recall the several suicides and disappearances that shook my college campus, and America, to the core. Most people would be surprised to learn that the majority of suicides don't leave letters for their family members or friends to read when they've gone. There's no letter to explain the pain away, for those still alive to read and feel a little bit better without the huge "why?" hanging over their heads.

I don't know if an explanation would make things better or worse. I can't imagine a suicide letter being very accusatory, but what if it was, and you were the cause of the hurt? How bad would that feel? In most cases, I can't see it being a good thing to leave a note. Nothing you say is going to bring you back, and nothing will make your loved ones feel better. The guilt simply sets in, leaving them feeling like if they'd said something more, done something more, you'd have stayed, pushed through, kept fighting.

Hearing "I love you" one more time would be good, but it would still be tainted by what came next. It's hard to believe that someone truly loves you when that person chooses to take their own life—not that that's a reflection on you, but we humans tend to internalize things, and in this case, it's impossible not to. But it's not about us.

Suicide isn't about your feelings. People who do it are more than likely not thinking about you at all. They're not thinking about much.

They're so focused on the pain, on the act of release from the pain, that all else fades away. It's selfish in the least malicious way. It's not about causing others pain—it's about ending their own.

And yet, it's devastating to those left behind.

Pain is energy. Energy can't be destroyed—suicide doesn't kill the pain. It only gives it to those left behind. Newton was right about that, at least.

The actress playing Rosanna is so halting and sincere, almost shy, that it's easy to believe she's not an actress at all, but someone who this happened to. Her story is brutally sad.

I pause to look her up online, and it turns out that she wasn't an actress—that these are real people who tried to kill themselves, although they have been directed by Antonioni, and in that sense have become actors. Some were real actors—or went on to become actors, which means this was their big break, coming off the back of trying to kill themselves.

I'm not sure if that makes it better or worse.

But that's the great thing about Antonioni—that it doesn't matter if they were actors before, after, or not at all. The story itself is what matters. How it makes you feel. Art should make you question, make you wonder, make you feel something.

They're not just talking about their experiences—they're acting them out to show the audience exactly what happened.

What must that have felt like, reliving some of the worst emotional moments of their lives? I shiver.

Another woman is almost militant in her descriptions of multiple suicide attempts and the ways people stopped her or she failed.

Another seems like she still wishes she were dead, but when asked if she is happy now, she says yes.

But in the back of her mind, is there always that escape hatch with the door swinging half open, invitingly, beckoning to her, soothing her while at the same time depressing her that it's there at all?

These films make smoking look so goddamn elegant, my fingers itch to pinch a slender white cigarette between them, exhaling warm smoke to make my breath visible to others. Another secret fantasy I've yet to explore with Jack. He hates smoking.

Is it impatient, languorous? Shallow, deep?

One woman has sleepy eyes like Lauren Bacall, and she talks of wanting to become an actress, but to do it properly through training.

The arts attract a great number of unstable types—some of them just hide it better than others. Maybe it's because, for those who feel things so deeply, it's easier to pretend to be someone else. They keep things clean and sober while on set, and it's only while they're at home, between parts, that the sorrow swells again, the doubt, the emptiness, and they try to drown it out with addictions and recklessness.

When you're being someone else, it's easier to look in the mirror.

In the crowd of people who initially filed inside to speak of their experiences, there were both men and women. But the only ones telling stories are the women. Why? Was it an intentional choice on Antonioni's part to only share the stories of a few of the people, and only the women, or was that just the way it worked out? Were women the only ones who replied to his call when he put out what he was looking for?

Was he trying to show the way the weaker sex reacts to love gone wrong? Was he making a statement—not necessarily a good one—that men aren't as affected by emotion?

He was said to have admired the authenticity and spontaneity of working-class women, and he loved and respected his mother. He wasn't exploitative.

And who were the men there with the women? Friends, family, lovers? Were they real people, too, or actors? A mixture of both? Did the women bring them along as plus-ones when they were told they could bring someone along, were they trying to impress the men in their lives by taking them to be a part of cinema? Come watch me while I talk about the time I tried to kill myself.

Hell of a place to take a date.

I restart the film from the beginning.

THREE

SOMETIMES THE BEST MOVIE SCENES happen after the lights have come on and the credits have scrolled out of sight. When you're shuffling out of the theater, disoriented because your mind's been shredded from the ride the director's taken you on. Then the screen flickers back to life and there's more, and you rush back inside, desperate to soak in a more complete picture of the message, but you're too late.

You miss the key moment that brings realization full circle to unlock the last puzzle piece of the film.

And sometimes, the superheroes just sit around eating shawarma.

Either way, you won't find out unless you keep your ass in the chair, business as usual, until the bitter end of the reel. And sometimes it takes more than one viewing of a film to pick up subtle changes in the story or character. Does the exposure change two stops when the character is happy? Or is the character spinning out of control, and her best friend is a symbol of her waning sanity?

Journalism is the same in a lot of ways. You've got to pay attention to things most people don't bother looking at. Find the little details that connect dots others miss. Get to the heart of the story and *make* people care about strangers. It's long hours fueled by a lot of shitty coffee—especially since I'm still at the beginning of my career.

And yet, there's something about the brutality of it all, the pure exploitation of the facts that's appealing. Freedom of the press is a fundamental ideal that's always drawn me in. It gets you in, gains you access to things no one else sees behind the curtains.

And then it's up to you to take that information and sell the shit out of it. Make the truth exciting—or bend the truth around a bit so it sounds more salacious and interesting. Facts are dry. You need to get people to give a shit—and these days that's easier said than done.

Written media is different from film, but the goal is the same: Make people see what you want them to, and evoke an emotional reaction from them. It's drier, as creation goes, but I've learned a lot. When you can't always rely on a picture to tell the story, you learn to get creative. It's not what I want to do with the rest of my life— ideally, I'll be a filmmaker in a few years—but it's relevant and a job related to what I want to do.

Maybe it's not a straight jump into film, but it's storytelling, and that's what I care about.

Besides, a job title of "Amateur Filmmaker" doesn't pay the bills. But one day I will get there—I've just got to hone my craft, make a few more contacts, and get more experience under my belt.

The late night finds me in the newsroom, discontent, stuffed into my crammed cubicle, staring at my computer monitor, scrolling listlessly through news articles hoping for something to widen my eyes and grip me. Work has actually felt like work for the first time in months. I've been searching for a story to write about for weeks, dredging up sources and past stories for possible updates when I should be looking for something new.

I probably won't know it until I see it, so I skim too many reports, stories blending together into a tapestry of macabre listlessness that settles over my shoulders and weighs me down. And yet, I sift through every grain of detail.

It's the same reason I'm meticulous with researching my articles. Film study taught me to look at things from different angles, to see the things I'm supposed to, and to focus on the things I'm not.

What subtext is hidden behind the subtitles?

The husband I knew was guilty when his wife disappeared, because of the way he kept trying to make any camera on him fade to black like he wanted to disappear.

The city planner whose corruption I exposed by focusing on the thing he refused to look at—his secretary.

I'm damn good at what I do, but lately there's just nothing inspiring me. A malaise has taken over like cold air seeping beneath the door, freezing my curiosity with it. I live in a different generation. Writers can't just build a career based on revolutionary reporting that brings justice or truth to the public. I constantly find myself having to fluctuate between the thoughtful and the trivial; otherwise, there is no respect.

For the past few weeks I've been more interested in my colleagues than in the next big story.

Offices are a strange microcosm of sexual energy, populated with people who should never have prolonged contact.

There's Mike, the obligatory hypermasculine reporter, who wears too much cologne and sees Hemingway's reflection when he looks in the mirror, but the closest he'll ever get to a war zone is the sample table at Costco. He's not-so-secretly writing a book (which no one will ever read because he's never going to finish it) and is the type to jerk off into the anal-retentive accounts receivable lady's coffee cup underneath his desk while thinking about his name on a Pulitzer. He's both a dick and a pussy—the dichotomy fascinates me. He despises fame, ironically, and would be the type to sue an influential filmmaker based on a story idea he had ten years ago but, you guessed it, never actually finished.

There's Sanders, the Ivy League graduate, one step above a dude-bro, who actually does want to be a serious journalist, but his perspective has been skewed by the flavor of silver on his tongue, and it will be another twenty years before that realization hits and he writes anything of value. In our limited interactions, he asks me probing questions with an earnest expression, but never seems to hear the answers I give. There are rumors that he has a fetish for flower flipping—that's not a sexual term, but sex is definitely involved when he can keep up. Good ol' boy Sanders has been heavily medicated on various antidepressants since his grad school days but fails to mention at his twice-weekly therapy sessions that he's not just ingesting the doctor's orders, but combining them with mushrooms and Ecstasy at an alarming rate. He throws parties and invites young money-hungry girls, some paid, some there for the free drugs. At a young thirty, he can hardly keep up, so he gets his rocks off by having them urinate on him. Plastic sheets and all. When the flowers are coming down and the girls get bored, he smokes a fat one before heading to the office. It's no surprise that his office smells like patchouli, cigarettes, and too much perfume.

There's Lucy, the pretty plastic darling, who got the job because of who her daddy's best friend is. She doesn't really want to be a reporter—she wants to be a star and be on television, but thinks she's above being the weather girl. This is a stepping stone for her career trajectory, which will be derailed when she's thirty-four and gets knocked up by one of the guys she features in a human interest story, and the network won't want her back because it's hard to retain dewy-eyed optimism when you only get two hours of sleep a night between breast-feedings. She works on a lot of fluff pieces. I hear she's been privy to a few flower-flipping parties, and I have to admit, I wouldn't mind feeling her big, firm breasts rub against my soft skin. I have this fantasy where she steps into the office late, as usual. I order her to strip her silk blouse off, leaving her plump breasts protruding from her expensive lingerie. I command her to give me twenty, which she can hardly do in her red-heeled Loubou-tins. She begs me to let her take them off, but I tell her she will need them. When she's shaking and sweating, I make her undress me and grind her tits all over my body, flicking each nipple with my tongue, slowly, before consuming both of her glorious breasts in my mouth. I order her to grind her cunt on mine, and when I'm done, I call the rest of the office in to fill her up. I spit on her, and then I get back to work while she finishes. There's something sexy about sexually degrading a cliché. I don't think she ever fucks, and by the cemented look on her face, I can tell she needs it.

The best reporters are the ones you don't really notice. They have a way of blending into the background like omniscient furniture. It's about as startling as a lamp suddenly speaking to you when they remind you of their presence by asking a question, making a comment to keep you talking. We've a few of those here, and they are the ones I aspire to emulate because their stories are deep and valu-able. Their words don't just entertain; they teach, strip back a part of reality and give you a peek behind the façade.

I want to do that as well. I want to be successful in my own right, but on my own terms. Breaking news about the latest celebrity baby name doesn't do it for me, though that sells papers. We're not an enter-tainment rag, but cute babies and celebrities sell.

And news is a business as well as a medium of information.

The strange story I find next might help me blend the two.

Inana Luna: Six-month anniversary of the provocateur's suicide.

The article is three months old, but had me at "provocateur."

As I read about the woman who disappeared, seemingly without a trace, something about the story resonates with me. Luna's sister, Lola, is interviewed. I find an article from shortly after Inana's disappearance in which Lola pleads for anyone with information to contact her, admitting that her sister's lifestyle seemed unstable, but that she always kept in touch.

The writer included a few pages from Inana's diary.

What is it about this? The tip of my tongue curls against the roof of my mouth. So familiar...

Flashes of Antonioni's *L'Avventura* hit me, though it's been years since I watched it. Black and white and tumbling ocean waves. That's why this feels familiar, for it begins with a desperate search for a missing woman.

Anna.

But it's hazy. Half-remembered.

Something primal crawls over my spine and caresses my scalp with goosebumps.

Antonioni's Anna connected Claudia and Sandro, then vanished.

Except my Anna didn't connect me to a person. She connected me to so much more.

For a moment, my senses are filled with the memory of her. The way she smelled, the way she laughed. Anna wasn't a temptress; she was a bridge to a dark place inside yourself that you had to cross of your own free will.

People like her remind you of those places, those bridges lying in wait inside every bated breath.

People like Inana Luna. I care because she also reminds me of my Anna.

Sitting up straight, I open another tab and google Inana's name.

There's a surprising amount of information about Inana Luna online.

She was not just any missing woman, but one of some fame and notoriety—an exotic beauty who led a scandalous and controversial life, dedicating herself wholly to the pursuit of sexual pleasure, in any and all forms, and documenting her experiences with a relentless honesty.

It caused quite a stir—one she seemed to revel in.

Right up until she took her own life in her Nevada bungalow.

I go back to the article that had pages of Inana's diary reproduced at the bottom of the page. Large, careless, scrawling script allows no more than a few words per line, but they're easy to read.

The trouble with judgment is that we're all woefully underqualified but too experienced, except when it comes to anything outside the box. Limitless limits. Even the word "limits" looks like people on their knees crawling after something like a human centipede. I don't want to taste someone else's limitation inside my mouth, feel it dancing in my body in a dance I never wanted to move to. I need my own means of expression. I'll invent the language if the words haven't been made for it yet. And when watching me, when seeing me speak it without sound, they'll recognize themselves and know freedom.

I bite my lip and go back to an interview the sister gave shortly after Inana was found—after she insisted her death wasn't a suicide at all.

When asked about the suggestion that her sister was a promiscuous wannabe actress who turned to pornography because she couldn't hack it in Hollywood, Lola explained, "It isn't pornography. She was an internationally successful model for major brands and magazines, but her art chose transgression as its medium, which most people don't understand because of puritanical beliefs. She had representation by a major gallerist, and had several collectors around the world. She wasn't spread-eagled for a random wrist manual, and to dismiss her based on that is demeaning to people who do choose that as a profession. Inana had a mission, and it was respected until her death. My sister was a free spirit and way more intelligent than most people will ever hope to be, but she was a good person. Just because someone's expression takes a form you don't understand yet doesn't mean they're sick, or damaged, or bad. It means people are judgmental. All this is detracting attention from the fact that my sister would never take her own life. She lived harder than most of us ever will. She'd never have killed herself."

The investigation into her death was closed pretty much immediately due to lack of evidence pointing to anything other than suicide—despite there being no note. In her case, with the way she documented everything in her life, I can't believe she left no prose behind for people to read and understand her reasons. Was it the one thing that was too personal for even her to write about?

I didn't even know her, and yet I can't picture this woman choosing not to experience every goddamn second of life that she could. Some people wring every drop of experience they can from life and then lick the bowl clean. Inana did that—after mining the clay from the ground and sculpting the fucking bowl.

The sister's eyes are hollow and shadowed in the picture included; someone wanted to make her seem like a shattered family member grasping at the straws of her sister's tainted memory.

How this woman must hurt.

I have no experience with suicide, so my heart shouldn't throb in sympathy for Inana's sister, yet it does.

To escape it, I search for the pictures of Inana that led everyone to believe she was reckless and hypersexual. Hypersexual—isn't that what men are every day?

In two years' time, she went from top model and ideal muse of photographers and filmmakers to a photographer of fine art self-portraits. From mannequin to goddess. Whether posing for herself or for someone else, she is a bitchslap to expectations of what eroticism should be. Looking at her portraits, I imagine she was trying to find her true being and essence. Slightly off-center, they're dark, atmospheric, but almost whimsical in the way the nudity and poses are juxtaposed with quirkiness. They take you by surprise, and you shouldn't find them sexy, but they're undeniably captivating. As you're staring at a gorgeous woman, there's a tragedy mask carved from light staring back at you from between her spread legs. It doesn't blend into the picture—you're supposed to notice it. It's supposed to feel jarring. You're meant to feel the "sin" and react to it. In another, she cups her hands, which are shaped like a triangle, symbolizing the female form, broadcasting the power and mysticism of women, screaming at you that she holds the power, with eyes half open.

These aren't lusty images. They're art.

These aren't tacky portraits for gossip rags to display with bold yellow type declaring "who wore it best." These are legitimate, high-culture art pieces. These photos are made to show you something—and you're supposed to shut your mouth while looking, because it's in silence that the understanding shudders over your spine, and you realize your likes fall so far outside the lines that there may as well not even be a fucking box.

The need to be in her head at the moment when the camera flashes went off surges over me like a type of mania. A madness.

An insatiable need to truly know.

Inana isn't the blazing bombshell I was expecting from the way people spoke of her, with pillowy lips and hungry eyes. She's extremely tall, and muscular. No huge fake tits for someone's dick to thrust between, angling their load at her vacant expression and bee-stung lips slicked with red lipstick. Her long limbs and wide, piercing eyes make her birdlike, and not of this Earth.

I click through photo after photo. With her history, there's a wealth of pictures online for the vultures to leer at. Paparazzo captured her on countless occasions as she gracefully and easily towered over the short rock stars and actors whom she called her lovers. As public as her exploits were, a groupie or one-track-minded model she wasn't. With her fame and effortless beauty, I'm surprised I never heard her story until now. But there's also a guilelessness to her, an open, raw vulnerability that makes my heart clench in my chest at the thought of anything bad happening to her. I want to protect a woman who's already dead. I want to know her, crawl inside her head and learn the things she learned, see what she saw. Her life was so public, but also a mystery. She speaks like a poet in the rare interviews that are accessible.

I'm pretty sure I've already felt what she felt—or at least had a taste of it.

My mouth is dry with wanting more, and I swallow the feeling back with a mouthful of now cold coffee. *Inana Luna.*

Also showing up in my search of her name: the Sumerian goddess of love, fertility, and warfare.

Inana the woman was almost militant in her desire to redefine passion, to discover herself through sex. She was following her namesake in a way. Bold, unafraid to go places that scared her, that should have scared her. Birthed by Venus and guided by Aphrodite.

I don't know if she was ever afraid of the journey or of herself, or scared of what she'd be at the end.

I need to know. In a way, finding out everything about Inana is like discovering what may have happened to me if I'd continued on my journey instead of deciding that what I have with Jack is enough. Sacrificing my own desires to protect the man I love, and to protect our relationship.

Part of me has always wondered what would have happened. This is a way to follow the yellow brick road while staying perfectly safe.

I return to the other browser tab, the Google search of her name, full of articles focusing on her fate, reduced from a bold life to grim details that are hard to reconcile with the eyes of the adventurous woman on a journey of self-discovery and expression that most will never dare to even think about too closely.

You know what I mean.

How many bestselling revolutionary lifestyle books have you heard about and thought might actually be the key to fixing your mundane life? If you could just Feng Shui harder, declutter one more room, juice your way into a shinier version of yourself, your problems would be solved. Your life would be absolutely perfect. Bigger, better, with more expensive shoes and brighter smiles, and more time to devote to those hobbies you never got around to.

But you never really commit to it. You'll vigorously attack the first three days of every new regime, then slowly fade back into your beige life because it's comfortable.

And beneath it all, most of us like being comfortable. Comfortable is safe and unchallenging. It keeps your boundaries nice and small so you feel like you're living large in a small life.

No one wants to be trapped on the roller coaster 24/7. Thrills are bad for the heart. If you actually took stock of your life and turned it upside down to be the type of person that takes your own breath away, you would scare the shit out of yourself.

Living like that is terrifying because you're finally on the other side of the fence instead of sitting around telling yourself that life wouldn't be all that sensational if you got there.

Maybe it isn't, most of the time. Life is what you make of it, and most people lack the imagination for anything substantial and exciting for long.

Look at those people who win giant lotteries. For most of them, the wildest thing they can do with the money is go on a spending spree. But there's still no expansion in being—just them with a fancier leash tethering them to the person they've always been.

No vision.

And they end up bored as fuck inside a year, trying to buy happiness. Fulfillment. But those aren't things you can buy. External things never are truly attainable. The thrill isn't in the having, it's in the pursuit of happiness. There's a pinnacle, and then what?

The fall from the lofty heights of expectation.

But if you've got a goal, a vision for your future that involves creation, that is when the real magic happens.

Some people have kids to mask their unhappiness, as if that will fix all their problems, expecting that birth to be the best there is.

But it's the birth of creation, of art, of mystery, of dreaming something up and freeing it upon the world that they should seek. Finding that one thing that burns from within—and it can't be attainment. It can't be accumulation.

It's not about making something. It's about taking a piece of your fucking soul, tearing it from inside yourself and throwing it out into the world so it exists outside yourself. It's not a legacy. Nothing that grandiose. It's a cycle. Using the experiences that have shaped you to create something that shapes others and spawns inspiration, that spawns that same hunger inside them.

It's what cinema gives me. It's the reason I ultimately want to make films instead of just watching them.

I want to know that people are reacting to the things inside of my mind.

I don't have to see the reactions for them to have value.

I just have to know that piece of me is out there.

Inana Luna was doing this with these photos.

I can smell the journey like it's my own. Shades of smoke and sex and come and regret.

Of passion half-fulfilled.

A year or so after she left the mainstream currents for the white waters of her vision, she went missing, seemingly without a trace. No photos exist of her from the four-month period she was gone.

Then, as suddenly as she vanished, she was back in her bungalow—found on the floor with a stomach full of pills and empty, unseeing eyes.

Gone again, but for good this time.

How does a woman go from being the insatiable, full-of-life boundary pusher who wrote those diary pages to a suicide victim? It feels off.

Maybe it feels off because I want it to feel off.

Anything to justify learning more about this woman whose dark eyes burn into me from surreal photos that captured something deep and dark and compelling.

Here was a woman who knew how I felt, because she felt it, too.

I fire off an e-mail to my editor, attaching a few of the more salacious pictures and high-profile articles to give weight to my desire to follow up on what happened to Inana, explaining my intent to do a piece going more in-depth than before. I give a few possible angles: abuse in the entertainment industry; was Inana a victim of her own celebrity hype; was it all a cover-up? My intuition tells me that there was a planned smear campaign against her. How did she go from being a revered model and artist to a "dirty pornographer," literally overnight? Her images don't look like the porn Jack and I watch together—or that I see in his search history. I have to dig deeper. To really hook my editor, I have to tie it in to the relatively new term for the phenomenon of suddenly vanishing from someone's life: ghosting.

I want to do an article about ghosting, and the effect on those left behind.

But even if he says no, I need to know more.

FOUR

∽ᴑᴑᴑᴍᴑᴍᴍᴑ

EVEN THOUGH HE SPENDS NEARLY every waking hour in Bob's company or dealing with things surrounding him, Jack still soaks up news about the senator like he's never met the man who's still his idol. Unflagging enthusiasm.

Despite the dark circles beneath his eyes from having been awake for nineteen hours, he sits forward on the couch, leaning into the television like a flower trying to reach the sun, watching the news anchor with wide eyes and coiffed hair talking about DeVille.

"We've just learned that Senator DeVille has scheduled an announcement for later this week. Speculation is running high that at this time he'll announce his plans to run for president, but as of yet that hasn't been confirmed or denied by his press office."

It shouldn't be a highlight, but it's been a slow week, and Bob's been making waves with his stance on immigration reform, among other things. Jack still idolizes DeVille, and the thought of him becoming more like Bob makes my skin crawl, but that's as unlikely as me sprouting wings and flying away. Jack is a good man; Bob is not. If I could have figured out a way to get Jack away from Bob without revealing everything, which would have torn the ground from beneath Jack—losing me, his mentor, his job all in one fell swoop—then I would have.

But as long as DeVille keeps his mouth shut, so will I.

Years later, I'm not without connections of my own.

At first, I fantasized about bringing him down and exposing him for what he really is. But time went by and we came to ignore each other better, ignore the memories churning beneath the surfaces of our skin. Besides, if it wasn't Bob, it would be some other monster—maybe one who was even worse.

You know that old saying, "Let sleeping dogs lie"? Well, I've got one I found in a fortune cookie a week after that night Bob and I had our hands around each other's throats, consuming one another like wild, hungry animals. "Never trouble trouble till trouble troubles you."

Sound advice that I've chosen to take as a sign, but maybe that was the MSG humming through my nervous system, making the synapses of my brain jangle. Either way, things have worked out for the best, and we each keep a respectful distance from the other as much as possible.

I tuck my toes underneath Jack's thigh, and he absentmindedly rubs up and down my shin, eyes still glued to the screen. "Is that true?" I ask him, surprised that he hasn't told me the "good" news.

"Is what?" He turns to me, and the wide-eyed stare is almost convincing, but there's a smile beneath the corners of his mouth.

"He's running for POTUS?" If so, this is news to me, but it makes sense with the insane hours Jack's been spending at the campaign office. "Isn't that kind of sudden? He's only been a senator for four years."

"You'll just have to wait and see," he says teasingly. I hate when he gets in this NDA mode about Bob, even if he does it good-naturedly. It makes me feel like an outsider, as though Jack, Bob, and Bob's wife, Gena, have made a new little family I'm not a part of. It makes me feel like Jack doesn't trust me with everything, when I've done nothing to deserve his suspicion. He's proud of all his hard work coming to fruition—I understand that. But he incorrectly thinks I love Gena and Bob, too, and that this is a wonderful surprise for me. He thinks I'd be excited and pleased for him to be working with the most powerful man in America.

In the world.

And I can't correct his thinking in that area, so I smile and play along and don't push about him not trusting me so I don't cause another fight.

I guess I should have expected DeVille to slither up that ladder as quickly as possible. He's perfect for the position, really, and Gena would be the perfect first lady—as long as nothing too taxing happened to tip her over her psychological breaking point. But she's easily managed with the help of her various little yellow pills—probably the reason Bob chose her as his partner.

Men like him seek out power to better exploit others.

The Juliette Society would love to have one of theirs in a position like that—all the perks and resources of the office at their disposal.

If they don't already.

That's something I never thought about. What if they already have him? Then again, I know that the POTUS isn't the most powerful man in the world, nevermind The Juliette Society, if he's one of theirs. Even if we have a female president in the White House soon, the gender is irrelevant in this case, and it always will be. There's always someone else, a committee of people, calling the shots from one level above. Who, then, is the most powerful?

And what would all that power and access do to DeVille? Would he go off the rails, drunk on his own hype, thinking he can get away with even more?

He probably would, but he's a puppet, too.

I want to know whose the hand is.

Climb high enough and there's one person who calls the shots, even from within a group, a natural leader, the one people look to before committing themselves to an action. That's the person I'd love to have an interview with.

"Hey," Jack says, frowning, "I'm only teasing."

"No, I know. I was just thinking about my article."

"Oh. Have you decided what you're going to do?" He smiles at me, and I love that he remembers how much trouble I've been having deciding what to focus on next.

"Not quite," I say, which is technically true. I still need more of an angle than "following up on a star who committed suicide." That's not going to sell papers.

"I could get you something with Bob. An exclusive." He sits forward, lighting up like a kid talking about his favorite toy. "How amazing would that be? I know he'd do it, too."

"I know, but I don't want something handed to me like that. I want to do this on my own. It's important to me."

He sighs but lets it go.

I stare at the television again to avoid saying anything. Not wanting to focus on politics is a weak excuse—most reporters would dream for something salacious or exclusive, and Jack doesn't understand why I'm not snatching up what could be a career-making opportunity, especially when I've been floundering for story ideas lately.

But sometimes, instead of boning you, life throws you a bone.

"Maxxy, pop's reigning princess, was reported missing this morning when her father and manager called the police, saying that his daughter hadn't been seen for six days." A picture of Maxxy flashes on the screen, but even people in Sub-Saharan Africa know who Maxxy is.

The beloved bubblegum singer went on a mission a couple years ago, trying to give back to the "global community." Really, it was a PR stunt to raise her profile as a serious humanitarian, the same thing that made people overlook Angelina Jolie's Billy Bob Thornton, blood-vials-around-the-neck, brother-kissing phase.

It would have worked, had an unfortunate choice not landed her in a place that had recently been ravaged by Ebola. Maxxy didn't understand that the area had been cleared of the disease and went from altruistic to hysterical. The whole conniption fit was recorded by an overworked, underpaid assistant. Maxxy looked like a deranged, stone-cold bitch, demanding the helicopter come back because "Screw the sick fuckers, my life is worth more than theirs! I'm the talent, get me the fuck out of here!"

It went viral.

And yet, she'd managed to claw her way back up to the top over the last few months. It's amazing what a timely new release can do for a tarnished reputation, no matter how deserved.

We loved bald Britney, but we loved her comeback even more. But her stability is boring and we've moved on to Miley.

The wildest thing Gaga's done in ages is be "normal."

We love an underdog trainwreck that keeps us on our toes. And Maxxy provides that.

"How the hell could someone like Maxxy just disappear?" I ask, turning to Jack.

"If she really wanted to?"

"With help. Exactly. People like her do not blend in." But did she want to? If she was kidnapped, there'd have been some demand for money or perks by now. But that means she's trying to disappear.

She wouldn't be the first celebrity to disappear. Sometimes stars get burned by the limelight or decide they've finally had enough and walk away. Rehab, private islands, darkened apartments filled with paranoia and regret. With enough money, disappearing isn't that difficult.

Garbo, Bill Withers, Salinger, Gene Wilder, Captain Beefheart. Terrence Malick. Hell, even Dave Chapelle. Some end up only taking a long hiatus, others never come back at all. Did you know that Cherie Currie left music to go carve shit with a chainsaw? She's pretty good, too.

The point is, Maxxy wouldn't be the first to want to get away from it all—maybe fake her own death if she wanted to get drastic with it. It's not even just celebrities that have longed to escape the spotlight—or enormous debts. I heard a guy once fled the country after faking his own death to escape an insane phone bill. Roaming charges strike again.

We all want to escape something—it's just that most of us never go through with it.

But even when it doesn't involve a fictitious death, people still willingly disappear every day.

You may have even been on the receiving end of a "ghosting" where the person you're dating up and vanishes, never to be heard from again, and you're questioning, after all the time you spent talking, whether they were ever really there at all.

Beats the hell out of that last awkward, "it's not you, it's me" speech, I guess, but I think it's pretty low.

At least Carrie Bradshaw got a Post-It.

But what about the people left behind? People like Inana's sister, or Maxxy's father. That's not even the end of it in cases like Maxxy's. She's not just a person, she's an empire. She's got an entourage. Her entourage has an entourage. How many people are directly employed by her with the sole aim of keeping that machine running smoothly? They've got loved ones and families as well who rely on Maxxy as a means of economic survival.

What happens to them while she's missing? If she never comes back?

I wander over to my laptop and open a Word file, entering a few preliminary ideas about the fallout for those left behind. So often people focus only on those who leave, not the ones who are left.

Jack's used to this from me—wandering away to write down an idea before it flits from my mind completely like a butterfly in a big wind—and after turning the television off a few minutes later, he heads into the bathroom.

A startling number of people have had high-profile disappearances—either unsolved, or that turned out to be ghosting and admitted as such, sometimes years later.

I lose myself in reading about their families and friends, interviews with people aching with the loss, not understanding what happened. And it's thin, but it's enough of a justification to tie Inana and her sister to something more than personal curiosity.

Jack startles me coming out of the bathroom, damp from his shower. "What are you looking up?" He kisses the top of my head.

I hadn't realized half an hour had passed, and I roll the tension from my shoulders. "Well, Maxxy reminded me of a story I read recently about this model, Inana Luna—she did quite provocative performance art—who disappeared as well before turning up deceased. It gave me the idea to do a story focusing on women who disappear—the ghosts in our lives—and the impact that has on those left behind. She has a sister who I think could be a great lead, but she hasn't replied to me."

He rubs my shoulders. "Do you want to…"

"I really just want to work on this now that I've found something." I brace for annoyance, but he just shrugs.

"It's good to see you interested in something again."

My smile is easy. "It feels good. I'm trying to look up more about Inana so if the sister does agree to a meeting, I don't look completely clueless."

"I won't convince you to come to bed, in that case."

"Not that you're in any shape for anything tonight. The bags under your eyes wouldn't make it onto the plane."

"They'd definitely need to be checked."

I tip my head back for a kiss. "Sorry."

His lips linger on mine for a moment, not erotically, but sensually, and I give his shoulder a squeeze before he heads for the bedroom.

And I fully intended to research Maxxy, but after a cursory search, my fingers type in Inana's name, taking me to a fan website as though my hands are haunted, possessed, in a fugue state that the ghost of this woman controls.

Her dark eyes seem to burn into you, no matter which picture of her you look at. No matter which scene from which experimental film. I guess that's one of the hallmarks of a great performer—such people always make the audience feel like they're focusing only on them. Looking into their souls, singing just for them, making love to them, dancing for them.

Yearning for them.

Inana's the same—charisma oozed from her every pore. She was gorgeous, talented, had the "it factor." There's never been anyone like her.

What was it?

I search for any content I can, but I want to look beyond the interviews and clips from the films and TV shows she shot. Cameos and bit parts from before she made it big. A couple of commercials from before she made it at all, hawking skin cream. Campy backstage photos from stage plays.

I'm down to the third page when I find what I'm looking for.

She's lying on the floor in the thumbnail. The link takes me to an obscure gallery website with a video excerpt.

Her hair's mussed, like it was styled against a pillowcase by a thorough lover. Maybe it was.

A single note is being plucked on a stringed instrument, but I don't know what it is. Bass, maybe, but high up on the neck?

The lights flash in a counter rhythm to the sound.

The camera pulls back, revealing her body covered in a blanket of hands. The shot pans out, and you see the arms, but not the people.

Oh, but what they're doing to her.

Ceaselessly kneading, rubbing, touching, hiding her body—everywhere except her pussy and breasts. They've made a reverse bikini with their touches, and she writhes, clearly desperate for them to get her off. But they don't.

It vaguely reminds me of *Pryings,* a famous Acconci piece that several filmmakers have paid homage to.

They don't stop.

Her eyes go wild.

I pause it, heartbeat kicked up in sympathetic frustration for her. All those hands and none of them touching her in the places she wants them the most.

I find another clip of her online, from the premiere for some movie she was in that I never saw. Big budget, big director, but I can't recall even seeing a trailer for it.

She's wearing a simple blue dress and red-soled Louboutins. Her hair's twisted back into a chignon and her makeup's flawlessly done, but it somehow detracts from the vision of her. Like she's hidden behind a layer of perfection instead of having her attributes accentuated.

She's smiling along with the interviewer, giving charming but flippant answers to his questions. Her voice is low-pitched and pleasant, with a sort of lilting cadence that's vaguely hypnotic. She's an old soul. She's beautiful, and if I hadn't seen the other video first, I might never have noticed that something's missing from her eyes. Inana's sparkle is dulled in this video.

I find another interview and watch it to be sure.

Again, it's as though she's breathing but not getting any air.

I click back to the performance piece, where she radiates.

Her movements are more languid, her eyes almost wild, but she's somehow more relaxed than she seems in the other footage, which should be ridiculous. And yet it's not. We're most ourselves just before we come, the most attached to our bodies, reduced to the purest we can be. It's needy, pure, and honest. Single-minded.

Interrupt a woman's orgasm, and you'll feel the wrath of God— you can see it in her eyes if you dare to look. Because in that moment of pure, blank desire, when we're stripped of everything else but that divine sensation—we're also gods.

Singular.

Everything else melts away.

And to watch this woman, so strong and sure, so gorgeously content and happy here, and then flip back to the other interview—it's just wrong on a primal level.

Inana was meant to be on a pedestal with light in her eyes.

Gifts being brought to her, the high priestess.

I go back to the first video, desperately wanting her to get off at the end of it, but it ends with her literal whimper, reminiscent of *The Hollow Men* by Eliot. The audience is supposed to leave feeling as unfulfilled as she is.

I search the name of the video and find Inana Luna's write-up about the video.

"Witnessing an unmet need is jagged to the soul—especially when you know what that need is like, but worse when you see how easy it would be to fix. Humans know touch, they know need. Most of all, they know discontentment. This piece is about complete decadent excess that is empty and ultimately dissatisfying for myself and the audience. So close, but never getting the thing we all wanted: release."

She got that right.

I flip between tabs, looking at her face, searching it for instability and answers. Before and after. Inana seemed alive during her search for sexual expression, despite her obvious "success" of before. She seemed happier afterward, not like someone who'd gone off the rails into harmful territory.

What was it about that journey that made people so uncomfortable?

Was it because they were jealous, or because there was something inherently wrong about it?

Right now I feel the former, even though a large part of me has accepted the latter as truth—even if my core rebels at the thought.

Success means different things to different people, the connotation more important than what the word itself denotes. It's all relative. Happiness is relative. There's a reason media and fashion are able to play our insecurities against us with the "grass is greener" marketing. If they shift the goalposts often enough, no one will ever have what they think they wanted, so there's no reason to stop striving for the next big thing.

Inana stripped it down to her body—her self—in a pure way that resonates with me. Her body, mind, and desires. Blowing limitations out of the water.

And I think it made people feel uncomfortable the way any self-improvement does, because they start to wonder if their goals are meaningless. If the things they've been fighting for, working for, slaving for in a job they hate for so long have been the wrong things, and it could have all been so much simpler if only they'd gotten out of their own way and stripped away the bullshit.

Or maybe she's a slut. But what is a slut? It's a judgment meant to keep women on their knees, which is really fucking ironic if you ask me. Stay on your knees, subservient for your masters, but God forbid you enjoy yourself while you're down there with your mouth open. Where's the line between art and trash?

Art pushes boundaries, but it's not infallible. It should forward conversation, thought, and social dialogue. There have been plenty of films made that blurred or crossed lines, but who decides where that line is? When asked about those boundary pushers, actors often say that it wasn't the controversial act itself that made them uncomfortable, but the blowback—no pun intended—they faced afterwards by the public, by the critics. What they'd thought to be a powerful scene in the moment, and even afterward, was viewed as something tawdry and cheap. People tried to reduce it to shock value and an attempt to drum up a little controversy when the reality was anything but.

The infamous unsimulated blowjob scene in *The Brown Bunny*, for example, but even that was only half-real.

That happened, but there are other things that we don't know are true. Did Tom and Nicole fuck in *Eyes Wide Shut*? Did Harvey Keitel really secretly come in Nic's hair? I find it hard to believe it's actually true. Real versus fake. Simulated versus true. Was it a fake blowjob on a real cock, or a real blowjob on a prosthetic dick?

Even if it's simulated, you've still sucked dick on camera, and that closes a lot of doors in Hollywood—while blowing others wide open.

It's a choice as to how far you'll go. Where you'll take it. Whether you want to be cast as the girl next door, or the one who steals her boyfriend.

But more than that, this is what I want to know: Was Charlotte Gainsbourg's prosthetic vagina modeled on her real vagina? If so, isn't that kind of weird? Maybe she should find someone to market it. I couldn't imagine ever using her prosthetic pussy as anything other than a coffee table ornament. Did Jane Birkin wear a prosthetic pussy in *Je T'aime...Moi Non Plus*? Did she have a "porn double"? Maria Schneider never wore a prosthetic vagina, I'm pretty sure about that.

Vincent Gallo definitely used a stunt cock in *The Brown Bunny* and made everyone believe it was his own, while Joe Dallesandro displayed his manhood proudly and with no sense of shame. But maybe that was just a clever ploy by Andy Warhol to distract from how wooden his acting was. Actors having sex in movies want to have their cake and eat it, too. They want to appeal to everyone, be as sexy as possible without jeopardizing any roles or alienating anybody. They want to make us believe that they're pushing boundaries, but they haven't got the balls (or vagina) to really follow through. Violence is fine, but sex still isn't.

And so they fake it.

They can say that it's because cinema is changing, society is changing, and to stay relevant, they've got to take more clothes off, kiss more passionately, grind a little harder. Maybe that's true. But it's putting a lot of energy into fakery, and a lot of special effects into making it the most realistic imitation they possibly can.

But then, maybe make-believe is better.

I've seen the Colin Farrell sex tape. It certainly looked real, but it seemed like he was faking it. Is it that a lot of male celebs have become so used to groupies doing all the work that they have no idea what they're doing anymore with a partner who isn't faking it because she's just so damn happy to be there? Girls like that will never admit how shitty the sex was, or that he hadn't brushed his teeth for three days beforehand, because that kills the dream.

And the dialogue in Farrell's tape was so corny, it made the pizza delivery boy in Eighties pornos sound like Samuel Beckett.

Off script, such celebrities are usually terrible speakers with nothing interesting to say. Not all of them, but a lot. The smart ones stay quiet to keep the mystery alive. Look at Ozzy Osbourne. Can you honestly tell me you look at him the same way, like he is a rock-and-roll badass, after you've seen him doddering around in his house, shouting about dog shit with all the pep and none of the charm of your senile grandfather?

That's what I thought.

It's not a burn on him. It's just that he should have kept things behind the curtain so the performances on stage were more believable.

The actresses who smirk like they're above getting a few fingers rammed up their ass while they swallow their lover's load, who promptly do it behind closed doors on the casting couch, really need to stop. Who hasn't been a whore for her dream at one time or another?

Sticks and stones. Objective morality.

I think that as long as you don't hurt anyone, and you're happy, then you're doing all right.

My inbox dings, and I check my messages.

And smile.

FIVE

I'M WAITING FOR ANSWERS SURROUNDED by addicts.

Brands define you in the same way that cattle are branded by the red-hot irons pressed to their sides. You start to identify with a certain product line as though it somehow matters whether you're an Apple or Android user. And within those types, everyone is chasing an ideal, in competition with one another to have the latest and greatest.

And yet, you can bond with someone based solely on having the same kind of car or phone that they have—or over the type of headphones they listen to their music with.

Tiny white buds or huge black ones that look like earmuffs.

You are what you eat.

You are what you drink.

Things give us status.

Status is a marketplace we carry with our competitive natures, lining the pockets of those at the top who have true status and privilege we've never even fathomed. The ability to make or break people, nations.

A product doesn't exist that isn't designed to ensnare our sense of need, and that hasn't been raked over the coals of a focus group and engineered to suck as many dollars out of our wallets as it can.

And if for some reason the targeting flops, a 2.0 version will show up in a few months with a new color, a new feature, and we can all forget about the last inferior model and the way it went horrifically sideways. Marketers count on short memories and eager hands to forgive and snatch up the next model.

And yet, despite the fact that you're a teeny, infinitely replaceable cog in the consumer machine, you still think you're unique. But even if you're sewing your own clothes, it's still usually with material that someone else made, working off a ready-made pattern.

Things end up being the same, like bearded hipsters trying desperately to be different—and ending up exactly like the rest of the special snowflakes trying to stand out in the exact same rebellion of identity.

Have you ever noticed how celebrities all start looking alike—at least, the ones who go under the knife? There's a reason for this.

Let me explain. There exists an ideal beauty formula: the golden ratio for a face to be "perfect."

It's based on math and symmetry. The more symmetrical a face is, and the closer to this ideal ratio, the more pleasing it is to us.

But only to a point. True symmetry can feel too masklike and artificial. It turns out that our brains like a little flaw—as long as it, too, is pleasing. We like faces to have "character." One of the teeth in our crush's mouth can be slightly crooked, but not totally black. Tiny flecks of gold in a blue eye can be pretty, but a blown-out pupil? Hell no. When they meet a person with heterochromia—two different colored eyes—people even tend to prefer one eye or the other. Producers make those actors wear contacts to correct that unsightly and distracting problem. But it always worked for Bowie—hell they wrote roles for him.

I bet you're curious about your face now, and how close it is to the ideal ratio. Go look it up, but be prepared to be disappointed.

Math is so cold. So goddamn heartless.

They say Audrey Hepburn attained it.

But celebrities, and anyone with the inclination and the money, carve away at their perceived flaws, aiming for that cold number of perfection. These changes generally have the same results, aiming for that ideal beauty ratio even if people don't realize why they find that appealing. Smaller nose, bigger lips, stronger cheekbones. Nevermind the body enhancements that are now available.

And it's not just women getting them.

For a price, fellas, you can have pectoral implants, calf shaving, and muscular sculpting done to achieve visual results without ever having to waste a moment setting foot in a gym. As well as wanting the best of the best, we all want it now, with as little effort as possible. It's why get-rich-quick schemes still work. It's why dodgy diet pills are still consumed by the handful—even though the side effects could include death at worst, and anal leakage at most mortifying.

But if it gets you looking like a waif, stinky seclusion for a few weeks seems preferable to actually dieting and exercising for months on end. So, again, these people are all cutting and pulling and twisting and reforming themselves into something that ends up looking remarkably uniform—not that it will really help their careers. Look at Baby from *Dirty Dancing*. That one "flaw" that makes someone relatable can be the difference between a leading lady and last year's one-hit wonder.

But I digress.

The glaring exception to the rule—the refuge, if you will, from cookie-cutter consumption—is at Starbucks, of all places.

I've never known two people to drink the same beverage at Starbucks. It's just another brand we all viscerally cling to, but a more personal one.

Our drink orders.

If you pay attention, people don't even treat it as a separate thing from themselves. The baristas either throw out a name, or they'll ask, "Who *is* the tall half-caf soy latte, extra hot, extra whip, with caramel?" and we just go along with it like cattle, as though we are our drink choice.

Because we *are* our choices.

Even the cup itself is a status symbol. You're not one of the hoi polloi who wake up early and make their own beverages. You're above that, too fabulously busy for something so basic. And the fact you go to Starbucks instead of another lesser chain says much about you. Even if you can afford the Louis Vuitton weekend bag, Cartier bracelet, and flamboyant Hermès handkerchief, that green straw is never uncomfortably plebeian, even for the elite. It's a fashion state-ment; it ties fluidly in to your accessories.

What is your drink?

It doesn't matter what mine is. All you need to know is that Inana's sister and I ordered the same thing that day.

Looking back, perhaps I should have taken it as a sign. It meant everything and nothing, wrapped up in a syrupy caramel bow.

But with that simple serendipitous detail, I knew it was her. It's a rule: I always let my subject pick the meeting place so they feel comfortable and in control, and this time it's just my hard luck.

Sometimes the universe is generous with its signs.

But you might not know what the sign means until later.

She stands and stirs and I wait for the sugar in her hand, both of us glancing around the coffee shop, waiting for the other.

When we realize we're here to meet each other, we drift toward a table in the quietest corner of the coffee shop and sit across from each other, taking each other in. I'm usually pretty good at ascertaining someone's age on sight, but she's got a timeless youth that could place her anywhere from early thirties to mid-forties. She dresses conser-vatively, but with a chic, understated quality that makes me think she has money but doesn't want to flaunt it. An insurance payout from Inana's death, maybe? That would explain it. It would feel like blood money, spending anything, if you thought your sister had been murdered for your gain—even if you truly needed it.

"Thank you for meeting with me," I say.

She nods and settles into her chair, accepting the business card I hand her. "I've done a lot of interviews, but I was intrigued by your message."

"I can imagine the requests have been unreal. Your sister was a very provocative figure. I looked up some of her visual pieces."

"And?" Her eyes harden. "It's not pornography."

"No, please don't get me wrong. Your sister was doing something unique and powerful. You can't help but react to them in a visceral way." I don't really see the resemblance between them, other than their small frames. But when Lola sits back and plays with the ends of her hair, trailing her fingers thoughtfully over her collarbone, the gesture does it. Inana did the same thing in an interview when she was lost in thought.

Funny, the affectations that we share with our families. My mom and I have the same rapid double blink when we're truly excited. I've felt myself do it, and I've seen it on her face.

It makes me feel like a part of Inana is here with us. Maybe connecting us.

"I understand what you're going through—to a lesser degree than you feel. It was my best friend, not my sister, who got wrapped up in something that swallowed her whole." I'm referring to Anna, but I leave it ambiguous to be more persuasive to Lola. I want her to relate to me, but surprisingly, it feels good to talk about Anna after so long. It makes it all feel real , and this time I'm the one sitting back in my chair, getting lost in thoughts of the past.

How much worse would it have felt if it had been my sister who went missing for months on end, then turned up dead?

For the first time, worry for my voluptuous, devilish, free-spir-ited friend fills me to the core. I look up at Lola, and she nods, seeing the fear in my eyes.

I worried enough about Anna to try to find her—and found Bob instead.

We are our choices.

I am denial.

You're incorruptible. Irreducible. You understand. Bob's words skitter across my skin.

Denial, denial, denial.

Lola's sigh cuts off my thoughts. "I can tell you understand, but it's still hard to trust anyone after everything that's happened. People exploited my sister while she was alive, and it got even worse after her death. Like cockroaches, people came crawling out of the woodwork, claiming to have known her—to have fucked her."

I cringe along with her, but mostly reacting to the things Bob said to me.

How they're still true.

I swallow hard. "That's awful."

She nods and her gaze softens. "It might seem like I'm a bit militant about my sister and her art, but it was important to her. And now that she's gone…"

"It's all you have left."

"Yes. And I hate that she's become synonymous with something she never stood for. Cheap thrills and whoring herself out." She grimaces and takes a sip of her coffee.

I see my opening. "Lola, I know it won't make things better—nothing could do that—but I can help you tell her story—the one she wanted to tell. Put that out there instead of the trash-talking and sensationalism. Our paper has a solid reputation and a credibility that the tabloids don't. If you answer some questions for me about Inana, I promise you I'll give you the platform to set the record straight."

She chews the inside of her lip.

"More than that, hers is a story I want to tell. It's personal to me, too, you know?" She nods once, decisively, and I decide to press on.

"What's something you wish people had known about Inana?"

"How smart she was. She wasn't manipulative, taking her intelligence to a place of cunning. But she could make you feel things by reducing them to their most basic fundamental ideas, stripping away the bullshit."

"Stripping away your expectations and preconceived notions," I add, remembering the hands on Inana's body, how she wanted you to think that the most personal touches would be on her breasts and crotch, but the most erotic part about that video was the anticipation—the way the viewer ached for her release right along with her.

"Exactly."

"I'm all in if you'll let me be. But the questions aren't going to be easy, and I want to warn you up front about that. What I want to do is get inside Inana's head. See what she saw, feel what she felt. Show the readers, I mean. To do that, I need to know her a lot better."

Lola holds her hand up to stop me, and my heart sinks, but I wait for her to speak. "I've got something that might help you out with that." She leans down and grabs her handbag from the floor, setting it into her lap in a smooth, languorous action. "But you need to promise me that you will protect this, keep it safe."

Whatever it is, I suddenly want it more than my next breath. "I swear."

She stares at me for a beat long enough to make me uncomfortable, but I don't look away.

I must meet her approval, because she suddenly nods and pulls a worn, dull red book out of her bag.

Inana's diary.

"This was her diary, Catherine." She slides it across the table toward me.

My hand twitches to snatch it, but I twist my fingers around unseen on my lap beneath the table, frightened by how close answers are. Frightened by how much I want it. "Are you sure you're okay with me reading it?"

"I think you'll tell the story that needs to be told, with sensitivity."
She's right about that. I hope.

It might be a little too close to home, like writing about the person I almost became.

Who I could still become, if...

"I know it's a sensitive subject, Lola, but why don't you believe that your sister committed suicide? You understand why I have to ask."

"Are you religious?"

I hedge. "I was baptized Catholic."

She nods. "No matter what else she did, said, or was, Catherine, my sister was a good Christian girl at the core. She'd never have committed suicide. Never." Her voice holds such certainty that I have a hard time meeting her eyes. She places a set of keys on top of the diary and jots down an address on the back of her receipt. "This is Inana's address." She taps the diary. "I'm giving you access to what was in her head. You might as well have access to the home she wrote the diary in as well. This is her life. I know you'll treat it with the respect it deserves."

I nod, and make my exit from the coffee shop with the diary and the keys.

SIX

A GOOD CHRISTIAN GIRL.

What does a good Christian girl do? The same things a good Catholic girl does.

She keeps her knees together. She keeps her hands clean.

She never has impure thoughts.

She drinks a lot of wine during socially acceptable hours and pushes out as many kids as her husband's penis can put inside her in the missionary position whenever he wants to do it.

Or...

Maybe she squeezes her thighs together while having impure thoughts about the new, young priest, imagining him taking her on the altar, using the rosary to rock against her clit the way I did. She imagines way more interesting things he could do with that anointing oil.

I couldn't understand how we weren't supposed to fantasize about him. If God made him beautiful, we were surely meant to see his appeal.

Even before I had had sex, my imagination was rampant with

impure thoughts and anticipation. Creative about the ways pleasure could be achieved—not that I found anything near satisfaction with a partner until Jack. My fertile fantasies were probably a huge part of the reason I was so let down. Until Jack, I was prepared to be underwhelmed unless I was alone with my hand. It's sad to realize that women are still conditioned to feel and think this way.

But this was before Jack, and before I'd had the chance to be underwhelmed by a partner in bed.

Good, Catholic, virginal Catherine.

I used to feel shame at my impure thoughts about the priest while at church, until I realized the whole place was teeming with sex.

I've said it before and I'll reiterate now—if there's something the good book isn't short of, it's sex. You can barely turn a page without people wondering when God will come, when Jesus is coming, when salvation cometh. There's nothing more transcendental than the rapture of an orgasm.

When you come.

Maybe Inana didn't know that. Maybe she didn't believe in anything except her vision anymore. But even if she no longer believed in God, she still couldn't entertain the idea of suicide.

Inana's diary radiates temptation from the passenger seat. At every red light, I reach over, running my fingers across the worn, red leather, a touchstone, to reassure myself that it's still there and that soon I'll get what I've wanted for days. Longer than that, if I'm being honest.

An unmet need will soon be met.

I'll get to know. To read her thoughts and see her world. Unfiltered by societal expectations and politeness. We're honest with our diaries, if not with ourselves. Maybe that's why diaries fell out of fashion, or maybe the language of expression changed. Selfie sticks are our new pens, capturing our lives with pictures instead of words.

Only now we post everything online for other people to see and care about, keeping very little to ourselves when we should be even more vigilant about our privacy than ever before. Cyberbullying, cyberstalking, cybersex. Why write your thoughts out when you can film yourself and put it online and go viral?

Be a star. No talent needed—just do something scandalous and people will pay attention for a few minutes.

But then, Inana was a real star and she wrote things down. Do other celebrities keep journals? Are they praying that they don't get out—or praying that they will, to revive stuttering careers with a little controversy? Dear little Anne Hathaway knows the invasive nature of her words being read by someone they were never intended for.

But then there are people like Anaïs Nin who intended for people to read their journals—they even revised and edited them. Hell, some people have only read Nin's journal, eschewing the novels she wrote about perfect fake characters to instead read about real people in her diary.

Did Inana self-edit, or let the truth speak for itself?

Good Catholic girls must not tell lies.

What kind of woman was Inana?

What kind of woman am I?

Most people think of Catherine the Great when they hear my name, but that's not where I got it. My parents had a thing for Catholic martyrs and saints and named me after Catherine of Alexandria. Born to a noble family, she found Christianity at a young age, as the people in the stories often do, through a dream where she was married to Jesus by Mary. To me, that reeks of teenage crush, but back then there weren't any demigods like One Direction or any Belieber groups to squee with.

She was very vocal about her conversions, and passionately converted others to the faith using logic and reason, to the point where she went to the Emperor Maxentius and insisted he stop persecuting Christians and personally convert as well. This went over slightly better than you'd imagine—initially.

Instead of immediately killing her, as they were wont to do back then, he predictably refused and locked her away, during which time he sent many pagan philosophers to try to convert her to paganism. Probably trying to make an example by getting her back on his team.

Maxentius underestimated Catherine's appeal, wit, and persuasiveness when it came to her faith, and she ended up converting an embarrassing amount of the pagans he sent to her. He had them killed. Back in those days, population control wasn't an issue—and we can all see why.

Anyway, eventually even the Empress herself got wind of this young woman and, intrigued by the things she'd heard, visited her in the cell.

You guessed it—Catherine converted the Empress, too, which went over even less favorably than her other conversions.

Maxentius had his wife, the Empress, put to death when she tried to intervene on Catherine's behalf and spare her life.

If I can't pray with you, nobody can!

Maxentius then decided to put Catherine to death on a torture wheel, but his plan was foiled by the supernatural. Apparently, Catherine Hulk-smashed it with her purity—at her touch, or an angel's, depending on the version you hear, the torture device shattered. And a few hundred pagans were killed as well, which seems to go completely sideways to Jesus's teachings, as miracles go. Catherine is one of the Fourteen Holy Helpers, and people still pray to her.

But, righteously pure or not, Catherine was eventually beheaded. There's still debate about whether or not she truly existed or was made up to help fill a virgin martyr quota, but the Church itself declared her story to be a legend, not fact. And yet, even as a legend, it still follows the rules women bow to under religious dogma.

Women in the Catholic Church only have two options: virgin or whore. Mary or Mary. Two sides of the same coin, even with the same name. Did they do that on purpose to tell us that it's all the same, really?

Catherine's feast day was removed from the calendar, then restored as optional, but she's still venerated by the Orthodox Church. And now there are fireworks called Catherine wheels. Because what better way to turn the frown of a martyr's life upside down than by creating bright bangs of ephemeral light to entertain the masses during celebrations? Her public tragedy becomes public entertainment to people who have no idea who she was or what those pretty swirling fireworks are called.

Beautiful, but macabre if you know Catherine's story.

It's said that when she died, angels flew her remains to Mount Sinai, and they're still with one of the world's oldest Catholic monasteries.

Obviously they aren't, since angels are just legends.

People still hotly debate the veracity of Jesus's existence, and yet that doesn't diminish his importance. What matters more: real teachings from a fake person that make people act better toward one another, or a real, awfully mistreated woman who died for no reason other than believing something different from others of her time?

So many people died for their faith over the years—and Christianity has a lot of blood on its hands as well; don't think I'm not pointing a giant finger at that machine. The Church doesn't do what it does out of the goodness of its heart—it's about numbers. Who's got more, who's got more money, who's mightier.

Because might still makes right.

These thoughts bounce around with me in the driver's seat of the car on the way back home, calculated to distract me from Inana's diary, but they fail.

Nothing takes my mind from the book. I imagine stripping naked and shrinking, crawling between the pages, nestling inside the half-closed cover, feeling the paper and ink across every inch of my body to absorb the words, the meaning of the words, the places her fingers touched when she wrote all of them down.

She was no more a whore than I am—was—the night after I

fucked a stranger in a mask, surrounded by a wall of flesh. When it's about experience, like Inana was going for, I think it transcends definitions of dirty or pure. Virgin or whore. Mary or Mary.

The only part of it that made me feel dirty was finding the money in my purse afterward, feeling that Bundy had taken an experience I wanted to have for myself and made it about gratifying someone else, turning me into Séverine. Belle de Jour by default. He took an intensely transformational experience and cheapened it by adding a qualifier: money.

Payment made it feel smaller than it was.

So no—I won't think of, can't think of, Inana as a whore, as less than someone on a journey of self-discovery, just because her medium is her body.

By the time I reach our apartment, I'm shaking and nearly feverish with the need to read the diary, clutching it to my chest and hurrying upstairs like a junkie with a fix, hoping Jack's not home early for once because if I can't wallow inside this right now I might explode.

No date. Just swirls of blue ink across the page, leading me one letter at a time on a journey I almost took myself on four years ago but suppressed. Desires I suppressed so I could save those close to me.

I flop onto the couch, curling my legs beneath myself, and read.

Hitting like a sharp, cold punch of an early snowstorm. Skin's still inside the sunlight, remembering that warmth, and it feels every flake on itself like the edges are serrated.

Knives of pain that radiate. Radiation that turns inward, transforming into pleasure.

I am transformed.

And yet, the same.

Truth isn't a revelation. Our reactions to it are. Our reactions are the world.

We make the world what it is through our reactions. We make more of it than what it is. We twist it to suit our purposes and the self-serving things we think we need to validate the things we think we shouldn't feel. Or like.

But we do.

Liking, licking, loving, loathing.

Living.

Some people think I should be repulsed by the things I've done and seen.

And I try to explain by giving them more, showing more, creating more, being more.

And most don't listen because they can't see.

Some don't wish to, actively closing themselves off to what's there. Shouting that they don't understand instead of listening.

But I say those people are the repulsive ones. What is repulsive? What is revulsion other than society's patriarchal norms clutching their pearls in terror that we'll find freedom inside the shackles of our choosing?

I want to feel everything.

If you're brave enough, life is easy.

I am easy.

I want to take myself further than I dreamed of going, soar to heights through the ceiling I didn't know was there.

I long to be astounded by the stretches of space between one limitation and the place I go next.

I want to be taken.

That which is freely given can never be stolen. It's impossible. Gifts are gifts are gifts.

The having and the taking are gifts.

Every breath is a gift.

Every gift comes with a price. Knowledge can't be unlearned. Self-knowledge can't be unlearned because lying to yourself is the hardest lie in the world to maintain and will poison you from within, spreading out like creeping mold, seeping into the rest of your mind like dye in a pool. Wet. Dark. Inescapable.

You get something, but something else is taken.

Knowledge for ignorance.

Something for nothing.

But things worth having are worth that exchange.

My heart is pounding in my chest reading the words of another woman who felt the way I felt.

The way I feel.

Deep, deep down, a ball of the things I pushed down and tried to forget about squirms free of its own shackles and spreads through my veins, humming inside me. Surging with every throb of my heart. In my head, my chest, between my legs.

I need more.

For a moment, I just run my hands over the lines of the page, feeling the indentations where she pressed the pen extra hard over certain words, taken over by passion, anger, righteousness, feeling them link us together over time and space, imagining her writing it, imagining her knowing someday I'd be the one with her book in my hands.

There's a picture of Inana lying on a white tiled floor, naked, hair held back from her face in a messy bun with wisps escaping above her ears and forehead, sweat dotting her brow and upper lip.

I sweat, too, when I see the contraption between her legs. It looks like a telescope mounted on a wide base with a dildo on it, half of which is buried inside Inana's pussy.

There's a handwritten caption beneath the photo.

I wanted to see what would wear out first. Human, or machine.

My lungs stutter.

I feel like I've seen this before.

Not something I could find online, no, definitely not. Not like the mechanical beasts that thrust and vibrate, making women burst into ecstasy, gushing with pleasure. This isn't the same, yet my fingers tremble when I search online for something that will match this, desperate to find more images, a video, anything more.

What would Inana be like with one of those machines?

This doesn't seem like staged, well-lit Internet porn. I search for keywords, maybe a gallery that might have showed a video performance. My mind must be cluttered, because all I can find are women vibrating and slithering like snakes, something that once simultaneously frightened me and turned me on. But compared to Inana, these women look like girls playing sexy. Inana radiates a more sensual awareness, as though she's had time to ripen and knows every inch of herself—and the things she could do to you.

The difference between a girl and a woman.

Knowledge. Experience. Wisdom.

Boundaries and limits that have been expanded again and again until the lines of possibility meet the line you should never cross. But maybe you can nudge it just a little farther away with your toe and become someone bigger than you ever thought you could be.

Frustrated to find nothing about the video of Inana, I look up the machine she's using to see the way it moves.

My pussy throbs in response to the slow—or fast—thrusts of the machine. I saw an oil rig once, and the slow, mesmerizing bobbing of the derrick was a lot like this. I'm sure there's a raging metaphor for the fossil fuel industry in there, but my wet panties are a serious distraction. The mechanical nature, the even thrusts of the dildo on the end of the contraption...Inana said she wanted to see which would wear out first. How long could a machine like that go for?

Hours? Days?

Being fucked and fucked, coming again and again, and it never ending?

How much pleasure can one person take? Did she eventually tap out and admit defeat, or, like Dorian Gray, did she break the machine? Did someone shout "Have you no shame?" at her if so? No, never. She kept this to herself, she wanted a secret. Maybe it was an unfinished project on a series related to stamina and pleasure.

I head to the couch and turn to the next page of the diary, apprehensive that it will reveal nothing.

The buildup becomes a refuge from the orgasms after a while. The aching need that makes you bear down hard, holding your breath and shaking toward God. The path is slippery and elusive. But today it's easy. Close your eyes and you're gone. Open them and you see your demise. Instead, the eyelashes become a filter for the ceaseless pumping. Sustenance, poison, darkness, bursts of light.

How long would pleasure stretch out with no other person, no fatigue to get in the way of our lust, our greed for pleasure? Forever? Would we all rut until we died, needing more, always more?

How long can I go on? How far would I go? Eight's as good as seven. Twelve is as good as twenty. What's one more hour when you've gone for seventeen?

The orgasm is as devastating as the asteroid hurtling toward Earth—it's just a more pleasurable way to die.

After the seventh hour I lost track of how many times I came. I no longer felt the pain in my lower back from writhing and grinding on the instrument of my demise. All I wanted was more. My name became Insatiable and I was the true devourer of worlds. We were made for this, made for fucking, for erasing the facts about ourselves. The things we think we know.

Take them all away, strip them from your bones. Become the pleasure you seek. I spit on myself. I imagine a Roman orgy, hands and bodies on mine. I imagine cuffs binding me so I have no choice but to receive pleasure. It was mind over matter.

After the twentieth hour, I imagined the machine could feel, too, and wanted more. I began moving my hips in ways that would feel good to it. I wanted to show off how steady I could be, too, match it thrust for thrust instead of lying there like a disappointment. It was a fat, stiff cock and I had to grip it tight. "Do you like when I bounce up and down for you, baby?" I started talking dirty to it, imagining that I made it come.

After the twenty-fourth hour, I forgot how to breathe. I popped a pill of Ecstasy to keep me steady. If the machine is artificial, I can incorporate something else man-made. After all, this is an experiment.

After the twenty-sixth, I forgot how to be.

After the twenty-eighth, I was reborn.

After the thirty-first, I knew the truth.

It lives in the insides of our eyelids when we're open enough to see.

I knew I could go longer. But I also knew the machine needed to serve its purpose. The machine needed to beat me, to fuck me into submission. But I'm a machine too, an extraordinary one, and no way was I giving up.

After the thirty-fifth hour, I lay still, taking instead of giving or responding. Passive as only a woman can be to see what the machine would give me.

More of the same. More and more and more. All the more I could bear and then some, but it needed me to direct it. Up, down, deeper, this angle, that. I had to make it make me come like a lover with the talent but not the direction. The potential without the skill.

I spent the next two hours actively fucking it. Coming three more times.

It overheated two hours after that. Woman versus Machine.

Woman on top. Woman on top with a voice hoarse from panting, but she still could talk.

And when I got home, I made myself come over and over again using nothing but my hands until I thought my fingers would break, until I passed out, as drooling and blissed-out as a drug addict. I slept for three days and dreamed the most surreal things that I'm still processing now, a week later.

Pleasure is a drug we all seek.

Bottle it. We're all addicts. Sell it. We're all dreamers trapped in nightmares. Give us something better and we'll buy our way into bankruptcy.

Fuck it all for as long as we can.

I did and I want it again.

Picturing the insatiable perfection of Inana, lying in bed after having come innumerable times and yet viciously finger-fucking herself, is too much.

I lay the diary on the floor and slide my hand beneath the waist of my jeans, not bothering to undo them. I can feel the wetness, waiting for me, waiting to be used, so I coat my fingers with it and slide it up, spreading it over my clit, feverishly working it across my skin.

How long could I take with the machine she broke?

How long would I last?

It's like the time in the mansion with Freddie and Dickie, and the masked man—DeVille, though I didn't know it then—but I push that

away as the sensate memories flood my body through the memories
the diary has unlocked.

*There's a wall of male flesh separating me from the rest of the room, as if
I'm cocooned. And I feel safe.*

*As some peel away, others take their place immediately. And I want that.
The more, the better.*

*I lose track of how many masked faces and anonymous cocks approach,
heads bowing as they move forward, begging for attention. I grab for everything
in my reach with everything that I've got and once I've got a taste I realize I'm
still hungry for more. The more I get, the hungrier I am, and it doesn't stop
until I want it to. And I don't.*

*The sex just keeps getting better and better and better. The orgasms get
more and more intense and just when I think I've reached the peak, another one
comes along that takes me even higher and I don't want it to stop, because the
pleasure is so intense.*

*It feels like my body is being jolted with electricity. Not just every time I
come. Every time I'm touched. Like I'm being hit with a taser, over and over
and over. I experience pleasure so intense it feels like pain. Dopamine floods
my brain, adrenaline courses through my body, and I lose track of time.*

*It feels like I'm fucking nonstop for twenty-four hours. And I figure if I
want to I could probably keep going for another twenty-four. My body would
keep going as long as my brain was stimulated. And here's the thing: The mind
never really gets tired from physical activity; it just gets distracted and bored.
That's when fatigue sets in. But if you can keep your mind focused, there's no
telling how far you can go.*

I move my hand faster.

How can you visualize what is limitless? Desire has no limit. If it
did, we would all be able to attain our desires and be entirely satisfied, but we can't and we'll never be able to.

My toes curl; already I'm racing toward release.

I've been there, Inana. I've been there, but with people instead of
a machine, a wall of bodies, of hands and mouths and cocks. Mine
were flesh, but I know how it feels to think you can go forever,

come forever, even though I never challenged myself the way she did. Bodies get tired, cocks ejaculate and go soft, pulling out and throwing off the rhythm. What would a machine be like, steady, steady, not caring what you wanted, only giving, giving, giving?

I slow down, closing my eyes and imagining the dildo pushing into me, imagining Inana watching me with those dark, soulful eyes, urging me to keep going, to make every stroke count. I slip my fingers down, shoving them inside as deep as I can to the rhythm of the machine in my mind. The cold, flawless rhythm of that machine made for pleasure.

I bite my lip and moan—so damn close.

But the machine doesn't know that and doesn't stop gently punishing my pussy with its motions.

"Cath?"

Jack's voice cuts through the haze, startling me away from my release, and I open my eyes to find him standing near my feet with a stunned look on his face. My lips part to speak.

SEVEN

‿ᴓᴓᴓᴓ‿

HE'S ON ME BEFORE I can get my hand out of my pants and he has me pinned to the couch before I even know what he's planning. His mouth presses hard against mine, kissing me hard and deep before I can squeak another word out.

His tongue strokes mine, plunging deep inside my mouth to take what he wants from me.

If I weren't already wet, this would have done it.

Jack—but hard Jack, alpha Jack, taking what he wants.

He slides a hand inside my shirt and up my belly. His nails dig into my skin on the way to my breast, and I gasp into his mouth. My right hand still trapped beneath his weight, pressing further into me, I use my left to frantically tear at his dress shirt to get to his sensitive nipples, pinching at them until he moans, too, the vibration playing on my lips like a song meant to be devoured.

Slowly, he rocks his hips into mine, pressing the back of my hand with his hard cock, and it drives me fucking crazy that I can't pull the fingers from my pussy so I can use my come as lubrication to stroke him hard and fast, but at the same time I want to drive them deeper inside myself, too. And he knows exactly what I want and is in complete control, overpowering me with his greater weight and my desire that's making me weak. My mouth waters for the taste of his come.

He uses his hips to move my hand, and it's so fucking erotic the way he's making me fuck myself, I shiver and moan his name. "What if I hadn't come home alone?" he asks.

With my free hand, I yank at his pants and underwear, and he shifts enough for me to slide them down over his ass, freeing his cock, ready for me, the tip glistening with pre-come. I slide my fingers out of my drenched pussy and grab him before he can deter me.

"If you hadn't come home alone? Who would you have brought?" I look him in the eye and slide my slick fingers up and down, and he groans.

"Maybe someone from the office. Someone new. Someone easily shocked."

I squeeze a little harder. "Yeah? Maybe she would only be pretending to be shocked because she likes it and didn't think you'd be into that."

"Into what?" he pants.

I picture him walking in with Inana, and my nipples ache. "Watching me finish. Watching you finish me. Or maybe even you watching me and her." I bite my lip and smile at the way his breath catches.

"Is that what you want?"

"I want this cock."

"Where do you want it?" He sucks just underneath my ear, hips rocking against mine, making me wish I had more than one pussy so Jack could make them all feel good.

"I want to lie here while you fuck my mouth," I say, leaning back.

He pulls my jeans down my legs, discarding them along with my panties, and then he gets up and crawls over my body until his balls are above my chin. I lick up the seam, leaving a trail of saliva. He pulls back and nudges the tip of his cock against my lips, coating them in his salty, tangy taste, which I lovingly lick away when he pulls back.

But it makes me think what could have happened if Jack *had* brought a friend back home unexpectedly, a stranger, someone I hadn't met yet. Someone adventurous—though it would have been more likely for his friend to be a man. God, I nearly purr at the thought of it, of Jack ordering me to my knees to suck his friend off.

I slide a hand along his shaft, squeezing near the root, and I pull his cock down toward my mouth, shifting up a little on the armrest to get my mouth at a better angle.

Jack's hands would shake as he undid his own pants and gripped his cock, jerking himself off while watching me suck his friend's cock, making another man feel good.

I swirl my tongue around the little hole, delicately, barely touching it, but his hips give a little jump anyways. It's only been a few days since we've fucked, but it feels like longer. I can never get enough of Jack. My breasts are swollen and ache with need. I cover my lips with spit and slowly close them around the head, tight, and take him into me, licking back and forth along the bottom of the shaft with quick, light motions, watching his eyes darken with desire. He pushes a little deeper, advancing along my tongue. Then withdraws.

Maybe he'd pull me up from my knees, pull my ass in the air while still sucking his friend's cock, and take me from behind, each thrust pushing the foreign cock further down my throat.

I like that.

"You like my cock in your mouth like that?" I lick all around the shaft, caressing his balls with my hand, focusing on one and then the other. I move to the base of his cock and work my way up like I'm taking slow licks of a melting ice cream cone until I get to the tip. And I lick all around it and put it inside my mouth. "Mm-hmm," I moan, knowing the vibration will make it feel even better.

He groans.

I want to feel my heart pound in surprise by being overwhelmed by him, by his cock filling my mouth so deep I can barely breathe. Today, I don't want to give pleasure to Jack.

I want him to take it from me.

I open wider, drawing his cock into me slowly, stroking the underside back and forth with my flattened tongue as it slips past my lips. I can feel myself getting wetter.

I take him deeper, and then withdraw, then deeper, then withdraw again when I feel his hips give an impatient hitch wanting more. His hands grab my hair, lightly fisting it.

I gag with a smile as his cock nudges the back of my throat.

I look up into his eyes, trying to smile with them so he knows it's good for me, and I bob my mouth up and down on his penis, loving the feeling of it filling my mouth.

I want more.

I feel his hands tighten their grip on my hair, sending little sharp zings of pain across my scalp, and I suck harder when he holds my head in place and begins to fuck my mouth.

I want him to come in thick bursts of sweet tanginess that fill my mouth as he unloads, but I want him inside me, too, pounding my pussy. I want him to be in me when he comes so that later I can stand and feel it drip down my legs and dry on my thighs.

He slips his hands down my face and slowly pulls out of me. I nod and spread my legs and he takes a few steps back toward my feet, settling between my thighs.

I watch as he takes his cock in his hands, his perfect cock, and guides it towards my pussy, then slides the head up and down a few times, coating himself, making his cock slick with my juices. I'm writhing now, desperate for him to shove into me, to slam home and fill me in a way my fingers can't.

He pushes in, just the tip, and smiles, knowing how torturous this is for me, but patiently teasing me. God, I love this man. He probes around the hole with a finger, spreading the wetness up to my clit, swollen with need, using fast, light flicks to torture me more, pulling back when I try to push against his hand.

"Jack, please," I say, the words a strangled moan.

"Do you know how sexy that was, walking in to see you like that on our couch?" With a smile, he pushes into me, slowly, his cock deliciously stretching my hole while his fingers graze my clit.

I shake my head. "Tell me," I gasp. *Take me, fuck me, use me.*

"I watched you for a minute. You had no idea I was there," he says, teasing me by sliding in a little more. "If I'd brought a friend back she'd have seen you rubbing that pretty pussy." His dirty talk surprises me—he's improved, but this is a new one. If there's anything that would drive him mad, it's the thought of me being with another person. "She'd have seen you at your sexiest and joined in with me. We'd all be naked and fucking right now instead of just you and me." When his lips utter these words, my entire body shivers down to my toes. He presses all the way in, his hard cock stretching against the soft walls of my pelvis, and he holds it right there, letting me feel how full he makes me, but he never stops rubbing my clit with his slick fingers.

I can feel my orgasm surging, building up inside. He shifts his weight and I can feel his cock move inside me and I'm going to come so fucking fast and I tell him that.

"I want to feel you come on my cock," he says, staring deep into my eyes.

I nod, licking my upper lip, tasting the saltiness of the thin sheen of sweat forming there and also him, still lingering in my mouth.

I'm going to come.

"I know," he says, and I must have said the words aloud again, but it's crashing over me in waves now.

Jack.

I'm coming, Jack.

So good.

I shudder and my hips buck and Jack grits his teeth and groans as my pussy tightens its grip on his cock, and I feel my limbs shake with the ache, with the release, but we're not finished yet.

Jack's still hard and inside me and starts thrusting hard, perfect stabs of pleasure radiating deeper than the clitoral stimulation did.

But the idea of Jack buried balls-deep in my cunt is almost as good as the actuality, and I stare down at it between us, watching it go in and out, my juices flowing harder, drenching my thighs and his balls as they slap against me.

I want to drown in the come we make together, feel it coat us like massage oil as we slide across each other's skin, because making love happens with every inch of our bodies, not just between our legs. Slathering each other with come. Modern art. Modern fucking art.

I grab his ass and grind my hips, wanting him to come so hard he can't see so that I'm the first and only thing he sees when he gets his vision back.

He growls deep in his chest, so male and turned on that I feel another orgasm unwinding my spine from within, and as he pounds harder, faster, deeper, it's torn from me like my mind's coming loose from my body, and I scream his name, shuddering around his cock.

A moment later I feel his cock twitch inside me, filling me with his hot come in thick spurts. His hot breath puffs against my neck when he pulls me closer and squeezes me tenderly, possessing me more with that simple gesture than with anything else.

I'm snuggled up next to Jack in bed, listening to his steady breathing, but I can't sleep. The diary's burning a hole in my mind, but I don't want to lose myself inside it right now. Some part of me wants to prove that I'm not obsessed with Inana yet, that I can take a break from the diary, so I slip from Jack's arms and pad into the living room to pop in a DVD.

L'Avventura. It's been niggling at the back of my mind for days, and I can no longer put it off.

For a while, I drift inside the visuals of the coast, the sea, the rocks. Everything seems more dangerous, but also more beautiful. I always rooted for Claudia. Monica Vitti was always a favorite of mine, and I couldn't help but want her to find a goddamn happy ending, though those aren't ensured or expected in serious films that mirror life.

Things rarely end up with neat bows.

Sandro tells Anna that words create misunderstandings and wasn't it enough that he cares for her?

Guess the Five Love Languages weren't popular back then.

He's got a point. Even now, couples continue to put arbitrary parameters on their definitions of love and relationships. Is monogamy natural?

No.

We're part of nature as well, and it goes against our biology—as well as our physiology—especially when it comes to reproducing. Men are hardwired to spread their sperm far and wide to impregnate as many females as possible to ensure that their genes are the ones to survive. Women are hardwired to want a mate who is bigger and stronger than the rest, hence why so many are attracted to the bad boy or the asshole—it screams back to the time of our ancestors, when those were the ones we thought could protect us and our future progeny from the very real dangers we faced.

Social monogamy is real, but oftentimes the children of supposedly monogamous couples aren't really the offspring of both partners.

The ladies looked elsewhere.

We're living in an artificial world. If we eschewed all of the things that aren't natural—air travel, makeup, synthetic fibers, spray cheese—our lives would be reduced to that of a granola cruncher living in a yurt in Tibet.

Monogamy can work, but it's a choice. We have to define for ourselves and our partner what it is we want from a given relationship, and then honor those definitions.

And yet, Claudia and Sandro were pretty eager to get together the moment Anna was out of the picture.

But it's not like she left. Or did she? The way it's written, we don't know if Anna ran off or was taken. If she's dead or alive. But that's not even the important thing. We're not meant to care about Anna—we're meant to care about Claudia.

It feels more like a Hitchcockian device that we're meant to believe, and as soon as we do buy into that idea, something bad will happen. I became protective of other people's truths, but was I really protecting them, or serving myself? Everything I do brings me closer to Anna. If I had continued searching I would have tarnished myself and brought everyone's private predilections into the public eye. Most of us chose selfishness over selflessness.

I turn the movie off, feeling tainted by my own past, and pick up Inana's diary again.

Here is another woman who burned like a meteor. She was never destined to be ordinary or to fit into society as a drone working from nine to five. I'm unable to reconcile the act of suicide with the woman in the pages of the diary, but maybe that's because she reminds me of myself. The similarities between what Inana wants and what I want give me a mild jolt.

I need to get inside the woman's head a little more. The best way to know her is to be her. In doing so, maybe I can know myself in a safe way, an acceptable way.

There's a quote underlined several times inside the diary. "I must explain this to her. If she loves me well enough she will understand. All things are possible in love. I will explain to her that I possess her at will without the loathsome absurdities of sex."

I search for the quote online and find it's from a book, *Fantazius Mallare: A Mysterious Oath*. The title reminds me a little of the infamous *Witch Hunter's Bible*, but I go back to the quote, reading it twice more.

Are all things possible in love? If someone loves you well enough, does that person truly understand? What if the things you want are slightly outside his or her realm of comfort or understanding?

Inana had fans, and yet a lot of them—as well as some friends— abandoned her when they learned about the new mission of her life. How is that friendship, love? Love is patient, love is kind. Love doesn't judge you when you embark on a public journey into BDSM and sexual expression and document it. Was her image so set as a muse, a representation of fashion houses, that they didn't want to lose the power she brought and gave?

Everyone's so goddamn ready to crucify each other, you'd think we lived two thousand years ago.

T Swizzle jumps from country to pop, most likely to launch that album even bigger, and some people scream that she's selling out. I think maybe she just got tired of being inside a big old sequined country box. But sometimes growing the way we want to, instead of the way someone else wants us to, seems like a crime.

The memory of Jack's horrified face flashes to mind, a memory I'd suppressed. He didn't understand when I wanted him to go further. To be wild with me.

To hurt me.

It turned him on to think of being with me and someone else, but when it's just him and me, he holds back—even when I beg him not to. There's no way he'd actually participate in a threesome with me—especially with another man. He's too straight-laced for that, and that's fine…for him.

I'm Inana without the journey—or rather, I put a foot through the threshold, then tried to take it all back and pretend I never did it. Pretend it didn't change me on a fundamental level. But knowledge acquired cannot be undone. And so, while living with Jack, seem-ingly content with the quiet domesticity of our lives, there is still something churning inside me: unanswered questions that trouble me, an ache to further my sexual experimentation and needs.

Simply admitting that to myself feels like a festering boil has been lanced, and some of the pressure is eased. I'm torn between the two versions of myself, the one that I am and the one that I could be. I adore Jack, crave the security and stability our relationship provides, and have made a conscious attempt to suppress my sexual desires for the sake of maintaining our connection and some kind of normalcy. Christ, his face when I asked him to hit me. I'll never ask him for something like that again.

I couldn't risk him misunderstanding, shrinking away again. I feel his love in words and caresses, but I want to be caressed and longed for the way Sandro looks at Claudia.

But at the same time, I still have the same feverish, hypersexual recurring dreams—a part of myself I can't deny.

It's not the same dream anymore; it has shifted to a point in the future, to a place inside myself that I don't recognize, to sexual scenarios that are darker and more intense—and that scare me, if I'm honest.

I dream I'm there again, and things make a certain stark sense. There's a perfect moment when you're on your knees in front of someone who can destroy a life, a business, a country without a regret, and the things you're doing with your mouth can make them forget how to breathe. Your roaming tongue stills theirs.

I'm talking about power. Real power.

Four years ago, if you'd told me I'd be masturbating in public, I'd have looked scandalized along with the other pretty pearl-clutchers.

But unlike them, I'd have had an interest that burned the inside of my skin, making me blush for a different reason. I'd have been dripping at the thought of doing something so audacious. So free. It's not that I was ashamed of my desires, even then. It's more that I thought I *should* have been, and that I was a little broken inside because shame flitted just beyond my fingertips.

I've been wet in public before, cold arousal lying against my crotch from panties I'd soaked earlier kissing Jack goodbye before running errands. Even better were the times we'd fucked and then I'd go out and his come would seep from my pussy, slicking my panties.

But the inappropriate thoughts coursing through my veins always made my "shouldn't"s rear up in outrage.

I shouldn't go grocery shopping before changing clothes.

I shouldn't like the heaviness of the damp fabric between my legs.

I shouldn't smile at the men who leered.

I shouldn't imagine how easy it would be for a stranger to glide up behind me, lift up my skirt and slide inside my pussy, using the wetness he had nothing to do with creating, to fuck me over the pork chops where anyone could see—not that he'd get the pork reference.

A stranger using Jack's come as lube to fuck me in public.

In my dreams, I'd shed so many goddamn shouldn'ts, like a snake rubbing against a rock to rid itself of too-tight skin, that I glowed. I was sleeker, faster, tighter.

Happier.

Making love doesn't do that. *Fucking* does. Anyone who tells you sex is only physical is doing it wrong.

In real life, I can't help but feel as though I've sort of…dulled. Now, sitting on our couch, remembering how it felt to be overwhelmed by possibilities, I shiver with dark delight and continue rhythmically squeezing my thighs together, muscles rippling over my clit.

Look, Ma, no hands.

Everyone's wound tightly these days, twisting themselves up into Gordian knots to protect themselves or to convince themselves that they're more complicated than they really are. Deep down, we're pretty fucking simple. We all just want the same thing at the end of the day:

More.

Maybe I can't have more of it without jeopardizing what Jack and I have built, are building.

But Jack's going away on a trip with DeVille for a week, which means I have one week to immerse myself in Inana's life and try to feel the things she felt. To dive in before shaking the droplets of interest from my skin like a wet dog.

And then I'll let it go.

EIGHT

NEVADA.

When most people think of Nevada, certain things come to mind. Sin City, twinkling in the desert like a sparkly tumor, malignant with its hunger to take all you've got. Sure, it's hungry, but it's like a cockroach, it's going to outlast us all because of its innate resilience—because nothing should be sustainable in such a harsh environment. If the water dried up for good, how long would it last?

And yet the show goes on decades after its prime, only now slathered in bronzer, with a few extra pounds changing the silhouette of its sequined jumpsuit into something the girls don't scream over anymore, but that people will still overpay to see.

Some cities in America are designed to trap as many tourists as they can, shamelessly, unapologetically, effectively. But some take care of their marks better than others, recognizing the symbiosis needed to survive, so they protect their livelihoods. I've only gone to Vegas once—and that was enough for me. I saw a few concerts, lost some money, and fucked Jack in a fancy hotel with windows that didn't open.

The whole place felt like it was starving. You walk down the strip trying to dodge the barkers who try to herd you into their place, handing you seventeen hundred flyers you don't want. You don't want to look like a tourist, but the place is designed to be overwhelming, bombarding the senses into going along with whatever they're trying to sell you. The glittering lies are there to entertain you and cover up the ugly truth: The sequins hide the flaws like a past-her-prime stripper coating her stretch marks with extra body glitter.

No eye contact is best.

But even dining out is brutal if you don't go to five-star fancy places. Buffets rule the world there to take the sting out of the cost of everything else. Who the fuck ever needs that much food? And yet I'm sure people would have gladly moved their chairs directly to the buffet tables and devoured until they made themselves sick, trying to make up for their losses at the craps table.

Balance doesn't work that way. Some losses can't be equaled in free breakfast sausages, but people are damn sure going to try.

It revolted me after a short amount of time.

I drive through it now, trying to see the beauty of the place, and the lights are pretty, but remind me of those predators that lurk in the depths of the ocean, using their shiny bioluminescence to lure in their prey. The prey gets a show, the predator gets a free dinner. It's malevolent in the most beautiful way. It's nature at her most gorgeously savage. Innovative.

Inana moved here about a year and a half before she died, and while she lived with a showgirl kind of quality, I can't see her loving it for long. She was all about truth and limits, and I don't think she'd have been able to get past the rot beneath the slick paint job.

The sheer opportunity for decadence was probably what lured Inana here in the first place. In places like this you can get away with more because it's expected. Locals play up legends and myths, dressing bigger, better, bolder for the tourists—the ones trying to scam you do, anyway.

The ones trying to make a buck aren't the only ones who make wildness possible. Because of the tourism, because of the number of people moving there to try to make it big in show business, you've got a huge rotating population. Other cities, too. LA, New York, and New Orleans have this transience to them that can make every day feel new—and also temporary, like things won't last.

That's as good or bad as you make it. Vegas has a short memory and lets you be as freaky as you want to be in ways you couldn't get away with in other cities. It can take you in and suck the marrow from your bones, leaving you haggard and disillusioned before your time. Cities like that won't remember your name, but they'll remember your flavor—has-been, never-was, model-actress, hooker-waitress. You taste just like the pretty little things it devoured yesterday.

But there's something worse lurking in Nevada than past-their-prime performers and predatory pushers. Harder than the city itself that fucks you without remembering your name. Something no one's talking about.

Asbestos.

Once used for soundproofing and insulation, among other things, we abandoned it and banned it when we realized it was literally killing people who breathed it in. But, you know—slowly. Anyway, it's dangerous as hell.

What's this got to do with Nevada? Turns out, the whole place is lousy with naturally occurring asbestos, blowing in the wind like malignant dandelion fluff.

It's not a secret; scientists have been trying to raise awareness about this for years, to the incredible resistance of the government. Tourism is their gravy. How many people would still flock there every day if they knew they were breathing in fibers that could potentially irritate their lungs into mesothelioma in a decade or two? It wouldn't kill the tourism industry—pun intended—but it could hurt it.

And in today's economy, you're damn right any news that could potentially harm income is immediately downplayed as much as possible. And the government gets away with ignoring it by falling back on the standard "More tests are needed," which is basically its version of the entertainment industry's "The check's in the mail."

Maybe it's easier to ignore because it's naturally occurring instead of an evil corporation doing the screwing—you can't sue Earth, even though our planet is constantly trying to kill us.

Earthquakes, floods, fires, tsunamis, volcanoes. It's a thrill a minute on good old planet Earth.

But here I am, flying down the road in my car with the windows down, breathing in the early evening air anyway. Knowledge is power, but becoming paranoid about the things that could kill us is ridiculous. We're dying from the first breath we take when the doctor slaps our ass anyway. I crank the radio and sing along obnoxiously loudly with the music, feeling strangely optimistic about things, like I've driven across the border into another life.

In a way, I have.

According to what I found online, when she first came to Vegas, Inana moved into a little apartment near the Strip, eager to immerse herself in the bustle of the place to research a mysterious project that I can't find any information on, needing to feel the pulse of Sin City. Yet less than a year later she moved to a bungalow a little ways outside of the city limits.

Her sister gave me the key, and her blessing to explore as much as I wanted.

I should feel guilty about the gratification I feel at being granted access to her place, should feel shame, like a stalker who gets *carte blanche* access to his victim's underwear drawer, but I don't. Satisfaction coats me like a second skin, and for the first time in a few days I feel like I'm close to something important.

Something voyeuristic, but cathartic.

Inana's bungalow sprawls alone on the left side of the road, a pale collection of modern right angles mixed with rustic, blocky fencing made of rough-hewn logs. There's no overgrowth blocking the way to the door—we're in the desert. Come, go, stay, it doesn't care and isn't going to try to cover up your presence. All that happens is that the wind blows more sand over any traces of life.

No tire tracks or footprints in the short driveway.

Lola says she hasn't been able to make herself come back here since Inana was found inside. Can't say I blame her. Maybe she should have sold the place and been rid of it, but perhaps it's a last connection to her sister. Even though it's empty except for bad memories, it's a connection. It's somewhere that Inana walked through, ate in, sat looking out the windows, touched things. If she sold it, what else would be left?

We never know what we'd do until we're faced with those decisions ourselves.

The door is heavy and shut tight, but I push it open and flick on the light, surprised to see a fine layer of sandy dust covering everything, muting the colors of the furniture and floors. I half expect to see an old woman in a ruined wedding dress waiting for her errant lover—or revenge—but it's as silent as a grave.

No carpet to absorb the dust, so the tiled floor is dull underfoot, and my boots leave faint footprints. The walls are a light buttery yellow, bringing a warmth to the dull emptiness, but I expected something more vibrant for Inana.

Then again, she herself would have been the brightest thing in any room she was in, no matter the décor. I guess she didn't want to compete with the furniture.

I wouldn't say it's in shambles, but it's obviously fallen into a state of neglect. Lola said I was welcome to stay here, but it needs some cleaning before that can happen.

People live differently in their houses. Some treat their place like storage, packing every spare room and drawer with things, occupying the space but not really living in it. With them it always feels like they're not unpacked, not staying.

Others use it like a rock band in a hotel room, wearing things out at an alarming rate—living in the space but not loving it or treating it as permanent. It's amazing how badly people will treat a space they don't have to clean.

Houses that are treated like homes feel different, smell different.

Despite the dirt and neglect, Inana's home is the latter. She lived and loved here. I want to see it the way she saw it when she was still living here, so I head for the kitchen and, sure enough, under the sink I find cleaning supplies. I get to work dusting every surface, cleaning the grime from windows. I tug the area rug from beneath the couch and hang it over the railing on the front porch to air out. Heading back inside, I sweep the dust from the corners of the floor.

I find a vacuum and set to cleaning the couch and two chairs in the dining nook.

Did Inana do this herself, or, like most stars, did she have someone in to clean? It's a little bit of a drive to get out here, but it's not like she couldn't have afforded it.

An hour or two later I've made it decent, and admire the subtle charm of the place now that it's restored. I wander to the window in the living room, trailing my fingertips over the sill, imagining Inana doing this years ago. I'm touching the place she probably touched. But she died here, too, I realize with a start, rifling in my purse for my phone to look at the police reports about Inana—when she was found.

No stain marks the place on the floor where her bright star faded to black, full of pills with her wrists cut—insurance in case the pills weren't enough to do the job, I guess. I sit on the couch, staring down at that blank space where she breathed her last breath. How did she feel at the end? Did regret seep into her consciousness, or did she look forward to whatever was next, no matter what it was, with the same lustful curiosity she had for everything else she tried?

I can't wrap my mind around her doing this. Ending things.

Macabre, maybe, but I get to my knees and lie down in the spot where Inana was found. Her heart stopped here.

Her life as we know it ended.

Why?

Is her sister right that she was murdered? But even if Inana did kill herself, that doesn't mean it was anything more than an accidental overdose. Except for the wrists, whoever did it and however, it wasn't an accident.

A small town's worth of people have jumped from the Golden Gate Bridge to their deaths. But did you know that almost thirty people have jumped—and survived? The common thread through all of their stories was that in that brief time between when their feet left the bridge and when they hit the water, they realized that all the things they'd thought were insurmountable—all the problems they hadn't seen a way out of—became nothing. Trivial, infinitely solvable. Except for one.

The fact that they'd just jumped off a fucking bridge.

Some prayed for God to save them and give them another chance. Others didn't have time.

What did they do with their lives after the "miracle"? That would make a good story.

Then again, worth is a relative concept as well. If someone gave up a high-flying job to become a turnip farmer in Arkansas because it made her happy, other people might think she was fucking loopy.

Happiness is relative as well.

Did Inana have a moment after the pills, after the cuts, where she regretted the choice to do it and would have given anything to take it back? Or by then had the narcotics turned her brain waves to something syrupy and slow, made her not care at all, made dying another adventure to be experienced?

What a waste. My heart aches for them all, and the sudden need to connect with Jack, tell him how much he means to me, presses close, surrounding me, and I pull out my phone and call him.

"Hello?"

I smile at the sound of his voice. "I love you, Jack."

"You got there safely."

"I did. It's such an isolated place for someone like her." I've given Jack a very stripped-down version of my story about Inana. He seemed a little less than excited about it, but he was going on the road with Bob anyway. It's not like we'd have been together at home if I hadn't decided to do this.

"Some people like the quiet."

"I guess so. How are you?"

A woman's voice murmurs in the background. Jack clears his throat. "Listen, Cath, I've got to go. Bob's giving an interview and I need to help prep him. Talk to you soon."

Annoyance at competing with Bob makes me hesitate and take two deep breaths before telling Jack I love him, but he's already hung up. I exhale frustration. Is it too much to ask for a little enthusiasm about what I'm trying to do? Maybe it's not as important to Jack, but it matters to me. That should make it matter to him too, right?

Maybe this story is as big as Jack's campaign. I just need to focus. I turn my head, my eyes landing on Inana's bookshelf across the room. It's only one shelf, nine small squares of equal size, but the books seem well-used. Some people keep books to be pretentious, hoarding trendy bestsellers—thanks, Oprah—and classics that they'll never crack the spines of. Rarely will you come across a true bibliophile who loves books the way most people love their children, and they'll hang onto first editions or favorites signed by authors they admire.

In today's age of digital everything, where we can download entire libraries to our phones, the physical books people keep mean something. Hundreds of years ago, people used to press flowers between the pages of books, flowers that were given to them by gentle suitors with good intentions and manners. Back when volumes were spoken based on types of flowers, colors.

I prefer the plain language of today, where we women are allowed to make our feelings known as well.

There's an unassuming black volume that I nearly don't notice, but the title grips me.

Fantazius Mallare: A Mysterious Oath by Ben Hecht.

The book Inana referenced in her diary.

I grab it and flee back to the couch, anxiously flipping through it to find the quote.

"I must explain this to her. If she loves me well enough she will understand. All things are possible in love. I will explain to her that I possess her at will without the loathsome absurdities of sex."

What did Inana find relevant enough about this quote to scrawl it in her diary and underline it three times? The quote itself suggests love not held to the strictures of physicality, but not selfless, either. Is it more about the mind? Sexy, complete dominance and ownership of someone even when sex isn't part of the equation? What are the "loathsome absurdities" of sex?

Sex itself can be hilarious when you stop to break down any part of it, but I don't think that's what he means. Is it that sex isn't enough? The way people attach other attributes and emotions, commitment and meaning, bondage of emotion, to something as simple as fucking. No one looks glamorous with a cock in her mouth, but it's not about how it looks.

It's about how it feels.

Maybe that's what resonated with Inana. She never gave a shit about what her journey looked like to others. It was about how it felt to her. Inana was using her body instead of words, but who speaks her language? Not many people, sadly.

I've got the rudimentary bits down, but I'm not fluent. Still, I speak enough to know she was onto something.

What she did, what she showed, made me feel something. Maybe that's all that she wanted.

Maybe that's enough.

But I need to know for sure. I need to know her thoughts, her angles. I need to see the things she did.

I find the quote on pages 71 and 72.

But there's also an address and the words *La Notte*.

I search for those online, and I'm somehow not surprised when absolutely nothing turns up.

Was this a favorite spot of Inana's? It's not late, 9:38 p.m., so I text Inana's sister, asking if she knows anything about La Notte and Inana's connection to it.

Her reply sets off a plan.

La Notte is where Inana worked for six months before she disappeared. It's a hotel.

And it's where I'm going to go tomorrow morning.

NINE

∽oℳℳℳ∽

REMEMBER WHAT I SAID ABOUT some hotels working on the same principle as testing military strategies? A means of making mistakes so they don't get made in the real world?

That's what this hotel is, too—the one I've come to, seeking answers. This was a model that was never intended to reach the market. It's a place designed to enable indiscretions that need to be hidden from the real world, appetites and perversions that need to be kept under wraps. A place for people who have something to lose.

How much? Inana lost everything.

There are no higher stakes than that.

I turn down a dirt road, following it through a little valley, and as I go around a turn, it comes into sight.

La Notte is a towering black monolith in the red desert, and it's intimidating even from a distance, the structure arcing slightly so that it appears sleek and graceful instead of boxy. Dangerous the way a crouching panther is before it pounces. Its darkness reflects back the panoramic sunrise, blinding me with everything I'm not looking at while I stare at the hotel itself.

The Burj Al Arab Jumeirah hotel in Dubai has got nothing on La Notte.

I pull into visitor parking, though nothing is labeled. Everything here is anonymous, I guess, which won't aid my snooping around, but it won't hinder it, either.

It wouldn't be the first time I've had to bend the rules a little for a story, but I wasn't expecting anything on this scale.

You hear "hotel" near Vegas and picture something way smaller, tackier, grimier than this. That aging showgirl, still flashy, but past her prime.

But my heels click on impeccably clean Italian marble stairs, and there's not a single crack in the flawless façade of the building. The doorman opens the door for me and I stride inside.

The lobby smells like wealth. You know what I mean. There's that certain indefinable yet undeniable scent that screams it.

Boutique designer shops in Milan—the ones where nothing has a price tag, because even when you're buying things, talking about money and prices is gauche.

The inside of a crocodile Birkin.

The inside of a Maybach Exelero.

The powder worn by some women whose great-grandparents were born with trust funds. The scent of never having worked a day in your life.

The aroma of entitlement. Class.

This lobby gleams with cleanliness, but you could stop by every hour on the hour and not catch anyone cleaning, because that defies the illusion of perfection—and there's no reek of vinegar on the windows here, just the elegant breeze of gently circulating air. They probably use the same air filters that hospitals do, the filters that keep the smell of death nonexistent.

Doors are closed, and the few windows are covered with heavy curtains.

No sneaky peeks to catch a glimpse of the Wizard here.

Lola told me that Inana was a VIP concierge here, which would have given her unfettered access to guest information and the hotel itself. It's a strange juxtaposition in secrecy and PR. The concierge is the one who is basically the face of the hotel, the one everyone sees, the one you're supposed to feel confident can grant all your requests, so she must be professional, competent, and appealing—someone you feel like you can trust.

But she's also the one in on the secrets. As VIP concierge, Inana would have been making things happen for celebrities and other high-profile clients. A supposedly sober rock star wants a bottle? She'd have been the one bringing it—or making sure it was sent by someone who was trusted. A married actress tells you she's got a "friend" coming by in the middle of the night? You shut your mouth and arrange the cab of shame when he leaves at three in the morning reeking of sex.

The VIP is a seller of security, the one who makes illicit dreams come true like a fucking genie without the lamp—because celebrities are what keep these places going. You're the face in the light when things go wrong, and you're the fleeting shadow at the bottom of the door, making sure things are going as smoothly as possible. Oh, concierges are never supposed to allow or facilitate anything illicit or illegal.

But celebrities don't color within the same lines as the rest of us. They have crayons in shades we've never heard of.

If a real celebrity takes a piss in your restaurant, you can capitalize on that for the next ten years. Even if no one else ever stays for a meal, you'll get tourists—or locals, celeb hunting.

But this place is different by its very nature.

Something tells me they don't give a shit about Yelp reviews or the general public. And for a business driven by tourism? That's hinky as shit. The clientele must be invited.

I skirt the front desk at the other side of the lobby, heading down a passage going off to the left. The hallways are long and well-lit without being harsh, but there's no activity, no small groups of people I can trail behind to gain access to an event or a bar. I stick out like the proverbial sore thumb as much as if I were wearing a damn trench coat and aviators.

But I manage to keep my cool when a slim young man, wearing a suit that subtly mirrors the hotel's black-and-gold décor, taps my shoulder. "Can I help you?"

"Are you the manager?" I ask, glancing at his chest for a name tag, but there isn't one. Not because guests will forget his name, but because it doesn't matter what his name is, who he is. What he does is all that matters to the people who stay here.

He frowns. "Are you here to apply for the position?"

"Yes." The word slips out in my breath of relief. This is my in.

"Follow me." He leads me back the way I came (disappointingly), behind the desk into a little office. Was this Inana's office? Did she spend a lot of time back here? "Have a seat."

I take the chair across from him. The concierge's office is roomy, but there are no windows. No prying eyes, except for a small security camera in a corner by the ceiling. I pretend not to see it, instead focusing on the painting on the wall. I know it's worth more than my car, or myself—and it's not a print.

"I'll take your resume now." I hesitate, and his brow furrows.

"I didn't bring one."

"You—"

"I'm sorry, but I can always e-mail it over later. See, it's been my experience that ninety percent of any job isn't about what's on paper. It's what happens when you're dealing with people. It's what happens when you have to think on your toes because things start going wrong and you're the only one who can fix them. Reading my work history will be impressive, but not as practical as if you see me in action."

"What's your name?"

I tell him, and he types it into the computer, likely doing a search on me. Learning that I'm a reporter will be a strike against me in a place that runs on confidentiality, but maybe that works in my favor, too—journalists know how to keep our mouths shut to protect our sources. Plus, I'm here. Knowing how to get here is half the battle. I hope I can bluff my way through the rest.

The phone on the desk next to him rings, and he holds a finger up for me to wait. His side is mostly murmurs of assent and exhalations, but a conversation seems to take place. He hasn't smiled or relaxed much, which isn't a good sign. Somehow, I've already managed to make a negative impression.

I mean, I'm not really trying to get the job, but it's the principle of the thing. Inana worked here. I want to know I could work here. And if I could work at her old job even for a day, that would provide invaluable insight into her life and a few more of the people in it.

Suddenly, nothing feels more important than getting this job.

My interviewer is good at communicating a lot while saying very little, but I use the opportunity to look around the room, feigning a casual demeanor.

As offices go, it's pretty standard, but I wouldn't mind a few minutes alone with the contents of the desk, or the computer that's in sleep mode right now with a screensaver of a black-and-gold logo turning slowly over and over. The desk, bookshelf, and cabinets are all a dark rosewood, or maybe mahogany. Like the rest of the hotel, there's not a speck of dust or a smear in sight, but this room smells vaguely of roses, and something citrusy but delicate—mandarin?

He hangs up, appraising me with his hazel eyes, his gaze lingering on my shoes—which I suddenly wish were fancier, but fuck that. I square my shoulders and stare him down, not giving a fuck about my clothes. Maybe a little princess could prance in here looking plastic and shinier than me and match the scenery better, but I've got skills he doesn't know about.

And tenacity to spare.

"And have you ever worked in a hotel, Catherine?"

"I've never worked in a hotel, but..." I trail off, taking him in, wondering how best to play this. I can't tell if his accent is the byproduct of having been born somewhere in Europe and moving to the United States when he was young, or if it's just a pretentious affectation, but either way, he's obviously got a modicum of power and takes his job seriously. I keep my expression sincere but serious. "I want to work for the best. I was told this was it." I shrug. "You won't find anyone more hardworking than me."

He squints. "You've never worked in this industry before?"

I shake my head. "No. But I know people. I've been around the political scene enough to be of use in the hotel industry."

"How does that translate to here?" he asks.

I smile. "I know how to keep my mouth shut, no matter how weird things get."

For the first time, he smiles back. "When can you start?"

TEN

TOMORROW.

I start work at the hotel tomorrow.

I'll see what Inana saw tomorrow.

Speak to people she spoke to.

Do things she did.

Be who she was.

Jack and I text back and forth for a while, but he's distracted and doesn't talk for long. I try to give him some sexy Facetime in the tub, but he's not into it, saying he's exhausted and had an early meeting. His job keeps him busy these days, but I'd hoped he'd talk with me a little more now that we're apart. Absence is supposed to make the heart grow fonder. He's not really engaged when I tell him about my undercover operation, trying to make it sound both more exciting and less strange than it is. Maybe the campaign isn't going as well as they hope, but something feels off.

We're still young, but our relationship is not as ravenous as it used to be. Is this where the comfortable phase of our relationship has taken us? I mean, we're both always tired now, and on different schedules, but what's the difference between boring and bored, between paused for a nap and paused for a break?

I guess it's all about intent. We haven't been fucking four times a day, and that's okay, too, I think. As long as the desire to is still there, and for me it is.

I know Jack loves me, and I've got nothing to worry about. He doesn't worry either, and sometimes the certainty of his belief makes me feel a little less desirable than I should.

As though he thinks no one would be looking to lead me astray. It's ridiculous to worry about something like that, but when have emotions ever stayed placid when passion is involved?

This quick vacation from each other will be a good thing for us both. Familiarity breeds contempt. Relationships need a little mystery to stay fresh, and besides, it's just a few days. I hope he ravages me the next time we meet.

Sleeping in someone else's bed always feels a little taboo. Even with clean sheets, you're lying where they've slept, dreamed, masturbated, fucked. These days, if beds were sentient, they would need a "see no evil, hear no evil, speak no evil" seal to counteract the memory foam's absorption.

Inana's bed is disappointingly benign. Medium-firm, pillow top. I was expecting something sexier. Four-poster, restraints, crimson satin sheets to keep things spicy for her debauchery at home.

But it's just a bed.

The kinkiest thing in her bedroom is me. The fact that I'm lying in her bed getting ready to go work her job tomorrow has got to be terrifically inappropriate.

Doing it while wearing her clothes? Even more so.

There's a saying that's not as common anymore, but most people will have heard it, even if they don't use it.

Dead men's shoes.

More specifically, waiting for them.

Sometimes, in the country more than a hundred years ago, people would hang boots over fence posts as a way to honor a recently deceased family member or hired man. Those boots could also be a sign that there was work available on the farm—at least one position per pair of boots had just opened up. I don't know if the new guys scooped the old guys' shoes off the fence on their way to replacing them on the farm, but it makes you think.

Predatory? Yes. Opportunistic? Certainly. But practical as well, in a less sentimental time.

Another explanation of the saying comes from good old-fashioned inheritance fights.

Your father or grandfather passes away, and what's his becomes yours—unless other members of the family want what he had as well; then you're fighting over "dead men's shoes." Things you want that don't belong to you.

There are a lot of superstitions regarding shoes. Don't put them on the table. Don't wear someone else's. Put things in yours for good luck.

Walk a mile in someone else's to see their point of view.

In my case, it's not shoes I'm in, but a dead woman's nightgown.

Now, before you judge me, I have to admit I'm terrible at packing and I forgot to bring something comfortable to sleep in. I wanted to feel something against my skin that had been against hers when I slipped between the cool sheets on her bed. The short, silky baby-doll gown shouldn't have fit me—Inana was much slimmer than I am—but it slid over my head and down my skin like a satin waterfall custom made for me.

There's no television in her bedroom, and I sort of like the stillness. I wonder where her cameras went. Maybe they were taken as part of the short investigation. I like the idea of this being her quiet space for reflecting and dreaming. Daydreaming.

I deny myself as long as I can before reaching for her diary, which I left beneath her pillow for safekeeping today when I went to the hotel.

Maybe it wasn't for safekeeping. It felt a lot like it was supposed to be there on her mattress, like it had been reunited with the place it was meant to be.

Did she keep it there? Did she try to hide it? Did she care if others read it? Maybe it was a conversation piece, like a coffee-table book set out for anyone who wants to pick it up.

I think Inana was the type of person who, if she let you into her home, let you have access to whatever you wanted. Her space was her sanctuary, and she wouldn't have let you come into it if you didn't matter to her. If you got past the door, you'd be comfortable raiding her fridge, borrowing her shower, reading her books, rummaging around in her closet.

She was open in ways I wish I could be, but have never learned.

Maybe that's why I'm white-knuckling her diary so much.

I open it up.

We look at rooms, but they look at us too.

Eyes with no eyes in places with no mind. In the night. Nuit. Notte.

I don't mind.

Sometimes faces are hard to forget, so it's better when there are only eyes. Less to see while they only see.

What is the purest kind of interaction?

Sound?

Sight?

Touch?

Some emotions are harder to hide, but with touch, you know.

Words aren't needed. Looks aren't needed. You can feel people's emotions in their touch.

I wish I knew more things. How does sex feel to blind people? What fills their heads when their lovers are beneath them? How is that for their lovers, being with someone who communicates in such a tactile way? What about a deaf partner, for that matter?

Note to self: Find more diverse partners to experience these things, to possess them and know them.

I was a statue once. Stiff, proud, gleaming, bored.

Admired.

Ignored.

Featured, yet only another part of the background. The décor. A decorated decoration, lonely in a room where all the eyes were on me—even the ones in faces that weren't there. The one face that was there but unseen.

Him.

I put on a show for him. It's still for me, but more for him, and what does that even mean when we can never get close? The ultimate freedom I've searched for within myself, but don't want with him. And yet, I'm stuck in his trap. It's all his. He's the spider and the web and the venom in my veins. But his aloofness makes me want more.

Is that all it is? All that glitters isn't Gold.

Gold is malleable if you warm it.

But he refuses my touch.

Who was this man who didn't want to be with her? Was he someone she pursued before her death? A lover, a boyfriend? Maybe he was married. If she was killed, could this be the reason why? Was this man connected to it?

There's got to be more.

Flipping through the diary in search of more references to the same man might be quicker, but I won't be able to get into Inana's headspace as well if I do that, and context matters. Her words are everything, her art was everything, and I know she wouldn't have left important details out. Just because I don't see names doesn't mean they're not there.

I've got to read it in order. Every word is a link in a chain, and who knows what I might miss if I skip things.

Superstitious? Maybe.

Or maybe it's being thorough. I take notes wherever lines rise to the top of her stream-of-consciousness writings as being more cogent than the rest.

But in the midst of that, she describes something she's done that makes my thighs quiver.

＊ ＊ ＊

During sex, everyone's focused on the same thing. Fucking for an orgasm. Chasing that kundalini energy through your spine until you blow up out of yourself and become more than what you are.

Come hard enough and you'll realize that our bodies are only half of what we are, maybe less.

We're stuck deep inside, but the best way to feel connected to your body is to fuck someone else's. And yet, that act in itself, when done right, is the thing that frees us from our bodies, shows us our souls. Reminds us of our essence so we can once again see the face of gods.

There are more than we even fathom.

Sometimes gods walk around in human bodies, fooling us into thinking that we're the apex of evolution when there's so much more staring us right in the face, watching, waiting.

Hungrily waiting for us to become more than what we are.

For them. For ourselves.

They used to call masturbation "self-abuse," which sounds frighteningly violent to describe the things you'd do to some of the best parts of your anatomy. But if you've ever watched someone get themself off, it is intense.

Men in particular look so angry, their movements almost furious in their quest for release, that it makes me laugh how they seem to devolve into the apes we share ancestors with. It's not sexy, and yet it's so animalistic it's hot. When someone goes that primal in front of you, on you, in you, you can't help but respond in kind.

You become the grunting moans.

The nails raked down his back.

You turn into an animal with him, and devolve into something purer than the person you pretend to be every day.

Sometimes the most civilized manners hide men who are one step above primordial ooze.

There's a golden god—nice to his friends, of whom there aren't many— who is a billionaire industrialist and playboy philanthropist. The man is so wealthy he can buy politicians, swing elections, and manipulate laws with a checkbook. The sole goal of his pleasure palace, which caters only to the elite of the elite in an environment that offers absolute discretion, is to help further his influence.

I got to see it. I got to be it.

Inside a chamber as wealthy in experience as any bank vault is in material riches, I gave something for nothing to a man who has everything.

I gave him a spectacular show.

I fucked his best friend. I want to fuck his greatest enemy the same way, just to see his pupils swell with rage, jealousy, and interest.

Maybe next time I will.

But the door doesn't open for everyone. The opportunity is as often not there as it is right in front of me. But I'm going to knock as often as I can until I no longer care about doors.

At doors of gold.

Was she being literal about fucking someone while someone else watched?

The idea is hot, but presents some logistical issues.

If I'm fucking someone, it's not for a show—it's because I am into fucking that person. How do you fuck someone to give a third person a show? Wouldn't it feel fake and pull you from the moment? I'm not sure if I could come if I were worried about how things looked instead of how they felt.

But maybe that's a part of it. Maybe the person watching doesn't want to feel like you're putting on a show for them. Maybe they want to feel like they're seeing a personal moment—or hour—between two people. The voyeurism being hotter than the things the watcher's seeing, or at least a huge part of the attraction.

It's not like I'm not familiar with the way being watched feels. The awareness of someone's eyes on me prickling gently at my skin. Any reasonably attractive woman knows exactly how it feels to enter a room and have every head swivel her way.

Sometimes you want that, you want the attention.

Other times you wish people would stop watching so you could hide in public, blend in with everyone else.

But Big Brother is always watching, even if the rest of the men in the room aren't, and it sees past the messy bun, flip-flops, and oversized sunglasses. The cold eye of the lens doesn't give a shit that your lips are chapped and you're trying to hide under an oversized sweater.

There are no pretty, colored filters on life.

They say we're filmed an average of a couple hundred times per day—and that's just by CCTV, by security cameras in stores, traffic, bars, and restaurants.

You don't even know how many people per day are taking intentional pictures of you, videos of you, when you're out and about your business. Why?

There are a few reasons.

Emulation. I love your haircut and think it would suit me. I take a pic to show my hairstylist the next time I go to get my hair cut. Or maybe I love your purse—and want to remember what it looks like. Or your shoes, or skirt, or coat. Maybe your nails are cute and I want my manicurist to do mine just like them later today.

It's not always a stalkery, *Single White Female* situation—imitation is the sincerest form of flattery, even when it's not about you. People see your purse and don't think of it as taking a picture of you—it's taking a picture of an object you happen to have. They take your picture and never really think about you again. It's not personal.

Except when it is.

It's not always malignant. Maybe someone just wants to snap a shot of you manspreading on the train so she can post it online to anonymously shame you and your gender into behaving the way she thinks you should.

Maybe someone sees you eating a bagel on the bus like someone's trying to take it from you and wants to laugh about it with his friends later—or post it online to anonymously shame you into being the lady he thinks you should be.

Maybe you're one of those people who dance in public, or sing, or do something quirky that could go viral—the jackpot of instafame. Flash mobs, Banksy, celebrities without makeup. Celebrities without makeup losing their shit at waitresses. People want to capture that to take part in it.

Then there are the times when people want to take a picture of you for weird reasons you don't want to know about.

Knowledge isn't always power.

On the next page of the diary, there's a sketch of something—a coin—scratched deeply into the paper in green ink, all by itself so it stands out. She pressed hard when drawing it, and I trace the emphatic indentations with my fingertips. It seems familiar, but I can't think why. It's got two faces on it, and they're looking toward the edges of the coin.

There's just something about it... Suddenly I realize: *Janus, of course!* The Roman god of gateways and transitions, who is visually represented by two faces turned in opposite directions, simultaneously looking to the past and to the future.

Janus has two strong contemporary links to sex and sexuality—one coincidental, the other deliberate. The most significant study of human sexuality since Alfred Kinsey's landmark research in the late forties and early fifties, published in 1993, was titled *The Janus Report*, after husband and wife psychologists Samuel and Cynthia Janus.

After my flirtation with leather and denim at underground sex clubs, I recall discovering stories about the Society of Janus, one of the very earliest American BDSM groups, a San Francisco-based, pansexual, sex-positive support network founded in 1974 by a woman named Cynthia Slater. She chose Janus to symbolize the dual nature of S&M sex roles—the dominant and the submissive.

I like to see the opposing faces of Janus another way, too: one deliberately looking away so it can't see what the other is doing. I don't know that it's as straightforward as us all having a dark and a light side, but most of us have that little voice of conscience that perks up with its halo when we're about to do something it considers untoward.

It's not like the other part of our id doesn't fight back. We're good at justifying things to ourselves. Self-preservation, self-confidence. Self-delusion. Self-interest. These are the things that keep us going even when it's smarter or easier not to. Look at me, in another woman's nightgown, lying in her bed while my loving partner hangs out with a man who might be the most dangerous president we'll ever have. If he's elected. What are the chances he won't be? Who's watching DeVille? If they dug deep enough, what would they find?

Does DeVille want me to be a ghost in his past? Maybe.

But what you do with information is where the power comes into play.

Do the ends justify the means?

I guess I'll find out soon.

ELEVEN

WHAT'S THE BEST PART OF knowing a secret: telling it to someone else and watching her face light up in horror, revulsion, or delight? Maybe she gets a gleam of admiration in her eyes, admiration that you were the one who possessed that insider information—that someone trusted you to reveal such a scandal to.

Perhaps the best part of a secret isn't the getting or the sharing but the having. Is it the way the knowledge burns inside of you, knowing you could tell anyone at any minute, but instead holding it inside to privately savor? Keeping it just for yourself. Knowing that information could change the way someone looks at a certain person or place if you told—but knowing you never will.

They say that if you tell a person a secret, that person will always tell at least three people, but maybe I'm an exception to that rule.

See, I like the power that comes with knowing something others don't. Yeah, it goes against everything about being a reporter, but it drives me forward in my search for information, like a magpie in search of something shiny. I want to expose the truth about things, but that's why I have trouble connecting with stories sometimes—if

I don't care to know a person or a company's secret, then what's the point?

Sometimes a secret meshes well with things the public will be interested in, and then I've got my story. I'm more than happy to share my toys.

But even when I'm writing the article, I'm inordinately pleased for those few moments, days, weeks where I'm the only one who knows about a certain fact or angle and if I stopped typing, people would never really know the truth.

Sure, they could find out from someone else, but for a while, I'd know. And no one would know that I knew. I'd live on with that knowledge stretching my mind like a cock sliding into my cunt. Secrets are so intimate, mindfucks, soulfucks.

Being a beat reporter makes me privy to all kinds of secrets, but this job in the hotel has real secrets. Juicier ones.

Everything from the real names of guests—based on the names on their credit cards—to strange diet requests—why does a certain indie rock singer staying by himself require nine room service orders per day?—to things the maids pass on with regards to personal hygiene. We know how many towels you need, how much toilet paper you use, whether you've slept in your bed.

Hotels seem impersonal, but we get to know our guests real well.

Maybe too well.

Everyone's got a secret. What's yours?

Are you sure no one knows it?

Who have you told?

Do you trust them?

Maybe it's not a secret that there's a Swedish supermodel staying on the twenty-sixth floor, but she damn sure shouldn't be wandering around naked. That may fly in some hotels in other countries—or cheaper hotels that want everyone to know they've got celebrity clientele—but in a hotel this prestigious, it's an issue.

I happen to catch sight of her on a security monitor at the right time, and I notice her erratic, disjointed behavior as she meanders down the hall. I watch as she settles into one of the stairwells, curling up on one of the landings like a tawny cat.

I grab a clean, fluffy bathrobe from housekeeping on the way to the elevator, and I get out on the twenty-fifth floor so that I can approach her from below in case she's gone mobile while I was making my way to her.

She's either one of those crazy hippie artsy types, or on drugs. If you don't know the person, the two options look suspiciously similar.

Both are remarkably unselfconscious, shedding clothes like skin cells.

Both speak in a narcissistic stream-of-consciousness pattern with a blatant disregard for what others around them are saying—sort of like Pretty Girl Syndrome, where they're so used to everyone falling all over themselves to hear whatever tripe they have to say that they begin thinking they're some sort of guru, dropping profundities like a herd of cows dropping shit in a field in Nebraska.

When I see she's in the exact same position she was in when I saw her on camera, I clear my throat to get her attention. Her head snaps up from where it was resting on her forearms, and she turns her head.

Her gamine features light up when she sees me. "Have you seen my room?" She leans closer, eyes unnaturally sparkly, and whispers, "I think they moved it."

Drugs. Definitely drugs, but Europeans tend to seem more boho than we do, with more relaxed attitudes toward nudity. We're desensitized to violence, they're desensitized to nipples. Their way seems better to me, but maybe if I had been born in another state, I'd feel differently. We're all the products of our births. This girl won the genetic lottery.

Up close she's even younger than I'd thought she was, maybe eighteen or nineteen at most, and I suddenly feel bad for her, alone and blissed out on something. People do drugs because their realities suck—what's someone this beautiful escaping from?

I hold out the robe. "I brought this for you."

"My favorite color is green. Do you have any green ones?"

"Sorry, we were all out. Maybe next time? This one's really soft." I pet it to entice her, and she watches intently before reaching for it.

"I want it."

"I thought you might." I help her shrug into it. "Now, let's see if we can track that room of yours down."

She docilely follows me up the hallway to the end. I employ the key card and let us into her room. The lights are still on, but thankfully not much is in disarray. I lead her to the bed. "Do you need anything before you go to sleep?"

"No."

"You don't have to pee, or need water first?" She hesitates, so I hand her a bottle from the minibar, and she gulps a few sips back. People on drugs make you feel like a parent when you're sober around them.

When she's had enough and begins tracing patterns in the condensation instead of drinking, I take the bottle back. "You're going to stay in your room now, right?"

She nods. "I'm sleepy now."

"Then you're in the perfect place." Something about her makes me feel like a big sister.

"I did a lot of things tonight." She stretches her arms above her head, then wiggles, making the robe gape open a little. "But the painting had eyes that watched."

"That's interesting."

She shivers. "I know who it was behind the face."

"Who?" I tuck the blanket around her, hoping that it will make her feel secure enough to stay in her bed instead of running amok again and getting into more trouble. Something about her is sweet, and despite the fact that she has no modesty and reeks of sex, there's a childlike vulnerability to her that makes me feel protective.

"Gold. Looking, always watching. He likes that," she whispers, turning her head on the pillow.

And I see it. A little smear of gold inside the delicate folds of her ear. My heart pounds as my mind flips the pages of Inana's diary, searching my memory.

Gold to his friends, of whom there aren't many, is a billionaire industrialist and playboy philanthropist. The man is so wealthy he can buy politicians, swing elections, and manipulate laws with a checkbook. The sole goal of his pleasure palace, which caters only to the elite of the elite in an environment that offers absolute discretion, is to help further his influence.

Gold has got to be Maximilian Gold, the elusive owner of this hotel.

It only makes sense. Maximilian Gold has watched Inana fuck. Through him, through his setup here, did her work and play blur together until someone took things a step too far? Did she herself take it too far, taking it somewhere she ultimately couldn't handle, and so she took the only way out she could find?

What could a person of his status and caliber get away with?

Murder? At the very least.

"Do you mean Maximilian?" I ask.

She smirks. "It's not the first time, either. That's what he likes." She picks at a flake of gold paint on her shoulder. "See? Gold."

Didn't Inana mention something about being a statue in a performance for the man she couldn't get enough of?

"What's this about Gold?" A man with a deep, silky voice speaks behind me, startling me into taking a quick step back from the bed.

The girl laughs and holds out the flake of gold leaf. "Me. I am gold, like a statue come to life." She flicks a warning glance my way, but covers it by smiling and making a show of handing me the shiny flake. "Maybe none of this is real. Maybe I'm not even really real."

I take it, looking at the man who spoke. He's anywhere from forty-five to sixty years old, hair slicked back from his forehead with something shiny but not greasy that only men that age seem to use.

He hovers near the foot of the bed, obviously not wanting to leave me alone with her. He's protective of this girl, but clearly not her father.

Why is it that men like him can't ever go for women their own age? Is it because they have to work harder to impress them and have nothing going for them except their money? Older women seem to know more about what they want—and know the shit they're no longer willing to put up with. Is it ego, that the men think they should have the biggest, brightest, and best of everything simply for showing up with their bloated bank accounts and even more bloated senses of entitlement? Naturally, they want what they no longer have—the beauty of youth. He possesses her with his eyes that want to be like Mastroianni's on Claudia, his lioness waiting for the throne, yet not ready to give up her youth-filled lust.

Maybe once in a while there's a love match. The ubiquitous "they" do say that opposites attract, but I have to wonder, what do an eighteen-year-old and a sixty-year-old have in common?

Not much, but also not my business, so I smile at him. "I'll leave you two alone. Ring the front desk if you need anything."

He nods as I pass but doesn't offer a tip. I'd have turned it down, anyway. He shouldn't have left her alone in her condition. Where the hell was he an hour ago when she really needed him to be there for her? This breach of protection isn't going to help her daddy issues.

But I also know she wasn't talking about whatever statue-play scene she was in before when she said "Gold."

She meant Maximilian. My boss.

I need to find out anything I possibly can about him from Inana's diary to arm myself with that information—and then meet him and see what I can find out about Inana. They were connected by more than just the employer-employee relationship.

The knowledge rides my shoulder like a tiny devil on my way to the lobby. Elias, the guy who interviewed me, is waiting for me at the front desk when I return, and he stands and jerks his head toward the elevator. "Come with me."

Reflexively, I wonder if the man fucking the young model got annoyed with me and decided to try to get me fired to hide something, but I force the paranoia down. I don't ask about Gold, either, but my tongue itches with the dots I just connected a few minutes ago. I also don't ask where we're going, because I'll see it soon, obviously, but also because that's a rank amateur move.

Words are cheap—politics have taught me a lot about posturing. Asking anything about our destination in this situation shows insecurity, and that the balance of power is on his side.

Elias sends me a few loaded glances, like he can't wait to see my face when I realize where we're going, but I keep my eyes focused on the elevator lights so as not to appear too eager or wary.

"Good job earlier, by the way," he says.

Big Brother is always watching. "Thanks."

"You'll be at the desk dealing with things, but a lot of the time—the majority of it, actually—you'll be taking care of the guests in this club." The elevator dings as we come to a halt, as if punctuating his words, and the doors slide open with a well-oiled alacrity that borders on sentience.

The beat hits me along with the darkness.

It's a club.

Bodies twine sinuously around each other. Men in suits, women in scraps of fabric. But there are half-naked men milling about as well.

The décor is lush, like something Louis XIV would have gone for. Even in low light, everything is gleaming and polished, giving the impression of wealth even though it could just be shiny from lube and body glitter—or could be if it were anywhere but here. Max wouldn't allow such an oversight in his hotel.

Everything is grand, high ceilings, big chairs covered in velvet—which is a bad choice when body fluids come into play.

Then again, it's not like Max couldn't afford to have them reupholstered every ten minutes when they started getting a little less than fresh.

This club doesn't just give the impression of wealth—it *is* wealth. I'm guessing that the pillars aren't granite but marble; the moldings not gold-colored paint, but actual gold leaf painstakingly applied by someone from Italy or France who knew what they were doing and had a team of assistants fluttering with their every barked command.

It reeks of the façade and fashion of BDSM, the flirtation, immersed in the imagery without commitment, understanding, or respect.

Staring across the expanse of space, I notice that what I took for huge works of art on the walls, hung in massive gilt frames, aren't paintings at all, but mirrors that send back images of us that look more like something Hieronymus Bosch could have painted than like a nightclub.

Mirrors are the favorite playground of the ego. Men and women like the ones here have egos big enough to fill these twelve-foot-wide mirrors.

It's not enough to have a good time and be seen having a good time. They need to watch themselves while they're seen having a good time.

Everything is carved and polished and decorated.

It's in direct opposition to the people in it. Hungry eyes, like they've never had a good time in their lives, set inside expressions showing the aloofness of those who have done it all.

But maybe it's just the Botox preventing them from emoting.

It's a fetish club inside the hotel. It reminds me of the Fuck Factory, but watered down, and it probably has a ridiculous name to go with it.

For a dizzying moment, I'm caught up remembering another time and place. A blond guy at a bar. Pressing me against the wall from behind. People crowding around to watch.

The same guy is sitting at the bar now.

But no, he turns and I see it's not him at all, but an androgynous woman. I take in the surroundings, taking care not to stare at some of the things happening in the corners—but really? This is Kink for Dummies, and tame compared to what I've done.

A memory quivers in my subconscious, but I force it back down, focusing on the tall dominatrix with G-cups and a flogger, flirting with a businessman and his table of lackeys. Again with the secrets swelling beneath the surface of my skin.

"What do you think?" Elias asks me. I almost want to speak, to tell Elias about the things I've done, things that are more shocking than anything happening in this room, that would raise his eyebrows and make him clutch his pearls.

I shrug. "The décor is great." It's nothing compared to my memories, compared to my dreams. But it's better to keep that inside. He's showing me this not so that I can try to one-up it with stories of my past, but to see my reaction.

But what else? Does he want me to make this a regular part of my days and nights? Is this to see if I'm into kink on a personal level? Men only want to know your proclivities if they want to be in the scene with you. You don't ask a stranger their favorite sexual position if you don't want to at least imagine them naked in that position, probably with yourself there, sticking a finger into an orifice for you to feel them from the inside. This isn't personal—it's a job, but something tells me nothing is one-sided here.

Instead, it's prismatic. Facets you don't know are there until someone shines a light into them.

And what is this place?

It's the club for tourists who *think* they're into kink. It's not what I want, but it's a pale imitation of it, and I'm happy to have this again in some capacity, even if only while I'm here investigating Inana.

"Did my predecessor take care of this place, too?"

Elias nods. "She did."

I clasp my hands behind my back and smile at this turn of events. "I can definitely handle this."

Elias grins. "That won't be a problem for someone like you, will it?" His gaze crawls over my starched blouse and prim pencil skirt.

The funny thing? Today my secret is that I'm not wearing panties to work.

"Not at all."

It's that sort of weirdly satisfying thing that I've been craving my whole life.

If this is going to be the average night at work, I can't wait to see what happens next.

TWELVE

I'VE HEARD IT SAID THAT people my age are part of the Entitlement Generation, and I believe it. We want what we want and want it now, with the least amount of effort expended. We were taught that we're all unique, that we're all brimming with limitless potential and can be anything we want to be, and society must make room for us at whichever table we want to sit at, because we're all equally special while also each being the best.

It's a load of shit, but it sure does engender a lot of false confidence, which feels pretty good when justifying the failure to get something you thought you were a shoo-in for.

That job, that promotion.

That free gift with purchase that sold out before you got to the store, and even though it was something you'd never in a million years want badly enough to pay for, you nonetheless feel cheated when it's taken away.

It goes back to what I was saying about our brands. Because you secretly think that those are the things that set you apart.

If you don't know a man like Will, you've seen one on television.

Wearing a man bun before they were trendy, the bearish beard he sports doing no favors for his attempts at cultivating the impression that he's a pussy magnet. He's a reality television star turned actor, or an MMA superstar turned musician, but he doesn't really do much of either anymore. No, now he's the king of cameos, beating what little fame and notoriety he gleaned from his fifteen minutes right into the ground, the gleam in his eyes getting brighter as his star fades along with his audience's interest.

He's a fabulous trainwreck about to happen at any moment.

He's the guy every bro dreams to be, and a publicist's nightmare.

The back of his neck probably smells like rancid pussy from all the wannabe models who he encourages to climb onto his shoulders to make himself seem desirable in his Instagram pics. He's loud and obnoxious, because he never learned to fake humility working his way up—his fame came overnight, and because of that, entitlement leaks from his every pore. He takes pride in not caring about anything, but like any squalling toddler, he sure gets upset when things don't go his way.

I've been maintaining a polite smile for the last ten minutes while he rants in my face about not being automatically upgraded—for free—to a better room because he's a celebrity. Somehow, he's under the impression that this brings up our profile and property value.

It doesn't. He's not a real celebrity; he's a pseudo-celeb, along with the other aging pop stars and D-listers who used to be somebody ten years, four rehab stints, and two chemical peels ago. Besides, even the cheapest rooms here put the best penthouses anywhere I've ever seen to shame, so any point about status or quality that he's not-so-subtly trying to make is moot.

His stale beer breath does nothing to win me over, nor does the lecherous stare he sends crawling up my body while bawling me out in the lobby of the hotel. He seems like the kind of guy who would fuck a Hot Pocket and brag about it for views on social media, like some kid did a while back.

I wonder what that kid is doing now. Where do you go with your life from there? Does that kid grow up into Neckbeard here? One day you're a regular horny teen, the next you're fucking inanimate objects in an attempt to shock and garner attention. Will that be his legacy? Crumbs of sexual controversy cling to his name like that warm filling did to his crotch.

Simulated sex, again.

But say the kid moves on with his life, gets serious, buckles down to earnestly make the world a better place for generations that come after him. He could build a better mousetrap, cure cancer, invent a new green energy source—and I bet the audience members at his Nobel Prize acceptance speech would still lean close to each other and whisper, "Did you know that he fucked a Hot Pocket once?"

Reinventing yourself is hard in the age of the Internet, where nothing is forgotten and knowledge isn't power, but a tool used to bring others down to feel better about yourself. Most people crave that insta-fame, but lack the constitution to get it. Maybe that's a good thing. Otherwise it becomes a crazy competition, people doing more and more outrageous things to one-up each other, top what their competitors are doing, until what's left?

The Pain Olympics? It starts out innocently enough, maybe with a contest to see who can drink the hottest hot sauce. But you know that meme, "That escalated quickly"? I can't see that without thinking of the video I saw of the Pain Olympics.

That shit was fucked up. Combine the male ego with the competitive spirit and you're left with trouble. The sizzle goes out of the room when someone cuts his own penis off, or another cuts his balls off and squeezes out the…maybe it was fake, but the videos looked pretty real to me.

Sad thing was, they weren't the only ones to cut something off.

The Internet means anyone can have an audience now.

"Are you even listening to me?" Pseudo-celeb Will snaps his fingers right in front of my face.

"Of course I am," I say with a bland smile. Speaking of cutting dicks off...

"So, what are you going to do about my little problem?" He crosses his arms in that way that insecure guys do, using his fists to push his biceps out in a vain attempt to look cut. It's the male equivalent of the chicks on Instagram who do the skinny-arm pose.

Stop doing that. You're fooling no one with your weird angles and unnatural contortions.

Will's little perceived problem has become a real one for me, and unfortunately, no one else is around for me to foist him off on, citing lack of experience. I can either let this asshole rant and rave some more, potentially upsetting any true VIPs who happen to walk by, or I can get him out of sight as quickly as possible. Even though he's an asshole, he's still a guest, and it's my job to keep the guests happy.

The key to bullshitting people is to make them feel two things.

The first: Special. Again, it harkens back to the idea that there is a unique snowflake inside of all of us, planted by grandmothers too eager to spoil, or parents who saw that you could play one note on a piano and got dollar signs in their eyes, eager to ride your ass to the top of Easy Street. So, you make the person feel like they're perceptive enough to have seen behind the curtain, seen past the lies, and you gather them close and praise them for being oh-so-smart. You make them feel like they're part of the exclusive club, and all of a sudden they're halfway to getting that stick of outrage out of their asses.

And the second thing you want to make them feel is like they're getting their own way. Everyone wants to be right, no matter how far off the mark they are, no matter how ridiculous the request they're making is. "What do you mean pomegranates aren't in season? I just had one last Thursday!" How dare you lie about this to make them feel stupid! Sometimes things like this are a real stumbling block, because you can't manifest out-of-season fruit out of thin air, but like a good magician, you pull out the misdirection. "Of course you did. And I didn't want to say anything in front of that other guest, but we've got something even better than those pomegranates: pears hand-picked by a virgin tribe of Tibetan acolytes to the Dalai Lama himself. Only three survived the trip, but we were saving them for someone who truly appreciates quality."

Sure, it's all a huge lie, but people love the warm, gentle swirl of smoke being blown up their assholes, because it feels good.

And everyone wants to feel good.

Especially Will.

I weave some bullshit legend about one of the rooms on the second floor, and how it was on hold for a notoriously reclusive A-Lister, giving sketchy half-details and letting him fill in every blank for me about who he wants it to be, but not confirming or denying anything. If he wants that actor to have been the one whose reservation was switched to next week instead, freeing the room for him, it makes my sale that much easier.

It's all a lie.

There are always other, better rooms available in hotels. Always.

I don't care if they've told you the American Olympic hockey team is staying and there's a sex-toy convention and three weddings happening that weekend. There are always rooms available, because they make sure there are always rooms available in case someone better comes along.

When it comes to celebrities, there's always room for one more.

Will found his way here, which says something—even if it was only through a friend. That may be the person we're trying to keep happy.

And I make goddamn sure he struts away from the desk to his new "upgraded" room with a smile on his face. The new room is exactly the same as his old one, but with a mirror-image layout and a small balcony for him to stand on and pretend he's someone important.

Pseudo-celebrities love looking down at people. Literally and figuratively.

I'm hanging up the phone, having ordered a small bottle of mid-quality Scotch to be delivered to Will's room on the house, when someone taps the desk by my hand.

Mr. Gold.

Max. I've seen him wandering the halls, never really seeming to be in a hurry, but always moving, like he's pulled along inside eddies only he can feel.

I've read about him in Inana's diary.

"I saw the way you handled that situation, Catherine."

It's the first thing he's ever said to me—the first time I've heard him speak at all. He's smaller than I thought he was, yet still imposing in that way truly confident and influential people are. They suck the oxygen from the air with their very presence, as if the very molecules rush to see what they're going to do next. His voice is low-pitched, but it sounds like he's trying to deepen it.

I keep a neutral expression, unsure if this is going in the direction of praise or recrimination. "You did?"

He nods. His skin is vaguely pink, like he's either suppressing emotions that he finds upsetting, or always just getting over a sunburn. His eyes are slightly too close together for him to be truly appealing, at least to me, but there's something about him that's compelling. He stares at me for a long moment before speaking again. "You did very well. Elias told me about the other day, too. We did well in hiring you, Catherine."

This is the man who watches. The man who owns. The man who Inana wanted—the man who may have driven her over the edge of obsession. "Thank you, sir," I say, emphasizing the last word to gauge his reaction, not moving away or fidgeting to betray anything.

"You remind me of someone," he says suddenly, and I lick my lips, hoping he means Inana.

"Do I?"

"I've seen you poking around room fourteen."

Shit. That's true. Inana had mentioned it, and I wanted to find out what was behind that door, but it's the one door that my all access keycard doesn't open.

Or the VIP section I know is somewhere, just out of reach.

I've been slinking around for the past couple of days, searching the hallways for doors without numbers, staircases that go up a flight too far, elevators that go sideways into the places I want to see—the land behind the curtains. I smile.

He looks at my hand but doesn't take it. "Come with me."

We walk for a couple minutes in silence. He breaks it. "You've already signed the NDA that's standard in all my hotels, but this isn't about forcing you to keep quiet about something. I already know you can keep your mouth shut, or I wouldn't have hired you."

Interesting. I murmur assent.

He spreads his hands. "This is about keeping our guests happy, and some of them have different...appetites than others. Certain proclivities they don't necessarily want the rest of the world to know about." A low buzz of excitement hums over my skin as he stops in front of room fourteen and puts a meaty hand in his pocket. "When you first walk into the room, you never know who you'll find behind the door, what you'll be required to do. You are given no prior warning, no privileged information. You enter naked. Metaphorically. This is the game. You have to adapt. Quickly. Think on your feet. To be caught out is to fail, to lose your place in the pecking order. It's all about the competition. Not Best in Show, Best in Sex. We fuck like dogs to win. Do you understand?"

This is a little too familiar for comfort, but I nod with a bland expression on my face. What's he going to try to get me to do? I thought he was only showing me something, a secret, not wanting me to fuck anyone. Swear to Christ, if he tries to get me to blow him in a broom closet...

He takes a black key from his pocket—not a keycard, I notice, and slides it into the door, raising an eyebrow at me as he does so. "What you're about to see will change your life. It's not too late to turn back, but soon it will be."

My body battles between wanting to roll my eyes and wanting to shove him out of my way so I can open the door faster and see what the hell is on the other side of it. Did Inana see this? Was this what she was talking about? Did she hear this speech on her first day, or did she have to earn it over time?

Was her journey of sexual self-expression the main reason Max hired her in the first place, knowing her voyage down this hallway was inevitable?

I smile. "It takes a lot to shock me."

His smirk is well rehearsed. "Don't say I didn't warn you." And he pulls the door open, revealing a second door. I step into the space between them, and he does, too, shutting the first door behind us. Though the space is cramped, he is careful not to touch me, which makes me feel simultaneously relieved and disappointed. He's odious, yet compelling.

He reaches around me, sliding another key into the next locked door, pushing it open to reveal a dark passageway thick with shadows. A sense of déjà vu rises in me as he waves at me to go ahead of him.

Maybe I should feel nervous, walking into the unknown with someone I'm vaguely repulsed by, in a place that's so remote and easy to dispose of a body in.

And I damn sure should be wondering why Max has selected me to see this, with me having been at the hotel for only a breath of time.

But all I feel is curiosity. Anticipation. There's a rush that comes with embracing the unknown, not with a reckless disregard for your own safety, but with a willingness to explore. And more than a small part of me wonders if Inana was presented with this same offer, this same temptation to walk through the door that was opened for her.

And maybe Max is trying to train her replacement in whatever capacity she served him.

I want to know what that was, so becoming her replacement in every sense is utterly vital. So when he opens this door for me, I wonder briefly if she'd have walked through it.

She'd have done it, no hesitation, only slowing to let the moment melt against her to better savor it and remember later in great detail. The thing I love about Inana's diary is the way she bombards every sense with description.

So it's with her in mind that I close my eyes and feel the cool air waft over my skin, taking a deep breath to catch the scent, but it's mostly the same as in the hall behind us.

A deep, pulsing bass pounds up toward me, faintly. The walls are thick, secure. Are there other entrances or exits? There have to be.

I want to find them all.

"Nervous?" Max asks, voice sardonic in the dark.

"The opposite, actually. I want to remember every detail of this. I know that it's important."

"Good girl. Welcome to the VIP section."

I step forward, heels clicking on the stairs underfoot. I reach out for a handrail and find nothing to support me or draw me along.

THIRTEEN

~oooooo~

THE MUSIC IS LOUDER AT the bottom of the stairs, filtering through the crack at the bottom of the burgundy door. Max is close behind me, so without hesitation, I pull the door open. Radiant lights and the deep bass of the minimal techno hit my body, ratcheting up my energy a few notches.

I'd thought the club upstairs was the only one we had.

Max lets me lead the way around the perimeter of the room. It shouldn't matter, but it does—this isn't about "ladies first" politeness. He's giving me the lead for a reason.

A muscular Asian man in black vinyl fetish wear sits in an antique clawfoot tub near the door with a red ball gag in his mouth and a sign taped into his bound hands that reads "Spit on me."

From the looks of his face, his body, and the inch of fluid in the tub, people have not only spit on him, but either poured drinks or urinated on him as well.

When in Rome.

I look him in the eyes for a moment and he tips his head back, smiling around the gag.

I spit on his face, and he moans and closes his eyes with a violent shiver of pleasure.

Max's lips twitch, in amusement or surprise, I don't know. I think both are a good thing when it comes to this man. Like the rest of the one percent, the worst thing they can feel is bored. It gets them—and the people around them—in trouble.

Millionaires are only slightly better than billionaires at keeping themselves entertained. When you reach a certain level of wealth and can have absolutely anything your heart desires, what happens next?

You stop following your heart and begin following your dreams.

And when those are done, your nightmares.

Or other people's nightmares. It depends on the person's character. Will you turn into Trump or Gates?

Will your creations aim to build or destroy?

Will you build a kink club beneath a monolithic, palatial hotel in the desert?

I turn to Max. "Interesting. Am I still on the clock, or is this more of an extracurricular activity?"

"It's a reward for dealing with Will—who knows nothing of this place. But maybe it's a test to see if you can handle it."

"Isn't everything?" In a way, I've sort of earned this, but they don't want to give me too much free rein in the fetish club, or he wouldn't have tagged along with me to observe. And he never said that I'm not on the clock.

Now this is a place that screams kink.

The club I saw with Elias screams wealth and class. It's a place where you could bring the snootiest patron, and they wouldn't find fault with the design or execution. This place is the polar opposite—and for a very good reason.

See, the people who this place is meant for already wallow in class and pomp. When they look to cut loose, it helps if they feel like they're slumming it.

So this place? The VIP section that has its own entrance, unattached to the main club? Gritty doesn't begin to describe it.

It's metal and concrete and black glass. Hard angles to lean against when you want a fix of pain—or want to inflict it upon someone else. That's your prerogative. It brings to mind city slums, red-light districts, seedy drug deals in back alleys.

It's meant to feel a little unhinged and dangerous. And it does.

The floors are black and the walls are dark with hints of color, like an oil slick. The music is bass to get your body and mind sedated; it's sludgier, more rhythmic than the trance that plays in the other club.

There are fewer people here, but it's a bit smaller, and though spacious, it doesn't feel empty. There are more alcoves for ducking into if you want a little privacy by yourself, or with a friend...or three.

There are various apparatuses in the vaguely octagonal room as well, and there are numbered doors that lead away from this main area. I open the door to Room 3962, the one nearest to us. Familiarity strikes like lightning when I see the man inside. Square jaw, short salt-and-pepper hair. Something about those perfectly plucked eyebrows...I know his face, but recognition doesn't come until his face relaxes in between strokes of the flogger.

No way.

Jack's favorite anchorman.

The man who, with a well-timed exposé, brought Bundy's skanky empire crashing to the ground like a wobbly Jenga tower. A man with no charm and even less authenticity: Forrester Sachs.

Him being anywhere near a scene like this would be shocking enough—but the fact that he's strapped, naked and spread-eagled, to a St. Andrew's cross makes my brain stutter for a moment.

They say context is everything, that you can run into someone you know well, but if you're in another town or country and not expecting that person, your mind will take a moment to recognize him.

Ding, ding, ding.

"More," he moans over his shoulder, and the tall woman sets the flogger aside with a smirk, liberally coats a dildo the size of my forearm with enough lube to fill an inflatable plastic pool, and shoves it home into his ass.

Vlad the Impaler's got nothing on modern BDSM.

I can't look away.

The best part is that the dildo she's buggering him with isn't a regular dildo. No, this is a model of Jesus nailed to a cross, the patibulum giving her a fantastic grip with which to shove Jesus's feet and legs on the stipes all the way inside Sachs's asshole.

At least he's crying out the correct name.

Jesus Christ, indeed.

I'd be lying if I said it didn't make me want to whip out my phone and take a video—a little souvenir to play for myself while watching the normally uber-composed Sachs as he's taking someone down in a supposedly impartial interview on television. But something tells me I wouldn't make it to the door with any video footage or photographs, so I don't bother trying to capture the moment.

What would Jack think about this?

Would he flip out to know I was here, or would he be as unaffected as he's been for the last couple of months when I mention my work? I push thoughts of Jack from my mind and move away from the cross, not liking the taste of guilt and frustration that's been introduced to my tongue.

It would make sense for Inana to have stumbled into the same secret society I did, wallowed in it for a while, then met resistance when she tried to get out. The things she did, the things she was interested in would have been compatible, welcomed, encouraged, but she was outspoken as well and had a medium of her own.

She wouldn't have been used to playing by anyone else's rules.

But TJS doesn't take no for an answer—and they don't like people they can't control.

It would be such a neat little package if this place was one of theirs, and she'd found it.

Designed to keep the rich businessmen happy when they're near Vegas on conference. They come here, feel like they're part of something elite and forbidden, and are happy to pay big bucks for the privilege of getting fucked.

Like Sachs.

Neat little bows don't exist in the real world. It's a messy damn place, and when we start looking for patterns, that's when things get dangerous.

We see things that aren't there.

We find the things we want to see, picking something out of nothingness. Order from chaos.

Fact from fiction.

But this is still a damn good place to kill an hour or two.

Why would I have been led here?

That's a question that has a clear answer—I just don't know it yet. I turn to ask Max, but he's no longer at my side. When did he leave? I scan the room, but he's nowhere to be found. Maybe he found a scene he wanted to participate in—or watch. Maybe he's hidden in a shadow or behind a mask, watching me.

What is this, really?

A reward? A test? Do they see in me the capacity for this, the interest, and want to see my reaction?

Maybe they'll be more surprised at my reaction than I am at the fact that this place has been pulsing beneath my feet the whole time.

A woman in a blue latex suit with her hair pulled back into a high ponytail sidles by, leading a lanky man crawling on the floor by a leash made of hair.

Maybe hair extensions—who knows what's fake and what's real in here? Other than the tits.

Fake.

I'm not supposed to like this. Women aren't supposed to like anything like this except for when there's a man on top leading the way to her sexual "awakening."

But I do. I still do. I may have left my leather and denim life behind, but that didn't stop me from indulging in fantasy online, calling it "research." I've found that the only female desires or fetishes we speak about are horrible, abusive pseudo-rape fantasies, and those are all that seem to be accepted by mainstream media, furthering the rape culture we so desperately need to cleanse. This is what has seeped into the mainstream media, rather than the true desires of women, because they've taken our power away.

Actually it's worse than that. They haven't taken our power away. We let them keep us down in the mainstream media when it comes to sex. They'll ask us, pressure women who aren't into anal sex into it but you express interest in pegging them and watch the lights come on and the audience run the hell out of the theater. Hypocrisy at its finest because men can't let themselves be in a vulnerable position.

But we could take all the power back if we realized we've got the reins in our hands every time we go online and connect with each other.

Why can't we share more stories of women and their sexual obsessions that don't scream *tacky* to serve as clickbait? I know there's a lot of clickbait. I know there are men who have desires to explore weird, dark, transgressive exploits—these fetishes can't exclusively belong to them; we have desires too. The hunger and desire to feel more, try more. Is it that men are more open to sharing their deeply rooted psychological desires, a fraternity that boasts about their sexual conquests? Women like to keep their kinks in a closet, the secrecy bringing more pleasure to their pleasures so we don't threaten the fragile male ego.

Really, it's more common to see female dominants—dominatrixes—than it is for a man to have a woman over his knee.

And virgins? That's more a fetish than a lifestyle choice. You know who likes fucking virgins, other than a sliver of the kink community?

Other virgins.

Virgins are terrible at sex because they haven't done it. It hurts for them, too, at least the women. The women who love sex right from their first time aren't common.

So I guess sadists could find crossover appeal, but the interest is limited, is all I'm saying. I think as long as you and your partner are into it—anything goes. Consenting adults are the two words that unlock doors inside yourself to places you never knew you could go.

What places in this hotel will I find?

Who will find me?

I want to explore every single room in this place, but being stationary has made me a little bit of a target, so I stride with purpose over to the bar in the corner of the room, illuminated from beneath with a purple-blue glow like a natural gas flame.

I get the feeling I'm going to need a drink to deal with what I might find. I lean in and wait for the bartender to get to me, keeping my eyes on the room behind me so as not to be sneaked up on.

This isn't the kind of room that I'd like to be surprised in.

"What can I get you?" the maître d' asks the woman next to me. The tiny smudge of pink beneath his eye stops me in my tracks.

The last time I saw him he was darker—skin and hair. Now he's got the look of a character from iZombie—hair a light blonde, skin paler, as though he spends all his time underground now literally as well as figuratively.

Maybe he does stay below the surface nowadays, if these are his new digs.

His hair may be different, and he's lost some weight, but I don't think two people in the world would get a fucking Krispy Kreme doughnut tattooed under their eye like a gangster devoted to type 2 diabetes.

Bundy.

Memories of four years ago crawl over me, thick and damp, making it feel like I'm breathing through a humid swamp.

The sound seems to get sucked from the room, and I do a slow spin, searching it with my eyes, hoping, dreading.

Hoping.

Anna. Is she here, too?

I'm bombarded by images, memories of my wild, free, reckless friend.

The bruises on her pale skin.

The way she'd lean in and make everything feel like a secret.

The unfiltered way she'd blurt out things about guys, sexual things that should have been too personal and dirty, but the way she said them sounded like she was reading facts from a spreadsheet.

Those green eyes I've missed, smiling at me with a glint, like we're soul sisters and two halves of the same whole, or two sides of a coin.

At least, we were until she went away.

She may have changed her appearance, too, but I still find myself searching for her blond hair and mischievous smile. What would I even say to her?

Where the fuck did you go?

Where the fuck have you been?

What the fuck are you doing here?

I missed you.

But the slow rotation reveals nothing but a room full of strangers, and by the time I finish the revolution and face Bundy again, I know Anna's not here.

It's stupid, maybe superstitious, but it seems like I'd have felt her presence if she were here.

I lean back over the bar, staring straight at Bundy Royale Tremayne.

"No need to ask what a guy like you is doing in a place like this, is there, Bundy?" I say over the throbbing of the music.

He freezes and turns to me, eyes lighting up like we're old friends reuniting on a daytime talk show.

Once in a while, the boomerang person we throw out of our lives circles back and finds us again when we least expect it.

When we're in an underground club.

Bundy "Boomerang" Tremayne.

He launches himself over the bar and grabs me in an uncomfortably tight hug. "Cate? I can't believe you're here."

"Catherine," I correct, pulling back after giving his back a couple pats. "And Sachs is here? Wasn't he the one who basically brought your career down?"

Bundy waves a hand. "Water under the bridge. Things were getting stale anyways."

A little bit of revisionist history, but seeing Sachs's asshole get plundered must give Bundy a certain sense of satisfaction and make it easy to be magnanimous. The last time I saw Bundy was in his apartment, which was crammed full of weeks-old garbage that still didn't smell as bad as his feet did. He'd admitted some personal things to me regarding pubic preferences.

He'd said he hadn't killed the girls in Sachs's piece that brought his life crashing to the ground—hell, crashing *through* the ground. He'd said he would never hurt Anna, that he'd done all those things trying to get closer to her, and I'd believed him.

But now? It can't be a coincidence that Bundy's here and working where Inana was. She's another woman who killed herself—like some of the girls did because of his amateur porn sites. The sites Sachs exposed in a news segment. More than one woman chose to end her life because of the videos Bundy took and posted online for the world to see.

Allegedly. But I still can't see him as a killer. He's a harmless horndog, not a diabolical genius, and most of what he shot was anonymous—and it was all with permission, whether or not they knew the footage would go up online and make him serious bank. Until it all came tumbling down.

"So you're here now? This is your place?" I ask.

He nods. "You know how it is. Haters gonna hate, and men like me will always land on our feet. What can I get you to drink?"

"Just a Coke. I'm still working."

Once I clocked that it was Bundy, there was no way was I letting him serve me alcohol.

He grins. "You work here?"

"Not here specifically, but in the hotel, yeah." I don't want him thinking he's my boss somehow.

"Well, welcome to the show." He grins and tosses a red straw into my glass.

I don't know what to do with my hands or my thoughts. It's like the past and future are colliding—here I am in front of Bundy, searching for a different woman, again. "How long have you been here?" I ask.

He squints. "Two years, give or take."

If he's been working here for two years, he was employed here when Inana was. "Do you remember a woman, Inana Luna?"

His eyes twinkle like a degenerate Santa Claus. "I know a lot of women, Catherine. I can't remember them all."

That's true enough, though I'm sure their recollections of him would be a little less mirthful. I remember the interview Sachs did with Bundy's mother.

"He drove those girls to suicide, Charmaine," says Sachs, and he's looking down at his notes nonchalantly as he says it, because he knows he's so fucking good at this that he could do it in his sleep.

"She worked here," I say. "Gorgeous, tall, dark complexion, dark eyes. Long black hair. She was into this kind of kink." I try to pin him with my gaze, but he's focused on his phone.

"Not ringing a bell, but I don't get out of here much. If she was down here, maybe if I saw her something would twig."

I sip my drink to avoid blurting anything out and betraying my unstable emotions, in case Max is still watching. "You'd remember her if you knew her." I need to stop talking about Inana, but the only other thing I can think about is what's behind the other doors in this room, and whether Jack could be somewhere just as nefarious as this.

Or if Inana ever made it here.

"What do you know about this place, Bundy?"

He leans closer and shows me a picture on his phone, of a grimy, green Chevy van in the parking lot with a dog sitting in the front seat. Since his national disgrace, he tells me, he's been driving the highways and byways of the country with a dog with no teeth in a Chevy van that he calls "the Fuckmobile," and somehow he ended up in the desert. He was in a local dive bar one day, and one of the old desert-rat regulars got to talking to him. Bundy says when he first walked into the bar—which is in Wonder Valley, nothing but abandoned meth shacks—everyone in the bar stopped talking and turned to look at him. They said to him, *Why'd you come here? Nobody comes here unless they're running from the law or fixing to die.* I guess that's what happens to Bundy; soon enough one of them had led him here. He walks into the bar and starts talking to people—and ends up in the same place as someone like me.

The VIP section.

I don't know if I should feel insulted by fate, or spooked by the coincidence.

Bundy shrugs when I say as much. "You made it here for a reason. Give it time and things will speak for themselves."

Things I don't want to remember, have suppressed hard in order to forget, force their way to the insides of my eyelids, waiting for me to relax and close my eyes and see them again.

I stare hard at Bundy.

But I've got to blink sometime.

FOURTEEN

AND YET, NOW THAT I'VE seen this, all I want is to see more.

I stay close to the bar for a while, wanting to keep an eye on Bundy and get as much information out of him as I can.

"So, you're a bartender?" I ask, a little surprised.

"The man who pours the liquor is the man who holds the world."

"Stop butchering song lyrics." I lean on my elbow, slouching so I can watch people more subtly. "I don't get it. It's all so open here."

"Open? We're underground."

"I mean that no one seems shy or worried about the rooms not being locked down." Sachs is a well-known figure. If even a single photo was taken of what he was getting up to.... "No one seems to care about privacy here."

"You don't need privacy when there's no one to hide from. It's open because we've already exposed ourselves to the bone. If we hadn't stripped our defenses, we wouldn't have gained access to a place like this. It's free, but the cost of admission is your protective skin that the rest of the world sees. Here we've shimmied out of it, and it's time to rub against each other with no lies or barriers."

I wrinkle my nose at his metaphor.

He laughs. "You're here too, kid. Think about that. Everything and everyone is contained within the secrets we've all bared to one another. None of us worry about how we're perceived, because underneath the lies we sell the world, we're all the same. If you think differently, well, look in the mirrors. It's safe. We've all done things to get here and answer the invitation."

Max brought me here himself, so maybe that can be considered my invitation.

"I don't believe there are people here with nothing at all to hide."

Bundy tilts his head. "It's my experience that people see what they expect to."

That sounds like a challenge, so I slide off my stool and head off to find another room of the club to explore.

Did we all heed a call to get here?

Are these people just like me on some level?

I find a door that's puffy and black, quilted vinyl with a large 3939 on it. Here's as good as any other.

I push inside. It's a large room, but the ceiling is low so it feels more intimate than it should. The walls are a dark forest green, and it smells smoky and sweet, like someone's smoking strawberry tobacco in a hookah, but the air is clear and warm. Fat white candles are lit on low tables that circle the perimeter, giving the only light, but it's enough to see everything.

It's quite a show.

A man's body is decorated with ropes, and he kneels with his arms bound behind his back, tied with more ropes in intricate knots and loops while a tall black woman—a dominatrix, based on the height of her heels and the leather outfit—slowly circles him like an affectionate predator toying with her meal.

A few people are gathered around watching, so I move closer and realize it's a side-by-side bondage demonstration. Next to the man, there's a woman, also in the process of being tied, but with delicate white silks. I can't help but notice that the man isn't tied up with anything that comfortably soft, but he doesn't seem to mind.

Naked, his cock juts up toward his face, stiff and aggressive.

A man loops the silk around the woman's arm, and the dominatrix stops him, adjusting the rope a little higher on the woman's bicep. "You've got to watch out for the arteries. We want to apply pressure, but not cut off blood flow or do damage." She twists the material and pulls tighter in the new spot, and the woman gasps.

The dominatrix addresses the group watching. "Keep in mind that if you suspend your submissive after this, the ropes will pull tighter in places. Adjust as you go along, but it's better to leave a little slack and tighten—you won't be able to give slack once they're in the hooks."

She calls over a couple of people to help her submissive guy up and into the suspension. He groans and shivers, a drop of pre-come glistening on the tip of his cock. Does it really feel that good?

Ropes and air and pressure. That's it. Is it the eyes of the people watching that makes it hotter?

Sex is in the mind before the body. The idea can turn us on as much as the touch, and when the dominatrix invites us forward to look at the rope marks on the skin of a woman she has tied up on the floor—a different woman, hidden from my view behind the crowd—I step forward to trace the marks on her body.

I'm not the only one. We surround her almost clinically, reaching out to feel where the ropes were. She shudders beneath our hands, eyes rolling back into her head, come leaking from between her legs onto the floor.

"She's in subspace," the dominatrix explains. "Every touch is overwhelming, no matter how light. Her body is trapped in a place where everything is good. Don't be fooled—not everyone who gets suspended reaches this place. For a while it hurts a lot. But if you gain their trust and do it right," she continues, trailing her hand over some indentations on the woman's thigh—the woman gasps and arches off the floor, labia quivering—"you can make them come without fucking them."

How erotic would it be if Jack tied me up like that, got me to that place and touched and touched and touched my body, bringing me higher and higher? Screw touching, how would it be if he fucked me while I was quivering at his every nudge?

I squeeze my thighs together, feeling how wet my panties are. I wonder if this woman does private instruction and how much she'd charge, but laughter flutters over to me from an open door on the other side of the room, and I head that way, curious.

What do people here find amusing?

The smell of sweat hits me just before I reach the threshold and step inside, gently fighting my way through the crowd to get to the center of the room where the action is—where everyone's eyes are.

A man—a titan, really; he's got to be pushing three hundred pounds—is tied to a huge pole in the middle of the room, his hands suspended above his head.

Every inch of his naked body glistens, with sweat or something else, I don't know, but around the gag in his mouth, he pants heavily.

A tiny blonde domme steps forward and grabs the base of his cock. It's so swollen, it's an angry purple shade. His legs shake and his eyes roll back in his head.

She leans in and whispers something the rest of us can't hear, but he frantically nods and moans.

She laughs and slowly strokes his cock—then stops and walks away from him, winking at the crowd.

"What's going on?" I ask a man in a suit next to me.

"Orgasm denial."

"Oh." Well, that seems tame.

He leans closer. "For the last four hours."

Oh. The poor guy. And yet, the warning "If you take this medication and suffer from an erection that lasts for more than four hours..."

flits through my mind, and I smother a laugh. The man next to me smiles as I turn back to the show.

The woman dances around the man, alternately stroking his body and his cock. She stops and fingers herself in front of him, and his eyes blaze, but he's completely helpless. All turned on and no way to fuck.

She grabs his cock and fists it hard and fast, but just when I'm sure he's going to come, she viciously pushes his cock towards his feet and punches him in the thighs, and he whimpers and tears stream down his cheeks.

I've never seen anything like it. Anticipation is one thing, but this has got to be torturous.

My cheeks hurt from smiling at this teeny little woman completely dominating this huge guy. I bet he'd do anything for her right now if she asked.

She starts rubbing his balls again, and a long line of drool strings from his mouth and hits the floor. He's vacant, nothing more than a body, nothing more than a need.

The tiny domme prances around him and asks us if she should reward him for being a good little slave.

We clap and cheer, most of us as desperate to see his relief as if it were our own.

It doesn't take more than ten seconds before thick spurts of come explode from his body.

I've never seen so much come, and we clap as the submissive cries with relief. He sags as she removes the gag and whispers in his ear, maybe congratulating him, praising him as the audience starts leaving.

A hand lands on my arm and I stop, turning to look up at the man in the suit.

"Want to try that?" He's tall and attractive in a wrong-side-of-the-tracks kind of way, and he's looking at me as though I could do to him what the dominatrix did to the other guy. He's looking at me as though I'm someone with power—and not just the privilege that comes with my job. I like that feeling more than I can say, but I decline, and I leave the club without another word.

Looking is one thing; participating is another. I love Jack and don't want to compromise our relationship, despite the heady temptation throbbing through my thighs with every beat of my heart.

FIFTEEN

GENA PACES, TREMBLING, FROM ONE room to another, even more brittle than the last time I saw her a few months ago. It's as if, because of the impending election, they've decided to lacquer her up and make her as shiny as they can. She was never going to be the relatable First Lady, comparable to William's Kate or Charles's Diana, even if age was on her side. She's not the type of woman who hangs out with the average woman trading parenting advice or witty jokes. In fact, she's not a woman at all—she's a lady, which actually makes her perfect for the job of standing around looking fashionable in photo-ops.

So, the team has gone in the complete opposite direction, making her as plastic as a doll.

It's a show of unrealistic perfection in the way only Southern belles understand. Fake tits, fake hair, fake smiles—and real claws beneath the fake tips. Because if there's anyone who will survive anything thrown at her, it's a girl from the South who has had to keep her poise and stay pretty no matter what life throws at her. Her purse matches her shoes, her feelings are always appropriately smothered, and she's unflaggingly supportive of her man, never overshadowing his accomplishments with her own, but complementing them.

There's a different tiny dog from the last time we were here. A constant rotation of dogs with brains the size of chickpeas have dragged their asses on the antique carpets of Gena's heart in the last four years.

I can't stop thinking about now juxtaposed with then.

Seeing Bundy did that to me. Even the ignominy and embarrassment of being exposed on national television apparently couldn't stop Bundy. He's been given another chance, a second act in his career as a disreputable scumbag, through the patronage of Maximilian Gold, who has given Bundy his own club to run in the bowels of the hotel. But why? Bundy was a laughingstock, a nobody, a shell of his already pretty low self. What was it about him that Max took pity on—or is it more? Bundy is a survivor. He's not altruistic; he's always going to look after himself. Maybe that's what you want in someone working for you.

Make him a part of the business, and that part of the business connected to him will always thrive.

Self-interests are the most strenuously protected—and Bundy has this way of being endearing, making you want to sit back and watch the show even when sometimes you think you should cringe. Now that I think about it, he could have been a temporary sacrifice for reasons unknown.

But what's the connection between Bundy and Max? Max and Inana?

Everything is mashed together like butter inside a French pastry dough, the two pressed up against each other and ironed together.

Jack called me away from the hotel to have dinner at Bob's house, but he's running late, leaving me with the past clinging to me like I'm wearing it as a toga. He's never late. I can't even make him late with a surprise blowjob before a meeting. Something's going on, but I can't figure out what. I didn't want to come back here, but

I missed Jack, and he wanted to have dinner with Bob and Gena. Now I'm frustrated and fidgety, and I wish Jack had met me at our place and fucked the tension out of me before coming here together with me.

It's not just seeing Bob that bothers me. I'm irritated at going back to being Catherine. At not getting to stay immersed in Inana's life. It feels like my authenticity, my depth of understanding of her is being stripped away with every minute I stand around in the uncomfortable clothes I'm forced to wear here because of Politics.

And this isn't where I want to be.

Not now.

Last night I was in the VIP club, immersed in things that most people will never see outside of a computer screen. I watched a ninety-five-pound dominatrix deny an orgasm to a guy three times her size until he was a crying, drooling mess, begging her for release.

It was amazing. When I walked in, I hadn't thought much of it except to think, "How the hell is this tiny woman going to overpower him?"

It was an amazing show of power—true power.

Seeing something like that every day would do wonders for the world we live in. Not just about what women can do, what we're capable of, but about the power of letting go and giving in to experiences to truly be present in them.

That's what Inana was trying to say with her art.

I was living it for a few short days, and now I've been snatched back into my own life.

At the best of times, my patience for Bob is on a very short leash, but right now, now that I've been living Inana's free life, living inside her head, seeing the way she does things, it makes it all that much worse.

The situation chafes at my skin like the tag on a shirt, rubbing, poking, distracting me. I want to tear it off and rub it better.

I want to go back to reading Inana's diary, tracing the words she wrote, focusing on the things she saw, staying inside La Notte to see what else is happening underground.

"Can I get you another glass of wine, Catherine?"

I'm surprised to see I've drained my glass. "No, thank you," I answer Gena with a smile. It's been twenty-eight fucking minutes. Where's Jack?

"I'll just nip to the kitchen and open another bottle for when Jack gets here, let it air out. He likes white, right?"

"Yes," I say, since she obviously wants a reason to drink. Airing out white wine? I guess it's the one socially acceptable vice to have, and she's going to milk the cork's teat for all it's worth before the election.

Can't say I blame her. Her every move will be on camera. Every smile, every frown, every outfit.

Every flaw and misstep.

It's exactly how I feel when I come to their house and make small talk.

It's worse now that I've seen Bundy again.

With Bob's political career about to go to the next level, I suspect he'll need another "event" like the last one they attended together. Considering how far he needed to go for stress relief last time, I wonder what he'd need to do now to feel better about everything.

The tinkle of ice hitting the bottom of a heavy crystal tumbler announces Bob's presence in the room. "I have it on good authority that you've recently started a new job," he says to me.

Why would Jack tell Bob about my new job? "No, still working at the paper."

"We both know that's not what I'm talking about."

"I don't know what you're talking about," I bluff, turning to where he stands near the bar, tumbler in hand.

His smile is bland. "Sometimes reporters get in too deep. Go native, as they say. Some stories hit close to home. It would be a shame if Jack found out what you've been up to."

"Excuse me?"

His eyes flick to the security guard standing in the doorway. "You heard me."

But there's no point lowering my voice. I'm sure his guard knows that Bob isn't just the typical sleazebag lawyer-turned-politician, and men like that know it's better to keep your ears shut, because the less you know, the better. "What I'm doing is exactly none of your business, Bob, and I can assure you that Jack knows—and any details he isn't aware of are harmless and insignificant and none of your business."

"Oh, but it's very much my business." His fake smile goes as brittle as Gena's, only it lacks the blurry softness of her eyes, and he walks over to me, a shark in a suit. "You're connected to Jack, who's connected to me. That makes everything you do my business. Especially in light of certain events."

I force my hands to stay at my sides, relaxed. "Nothing I do is your business."

How does he know—what does he know? I'm not stupid enough to admit to anything.

"Don't think your latest...obsession has gone unnoticed," he says. "I have reach you've never dreamed of, friends higher up—"

"And lower down?"

"—than you could imagine. People like you disappear all the time, Catherine."

Instead of shrinking back when he invades my personal space, I force a smile, hoping it's as cold as my hands suddenly are. "Yeah? Should I be flattered that you're so obsessed with me, even after all this time?" It's occurred to me that I never revealed anything about Bob, but he also never took action against me, despite my knowing all about his proclivities.

Maybe that wasn't just out of fear.

The thought is chilling, and goosebumps form on my skin.

His gaze lands on my throat. "Maybe you're the one who could never forget about that night." He takes a sip of the amber liquid in his glass, grimacing at the burn.

"Did you forget what happened? Only, I seem to recall that one of us nearly didn't get back up. Who was that?" I tilt my head.

"I wonder what Jack would say if he found out about that."

"It's Jack's reaction you should be worried about, not mine." It's the truth.

He grins, the first genuinely pleasant expression he's made tonight. "Jack? I think you'll find out that the one he's closest to as of late isn't you."

What the fuck does he mean by that? I keep my cool. "Don't flatter yourself into thinking you're more than what you are to Jack. You're his boss, not his father, Bob. I'm Jack's priority, not you." I take a step toward the table and settle into my seat, fussing with the napkin like I don't want to stuff it deep in Bob's mouth until he chokes on it. The truth is, lately it does feel like Bob's more important to Jack than I am.

"And what about you? What am I to you?"

I don't know. "Inconsequential."

His eyes darken, and he moves close to me, looming over the back of my chair. "We both know that's not true, and so do our friends in the Janus Chamber."

My mind flashes to the image of the coin in Inana's diary. A full-on body shudder claims my bones as Bob places a hand on my shoulder, so lightly I think I might have imagined it, because when I look up, his hand isn't touching me.

"The Janus Chamber?" Part of The Juliette Society, or something deeper, darker? "In Gold's hotel," I say, realizing. "That's what it's called." It makes sense now, the drawing of the Janus coin.

He nods. "Do you like it there?"

I keep my mouth shut, refusing to give him anything to work with and twist into being something it isn't. Of course I like it there. Part of me feels like it's home. "Do *you* like it there?" I counter.

"What's not to like?" He takes a sip of his drink and exhales, the alcohol sweet on his breath.

"What is the Janus Chamber?"

He looks me hard in the eye for a moment. "Whatever you want it to be. It's the place where desires are born and inhibitions go to die."

Has he been there recently?

Bob takes a step closer to me. "People like us naturally find places like that, Catherine."

"People like us?"

"People who need more than what others give us."

I shiver.

And here's where Jack should come in and see Bob looming over my body, making me uncomfortable. He wouldn't need to ask what's happening, because he'd see it on my face and know that whatever's gone down, Bob is the one in the wrong.

He'd pull me from my chair, possessively, tuck me protectively behind him while he rails at Bob, quits his job, walks us from the mansion.

And we'd never look back.

But Jack doesn't walk in.

Instead, the uncertain tapping of Gena's heels announces her arrival just outside the door, and Bob smoothly moves away from me, composing himself before his wife enters the room with another bottle of white wine and a tray of flaky rolls she made herself. What is it about a lush drinking white wine like water?

White knights only exist in the movies, and mine is running late. Mine's been texting me instead of phoning me just to hear my voice the way he used to.

Gena wanders to the window, looking out across the lawn, saying something about topiaries that I can't focus on. Bob sits at the head of the table, spreading his arms out like Jesus at the Last Supper.

I suppress a smile, reminded of Sachs, imagining Bob in his place.

If I could do anything to Bob, what would I do?

Blackness crowds the corners of my vision in a rush of blood and ideas.

Sharp instruments, meant to hurt, flay his flesh from the bone, but too soon the blood fades to reddened skin and rivers of melted red wax, the macabre scene taking a sensual turn. I climb on top of him, feeling the hair on his thighs tickle the sensitive flesh on the inside of mine. The melted wax burns my belly when I press close against him, sealing us together. My hands wander up his chest, viciously pinching his nipples on the way to his throat, and I squeeze hard as I slide down onto his cock.

Bob morphs into Jack, and then I'm choking Jack while he fucks me from below, desperate to come before he passes out.

His eyes are wide and trusting, and he comes with a gasp, filling me so full that I can't hold it all, and it drips out of my battered pussy, mixing with the red of the candle wax or blood or whatever it is staining our bodies.

I want to lick it off of us.

I squeeze my thighs together underneath the table, desperate to go finish this rhythmic pulsing off in the bathroom, but that's when Jack finally arrives.

I hug him slightly too hard, breathing in that clean scent that clings to him, wholesome and slightly citrusy. "I missed you," I whisper, and suddenly all I want is to be alone with this beautiful, good man and never think about the world outside again.

"I missed you, too." He gives me a quick squeeze before letting me go and nodding at Bob. "Bob, Gena, how are you?"

"We're good, son, how are you?"

We sit down, separated, and I want to seal us together again, reaffirm our connection after what feels like more than just a few days apart.

But first I have to get through supper with the DeVilles.

Jack makes small talk, catching up with Gena and Bob even though it's me he hasn't seen in days. Bob keeps shooting me meaningful glances over the table, as though this proves I'm not the one Jack cares about most.

I refuse to let that seed of doubt bloom into something more problematic under DeVille's insinuations. He's not a good man.

I ponder the true nature of evil over my creamed asparagus.

It's all subjective—morality isn't absolute, though I do think it's innate. The vast majority of us have that inner compass that points us in the right direction when we veer off course and fuck up, doing something truly mean or petty.

Or worse, something actively harmful to another person.

I remember one time, when I was about seven years old, I was riding my bike as fast as I could to get home on time—I'd stayed at my friend's house a little longer than I should have and was going to be late. My mom had warned me that the next time I came home late, I'd lose privileges—a vague threat that my fertile imagination was only too happy to take to the worst possible scenario.

It had rained hard that morning and was still a little drizzly, but there weren't many puddles.

I heard the squelch of my tire running over something before I saw what it was, and I'd made it twenty feet farther on the sidewalk before stopping my bike, dread forming into a knot in my guts, making it impossible to continue home until I'd seen what it was I'd killed.

I knew it was a baby bird. I just knew it.

I didn't want to see, but I couldn't blithely bike home at the same pace as though nothing had happened. Even at seven, I knew I owed it to the life I'd snuffed out to bear witness to its demise.

So I'd put my bike down, steeled myself, and walked back to the scene of the crime, feet heavy with the knowledge that I had killed something.

When I got there, it wasn't a baby bird at all, but the biggest, fattest worm I'd ever seen, writhing around, nearly crushed in two.

I felt relief and then resentment that I'd been so upset over a worm. It wasn't until I was zipping toward home on my bike again that I wondered why it mattered when I thought it was a bird, but not a worm. I'd burned ants with magnifying glasses on hot summer days with my brother, but the thought of running over a baby bird made me feel terrible, sick to the pit of my stomach.

Was it the jump across phyla that caused my feeling of relief, or did it come down to the fact that it was accidental? Why should that have mattered?

What makes an act evil, or immoral, or even wrong?

Perception of value? The bird would have been "worth" more than the worm.

Permission?

And what does any of that have to do with good or evil?

Jack nudges me with that look he has when he's asked a question and I've missed it, and that annoys me, so I nod like I know exactly what they've been droning on about for the past few minutes.

It turns out I just agreed to stay overnight here instead of going home. I could kick up a stink, and we'd go home, but I know Jack would give me shit, mortified at my refusal of Bob and Gena's hospitality.

Maybe it wasn't evil of Bob to offer or Jack to accept, but it sure feels intentional in this moment.

SIXTEEN

STAYING OVER AT THE DEVILLES' mansion isn't the worst thing in the world, but it feels like trying to go to sleep inside a burning building. My every instinct tells me to run, that it's not safe, that sooner or later I'm going to get scorched.

Maybe not a burning building, because that would leave nothing but nice, warm, clean ashes behind.

This is more like being trapped inside a building that's getting flooded with brackish water. Eventually I'll drown and the water will drain, but by then I'll be alone, with nothing but mold to keep my bloated corpse company.

The last time we spent the night was the time before the night Bob and I...

I shiver at the memory and slip beneath the cotton sheets, snuggling down in an attempt to get comfortable next to Jack's warm body, but he's facing away from me, still tapping notes into his phone with his thumbs.

He turns toward me, propping himself up on one arm. "Cath, there's something I've been wondering for a while."

I still smell the dampness from my imagined flood, and I suppress a gag as I walk my fingers up his chest, trying to lose myself in Jack instead of the memories of DeVille.

"Is it how my pussy feels from the inside? I know it's been a while, but you can't have forgotten already," I tease, half-desperate for a distraction before I go too far inside the memories I've pushed back for so long.

But there was something else. Something about a coin.

Jack captures my hand, toying with the engagement ring on my finger, but I can barely feel the touch of his hand on mine. "I want to set a date to get married."

"Oh." And just like that, I'm flung back into this moment, here, with the warmth of Jack's body next to mine, his eyes smiling down at me with something akin to shyness. I'll always be safe with Jack.

He squints at me with a grin. "Is that a good *oh*?"

Guilt squirms through my guts as I think of La Notte and how deeply I'm entangled in things over there—and how much further I'm willing to go for the story, for Lola's closure.

For my own.

What would he do, how would he look at me, if he knew every little detail about the things I've done? Then again, I haven't done anything that compromises our relationship. If Jack had done everything I have at La Notte, I'd be okay with it. I haven't crossed any lines.

Do I know every little detail of who he is and what he's done, too? I decide that it doesn't matter, but I still want to know why, after all this time, it's this moment, this bed, in this house, that he's chosen to do this, especially when he's been so distracted lately with work. "What's brought this on?"

He shrugs. "We've been engaged for a while. I love you."

"Is that it?" My heart sinks in my chest. "Because it's time?" Gee, how romantic.

He shakes his head. "It's not about a clock—though it *is* time. No, I want you to be my wife, and I want us to be that crusty old couple disgusting their kids with public displays of affection, and we can't do that until we make it official."

I press my lips to his, overcome that this perfect man wants to grow old with me. I needed to pursue Inana so I could close that chapter on my life and move on with Jack. It's helped me grow, and it's helping me learn more about myself. What if I'm not enough for him in ten years? What if... "You choose the date," I say between kisses. "I love you, I don't care when we do it."

"July 7?"

"Why the seventh?" I pull back.

He grins. "Because it's lucky."

Although I'm pretty sure there are cameras everywhere, I can't stop myself, and I tear the sheets out of my way to get to Jack.

One piece at a time, we remove the cotton barriers from each other's bodies, slowly but surely. I wrap my arms around his body, curling myself tight against his chest to let him heat me up with his skin and then roll on top of me. The way I feel when he's pressing me into the mattress is safe and comforted and wanted. It's like coming home.

God, I've missed this.

I gently scratch my nails down his back and cup his tight, strong ass, squeezing it hard. He kisses me deeply, thrusting his tongue into my mouth when I grind against the base of his penis, feeling him go from semi-hard to thick and solid against my crotch.

It feels like it's been forever, and I want Jack's cock buried deep inside. I don't care if there are thirty cameras catching every inch of space in this room; I need Jack now.

I swing my leg across his body, bracing my hands on his chest to hold steady as I straddle him.

He pushes the blanket and sheets out of the way, exposing me further, but it doesn't even matter.

Part of me is getting off on the idea that Bob is watching us right now.

Watching me fuck Jack—the man he considers the son he never had.

Watching his "son" fuck something he can never, ever have.

Jack diddles me with his thumb, and I'm soaked in a few seconds. Let's hear it for the Xbox generation of guys with nimble fingers. I slather my juices all over him, and he lets out a moan that makes me want to do it again.

So I do.

And then I guide his fat cock to my tight little hole and gasp at the way my pussy opens up to accommodate him, seemingly tighter after even a few days apart.

He's practically nudging the back of my throat, he's so deep, and I'm riding him, swiveling my hips along with his like we're churning butter.

I want his cream in me.

His hands find my tits and caress them, pinching my nipples, and I lean forward over him to grant better access as I slide up and down his cock, keeping the rhythm going to give the cameras a nice show.

I imagine Bob sitting in a cramped room, basted in the glow of monitors and his disappointment, stroking life into his penis, watching me fuck Jack, wishing he was with me doing something else.

"Fuck me harder, Jack."

And he does, back arching, legs shaking to slam himself into me, but I want more power and so does he, because he grabs my hip and rolls us over, pulling out so I can get on my knees for him to take me from behind.

I brace myself with wide-spread hands, arching my back and waving my little ass in the air, taunting him with my pussy. "Are you going to fuck my tight little hole, Jack?"

He spanks my ass once, and I cry out and smile over my shoulder at him. "I want you to come inside me and then use your come to fuck my ass next. I want you to pound into me and make me scream."

He jerks my hips back on the bed, burning my knees a little with the friction, and he spears me again.

I can't stop smiling.

He's ramming into me from behind again and again and again, like he knows we're part of a show, too, but the fact that it's just me making him this hot makes me wild, and I push back, listening to the smacking of my ass against his body.

This is what we could be forever. Him and me and our bodies and our love.

He pushes me to the mattress and clasps our hands above my head, twining our fingers together as though he feels the same thing I do. Our connection. Our love. And Bob jerking off in the closet watching us.

I can feel myself starting to come, spasms turning inward like a flower deep inside, and I spread my legs until I swear my hips will dislocate just to feel his balls slap against my clit and his breath quickens and his hands spasm in mine and I know he's about to come inside me. "Bob could be in the closet right now watching us, jerking off."

He tenses and goes still while I thrash underneath him, trying to get him off with the vibration of my body, wanting him to feel the depth of my orgasm squeezing the insides of my pelvis almost painfully. "What the fuck, Catherine?"

He pulls out of me and moves away from me, tugging the sheets around himself like a barrier.

I sit up. Shit. There's no way to explain that train of thought, so I spin it into something else I've thought about. "There's something about the idea of being watched—or watching you that turns me on."

"Are you serious?" Unfortunately, his inflection is incredulous, not exploratory.

I pull my legs beneath me so I'm sitting like a mermaid, trying to look suggestive. "You don't think it would be hot to bring a woman to our apartment and ravage her while I'm in the bedroom watching, and she has no idea I'm there?"

"And what, you spring out of the closet like a damned jack-in-the-box?"

"I thought you would be into that."

"Well, I'm not. You're fine with me fucking other people? What does that say about you—have you been sleeping with other guys behind my back?"

"Jack, no!" God, this is so far from what I wanted to happen. "I swear."

He shakes his head. "Sometimes it's like I don't even know you. I mean, these ideas are one thing when you're a teenager, but right now we're supposed to be getting serious in our lives and careers, and you're off pretending to be a rogue femme fatale or whatever—"

"Stop pretending like our sex life and work life need to be the same! Your fantasy about coming home with someone while I was masturbating is acceptable, but my flirtation with the same idea isn't? You're being an enormous hypocrite about fantasies."

"Bob is like a father to me. There's a huge difference."

"Fine, but this isn't just about fantasies. You're belittling my job. I'm a reporter. I'm writing a story, not playing at anything. You're not respecting us, or my work!"

"I've offered better stories for you."

"Maybe I want to do it on my own. I don't have DeVille giving everything to me one silver spoonful at a time."

He glares at me. "And I do? I work damned hard at my job and work insane hours to do it, and now that my efforts are finally paying off, you expect—what? You want me to take more time out of my day to chit-chat with you about some dead pop star? It's not worthy of my time."

"First of all, she wasn't a pop star, and second, what, I'm not worthy of your time? What's that saying, Jack, that your job is more important than mine?"

"Yes. A few minutes ago, we were talking about setting a date to be married. That's the ultimate commitment, and then while we're making love, you talk about how my boss, my mentor, could be watching us, and wouldn't it be hot if I brought another woman home and fucked her while you watch? Grow up. If you were really serious about reporting, you'd have taken my offer to ask Bob for something. Obviously you're not ready to be an adult."

His aloof manner and this overreaction click things into place—a horrible place I don't want to go, but have to. "Is there someone else?"

"No, and I can't believe you'd even ask me that." He rolls away from me and angrily rearranges the covers. "I need some time to think—and you need some time to grow up, obviously. Forget about July. We'll talk about it again when you're ready to settle down."

Relief fills me at his denial, but it still doesn't fix things. "You can't take it back!"

"I'm not talking about this any more tonight, Catherine."

I try a couple more times, but he's stonewalling me, and I lie back confused and hurt at the casual way he belittled my job. Even if he was just shocked at my timing, he's gone too far and spoken to me as though I'm a bad child instead of a partner.

It feels like I'm trapped in a bed with a stranger and trapped in a house with my enemy, DeVille. And the fact that maybe Bob was right about Jack's allegiances hurts worst of all.

That night I dream about that ruby-red silk robe with the gold embroidery that I wore when I discovered the man in the mask that I was fucking was Bob. I'm walking along a beach, somewhere warm but not hot, tracing the golden threads with my fingertip.

Someone gently takes my hand.

Her skin is brown, darker than mine, and I follow her forearm to her bicep to her shoulder, the world dissolving as I see her face.

Inana.

She smiles, and color floods my senses in a strange way—as though sound has flavor, and color has scent, and the world is made of a light we can feel if we listen hard enough.

"I'm all alone. What happened to you?" I ask, squeezing her

hand tight because I know how this works; it's only a matter of time before my logical mind realizes this is a dream and pulls me back into consciousness. I need her answers.

"I went deeper," she says with a smile.

"Should I go deeper?" I ask in a small voice.

"Are you ready for the answers?"

"Yes. Tell me."

But Jack shifts in his sleep, shifting the bed, and I wake up before she can answer me.

SEVENTEEN

~oollloo~

PEOPLE-WATCHING HAS ALWAYS FASCINATED me. Now even more so when I'm using it as a distraction from Jack saying he needs a break from us. From me.

His words feel like a burr stuck inside my throat that I can't swallow down.

I deliver a tray of specialty coffee to a woman whose smile seems a little forced, and I can't help but notice the superficial resemblance to the woman I saw wearing a mask, lying stretched out on the top of a table where people used her body to eat off of. Maybe she's worried I'll say something.

Maybe her smile is forced because she's a misanthrope or has social anxiety or hates my perfume.

If it is her, I saw a few people snorting off of her body, too, but that's none of my business. Something tells me Health and Safety would never make it through the front doors of the hotel. Not that they'd ever come that far. Max would have vigorously crossed that *T*.

The man I pass on the twenty-fourth floor looks like the one I saw getting paddled until he screamed. His come had the consistency of raw egg whites and coated his belly.

A man clears his throat in the elevator and sends a shiver of recognition through me. I know that cough—but from where? Are they the same people, or is it that I'm expecting the VIPs to be every-where now that I know the club is there?

I'm looking at all the guests differently, wondering which ones know about what's underneath their feet. Not all of them are into the same levels of debauchery, but then again, the people who find their way to the VIP section all got there for a reason, a common denomi-nator uniting them all in some strange commonality.

The one thing linking us together isn't something I can comfort-ably ask people about—even if I weren't part of the hotel. I think I recognize a few people from the club, but I'm not sure. Max stops by the front desk at 1:13 p.m. and waits until a man with a neatly trimmed black beard and outrageously long eyelashes stops by.

They leave without saying a word to me or each other.

He's familiar, and I need to know whether it's from my own expe-riences years ago, or something from my diary.

The rest of the afternoon drips by way too slowly, but ten o'clock comes around, and I smooth my skirt and make my way down to the VIP club.

Being overdressed makes me stand out, but more in the sense that I might have a particular kink, like I might enjoy getting off on having my blouse torn off—rape fantasies—or maybe I'm here for the men who are into tearing blouses and fulfilling rape fantasies and marking up pristine, starched women as though they're just another prop. So while I get noticed, I guess I'm not really standing out much after all.

I search for any familiar face, hoping and dreading I'll find one.

Confused?

You come to places like this to be someone else—yourself—the authentic face behind the pleasant mask you typically show to the world. Seeing a familiar face shatters the illusion and pulls you from the escape.

Have you ever run into your gynecologist while out and about in public? You can shake her hand and chat, but at the back of your mind you're wondering if she's thinking about your vagina, remembering how it looked the last time you saw her.

You wonder how long ago she washed her hands before she touched yours.

Fresh hell.

Anonymity is incredibly freeing.

Have you noticed how far people will go at masquerades when they think no one knows who they are? It's not the masquerade, specifically, but costumes and disguises that give the security to go further. It's an inhibition-killer without liquor.

Who you are when no one's looking is who they say you truly are.

Who are you when you think you can get away with anything?

What would you do?

What would you try?

Who could you become if there were no consequences for your actions?

That's where it gets sketchy when it comes to religion and moral absolutes. The Ten Commandments didn't cover everything, so does that mean those things are okay to do? Do you avoid running out and raping, murdering, and stealing only because your religion tells you it's wrong? Or is it because inside, you know when something feels off?

You hear people talk about morals and values as though there are strict guidelines beyond the "thou shalt not"s and the justice system, but there are gray areas everywhere.

Being an asshole isn't illegal.

You can toe the line between abuse and free speech, offend everyone and their neighbor, but the lines of propriety and rights are more flexible than people think. It goes the other way, too—

self-defense versus opportunistic motherfuckers trying to get back somehow for a perceived slight against them.

Politicians can't seem to shut up about traditional values, desperately trying to convince John Q. Voter that they're just like him—because who doesn't want to see himself inside that Oval Office? You want someone who you think holds your values, because you assume they'd do all the things you want them to, legalize all the things you want them to, ban all the things you think they should. It's comforting to think that your worldview won't be challenged by someone whose opinions differ radically from your own—especially when that person is in any position of authority.

It's an ego-jerk. Same reason why people get so emotionally invested in their sports teams.

But again, value is all about perception. Everything is worthless except for the value we place upon it. Why are natural diamonds more expensive than man-made synthetic gems that are truly flawless? They're just lying around in the ground. Where's the value in that?

What's so special about it? The chase? Finding them?

We've been taught they're worth more.

That's all.

The most valuable thing about diamonds is the lives lost in the mining process, but it's not like the companies care.

Corporations are machines run by machine-like people.

Diamonds are worth more to the corporations than the human lives of the people mining them.

Value is set arbitrarily based on what people in positions of power want you to buy.

Think about it.

When something is discounted, even if it's your favorite product that you've been searching for for ages, what's your knee-jerk reaction?

It's a scam. There must be something wrong with it. It's broken/faulty/expired, or a reproduction made in China at half the price and filled with lead.

Authenticity is another concept sold to us, and we buy it.

In a place like this, nothing is for sale—but everything and anything is up for grabs.

No money exchanges hands. Instead, it's a power exchange. Now it becomes a different type of indulgence that few can afford.

Remember brand exclusivity?

How does Max keep this place up and running?

Are the patrons attracted to the VIP club itself? How do they find out about it? I can't imagine it's mentioned in any in-room brochure.

Is it a side attraction of the hotel, and not the focus at all? Perhaps I'm looking at it in reverse only because it seems like the hotel was built around the club, when the opposite is true.

That feels incorrect.

If I told you how much it costs to stay here for a night, you wouldn't believe me. If I told you that the majority of our guests stay for no less than seven days, your eyes would bug out at the amount of zeroes on the price.

Perceived value.

What does Maximilian Gold value? More importantly, what does he get out of all this? Men like him don't get off on money. The ones who do operate in the open, going as flashy as they can with their possessions. Car, clothes, watches, girlfriend's fake tits. Those men are the ones who make a show of it because they want everyone to know what they've got.

They're like the people who win those huge lotteries and become the nouveau riche—and buy the biggest houses and a different car for each day of the week. They end up broke but have a lot of flashy toys, and resemble the Beverly Hillbillies.

Have you ever noticed that billionaires, people with true fuck-you money, have a uniform?

True wealth outside a suit.

It's khakis and a polo shirt with a pocket in the front that's always got a pen in it.

They've got scrawny legs and boat shoes—something with tassels. Good teeth and bad hair. They don't care about style or showing off—they don't want their assets known. They care about things other than getting their pricks sucked. If that's all Maximilian Gold wanted, he'd have had me on my knees by now. I've been propositioned harder at the newspaper than I have been here.

I think Max Gold disdains the physicality of sex but has created an environment to facilitate it in all its forms. His fetish is voyeurism, observing fetishes, but he's not a very sexual person. He looks but doesn't act, even if he seems to like what he sees. He enjoys the power of creating the environment. He's not the kid with the ant farm, he's the manufacturer of the ant farm who likes seeing the kid play with it.

He's not asexual, but he seems like a singularity.

If he was looking for a show, Inana was the best one he could have hoped to find.

They were connected when she was alive. I need to know if they were connected beyond that. Because if she was more to him than an employee, what would he do if he discovered she wanted to leave? His tastes are very narrow, and the woman I suspect was his favorite was taken or took herself out of the picture.

That means there was an opening in more than one area.

Jack's words bounce around inside my broken heart—despite my pleading in the morning, he remained stony and cold. We're on a break and I don't understand why.

Gold likes a performance.

And if he wants a show, I'll give him one.

I'm drawn to the VIP club like there's a string hooked from my clit to the pulsing behind that door. I want to press up against it and get myself off on the vibrations, but it's uncouth for the VIP concierge to be found humping a doorknob in a hotel hallway. And anyway, when I press my palm against it, I know the pulsing isn't as strong as the idea of it.

The vibrations aren't enough.

Anonymity. Bundy knows me, but there are enough nooks and crannies in the VIP club to get lost in. Besides, Bundy knows I'd never touch him, and he's sleazy enough to know when to cut his losses and move on to other ground.

Ground that will spread its soiled legs for him.

I'm not worried about him.

Down a hallway, not quite in the corner of a room, I walk through a scene where a man shoots women with paintball guns and they dodge and duck and shriek like a flock of birds. Jack went to play paintball once; I stayed home because it wasn't really my thing, but seeing it now is different.

Then again, it's not like Jack would have been shooting at a group of women in white lingerie—the better to see the paint splatters with. Some of the women wear huge smiles; others seem like they're trying very hard not to get hit, hiding behind the rest like they're on a group date gone horribly, horribly wrong, while still others stride for the front of the pack, trying to get closer. They all want to be here, but some enjoy the process as well as the results.

One of the girls licks at a blue splatter on her forearm. "Blue raspberry," she says to the girl next to her.

Edible paintballs.

Taste the rainbow?

Simulated violence makes no sense to me. I can't find it sexy—maybe because the only type of guy who is into it is like my ex, Macho Will, someone who owns too many guns, and there's something about that I find innately shady. It's like they're protesting too much, or compensating for something.

Wink wink.

These kinds of guys are fun or silly to fuck, but annoying in the real world. Who wants to stroll around town with a caveman on her arm?

I like the idea of safely playing with these paintball guns, especially because it's edible paint, which implies that someone's going to lick it off and bring it back to sensual instead of brutal. The women all seem into it.

Half of them form a line near a wall, angling their asses up for easier shots. Most of them wear their hair in high ponytails that swing back and forth as they prance around waiting to be shot.

What are female bronies called? Is that even a thing?

The rest, not lined up, surge toward me at once. I duck out of the way, trying to stay clear of the scene, skirting the edge of the group, but a snapping pain on the back of my thigh makes me suck in my breath through my teeth. My dark skirt hides the evidence, so at least I won't have to change clothes, but I still glare in the direction of the man with the gun before schooling my features into something more professional.

"I'm not a part of this scene," I say, trying to keep my tone pleasant, since he's still a guest of the hotel.

He's about thirty-five, blonde hair combed back from his face and ending in a boyish flip, the ends curling around his neck. Muscular but not meaty. Physically, he reminds me of a baseball player, or maybe a soccer player. He grins and holds up the gun. "Do you want to be?"

I glance at the other women, covered with blotches of paint, and am flattered because each of them radiate with beauty, putting my young model friend to shame, but I say, "No, thanks."

"Are you sure?"

I decline again and keep moving, but there's something so intensely erotic about him shooting the women interested in being his companions for the night that I get a little bounce in my step. What would that be like?

I realize it's not the jostling for a position, wanting to be shot that interests me, but the idea of gunplay, the fantasy of risk, without putting myself in harm's way.

I want to know how that feels, so I walk away from the temptation of it. It's packed here tonight—the place sticky and thick with bodies, the air tangy with sweat and sex and lemon slices tucked onto the edges of glasses. There are no drink minimums or maximums. People do whatever they want, however they want, and if anyone has a problem with it…let's just say that management isn't sympathetic to your complaints.

"Hey!" A hand shoots out of an alcove, latching onto my arm, pulling me into the darkness before I have time to be scared.

It's my golden goddess supermodel friend. "Hi."

She squeezes me into a tight hug, wrapping herself around me in a way that shouldn't be possible based on how tiny she is, but models tend to defy the laws of physics. "Thank you for helping me," she says.

"Don't mention it." I pat her back, and she sighs.

Definitely on something, probably Ecstasy, based on the size of her pupils—dilated until only a slim ring of iris colors the edges with icy blue. "Will you join me for a minute?"

I shouldn't, but her breath smells sweet from her drink in a way that reminds me of the paintball gun, and I find myself nodding and sliding into the booth next to her. "Where's your boyfriend?"

"He's around," she says with a dismissive wave. "Try this. I invented it myself. Tell me what you think."

I take a sip, and then another deeper one because it's sour like a cherry and sweet like honey. "It's very good. What do you call it?"

She pushes her lips out in a pout and takes a deep sip, considering. "I don't know yet. What's your name?"

"Catherine."

"That's too old-fashioned for you. You need something more exotic and fresh. Catherine is old."

"Catherines can be sexy. Catherine Deneuve. Catherine Zeta-Jones. Hepburn." I bite my lip, trying to think of another, but that's about it—I've exhausted my list of sexy Catherines.

"Yes, but you are different from them. Everyone should have a name that matches her face."

I like her accent and the way it lilts, making her sound sophisticated because she's different, even though she's so young. So young and so very stoned. "And what would you rename me?"

"Claudia."

Chills cover my body, for that can't be a coincidence. Claudia—in search of her friend Anna in *L'Avventura*. Anna, who, like Schrödinger's cat, both left and didn't leave the island; who both lived and died. She is and she isn't.

She wasn't and she was.

"Why Claudia?" I ask, stealing another sip of her drink, now because I need it instead of just wanting to taste it.

She smiles, playfully flicking my hand. "Your eyes remind me of hers."

"Monica Vitti's?" I ask.

She frowns. "Claudia Schiffer's. Who is Monica Vitti?"

"Just an actress. I must have misunderstood you. Please excuse me."

I slide from the booth, shaken, needing something. My skin's hot, not quite feverish, but approaching it like a car merging onto the freeway with reckless disregard.

I've heard *L'Avventura* referred to as moody existential ennui. Cool detachment. And that's sort of how I feel, only instead of it being fine, I'm trying to dig in with my claws to stay tethered to something I can believe in. It's not about being detached. It's about realizing that in life, there are very few things worth fighting for and believing in. It's about sorting the wheat from the chaff and focusing your attention on the things that actually matter.

It's about asking yourself what's truly important in life.

I want something to believe in.

I believe in love. But I feel like the definition is being rewritten from the corner of my eye, where the rest of the revelations live. If I could turn my head fast enough, I might catch sight of one.

I'm beginning to believe there was a special ingredient in that drink, and the fact that I'm not worried or even concerned about that only strengthens my hypothesis.

I hadn't noticed how terrible some of these people are at dancing until now. Their movements are too jerky and contained, like they're afraid of their own bodies, scared of occupying more space than is necessary, which is ironic if you've ever seen a fifty-something man parade around the boardroom like he's Baryshnikov, aching for every eye in the room to be on him. What is it about dancing that makes people feel vaguely ridiculous? A man's getting a dildo rammed up his ass in the corner; a woman's nipples are clamped so hard they're almost purple as she has two men take turns on her with a riding crop, and yet people are worried they'll look undignified if they bust a move?

Oh, the things that go on in some people's heads.

But now I know what this place is. Once, when doing a story about surprising British tourist traps, I learned about this place called Magaluf, in a part of Majorca. There was a huge scandal there a few years ago when a girl gave several blowjobs for what she thought was a free holiday, but turned out to really only be a free cocktail. She was irrationally angry, which I find hilarious, like she was offended that she wasn't receiving enough payment for her sloppy blowjobs on the dance floor.

The locals call it *mamading*, but it's classic bait and switch, and capitalizing on the ignorance of a tourist. Not all places take care of the tourism industry—they see the foreigners as marks, free for exploitation in any way necessary to get what they want. And like in Magaluf, right here everyone is doing the same thing. It's all about getting what they want.

This place filled with heavy drinking and sex is a safe place where people can let their desires thrive instead of hiding them. It's *mamading*, but everyone knows the score—and welcomes it. There are no tricks. I flow around the dance floor, determined to show everyone how it's done—to prove that I can move despite the clothes that would suggest I'm stiffer than I am. By the time three songs have passed, I'm sweaty and have gained an audience, and I've migrated back to where the guy with the paintball gun is hanging out.

And one of the girls is pulling his already hardening cock from his pants. He's sweaty, and I wonder if he smells like the leather pants he's wearing. He groans when her tongue swirls around his head.

He jerks, and at first I think it's because of her technique, but then I realize he's begun shooting the women with the paintball gun again.

She grazes the skin of his cock with her teeth while he uses the gun to shoot at other women—and the other women are so into the blowjob, I can tell, that they press closer, wanting to watch him get off. But all they get for their efforts are brightly colored splotches of brilliant paint, because they're making easier targets of themselves.

I'm watching them watching him, and it's sexy as hell.

His head tilts back and his jaw opens as his hips pump in rhythm to the girl's ministrations. One woman gets too close, and he shoots her in the thigh. She lets out a squawk of pain and surprise, scuttling back to the relative safety of the group. Silly girl. That's not going to get her noticed in a place like this. She's not a predator; she's the prey and needs to know her place.

Feeling my skin get flushed with heat, I unbutton my blouse and the front-clasping bra beneath it, and rock back on my heels. She pinches the back of his thigh and he shudders, sending thick jets of silvery come all over her face and tits, knocking her hand out of the way in his rush to continue pumping himself, draining his balls of the last drops, soaking her with his essence as the gun goes off—this time the paintball slaps me just above the left breast, and I cry out, with a wince he doesn't notice.

But one of the girls does.

A tall brunette steps forward from the crowd and stands in front of me. "May I kiss that better?"

I nod. I don't know whether this is the type of behavior that will get me fired or get me a raise, but she caresses my cheek, so at least I know I'm doing something positive for customer relations.

She's wearing a white silk camisole covered with paint, and a light gray pencil skirt—clothes that do nothing to hide her ample curves. Her tongue is small and catlike, darting out to clean the paint with slender, warm licks. Her mouth is so soft against my skin, it's not like anything I've ever felt. Men's kisses tend to be rougher— even when they're gentle, a lot of the time their stubble will lightly scratch you anyway, taking it from soft to lightly abrasive, unless they're barely twenty.

It's nice, but different from this silken mouth lapping at my chest. She makes it erotic instead of utilitarian simply by lingering, taking her time, and looking me in the eyes as she cleans the paint from my body.

She likes this.

Is this how it looks when I'm getting Jack off? The gentle teasing in her eyes, the shyness even in the knowingness. Screw Jack and his bullshit "break." The things I want to do to this woman would be crossing a very big line.

My legs shake as she takes me by the hand and pulls me through a silver door into a nearby room, quiet compared to what we just left behind.

The room is darker and smells like cinnamon and some sort of sweet musk. It's smaller, more intimate, and I realize there's two other women already here together. The woman who brought me here smiles and leads me to the corner of the room, where a silk screen hides a large wardrobe, but I can still see the other women from this angle. Their whispers and exhalations enhance my anticipation.

I've never been with a woman before. What's she going to do to me? While the other women build up their excitement, I try to listen to what they're saying, how they're interacting, but can't understand the words. It takes me a moment to realize they're speaking French.

My guide turns my face back to hers with a gentle pressure, biting her lip as she slowly strips my clothes from my body.

Her fingers don't fumble over my clothes the way men's do— she's undone as many bras as I have, unfastened as many tiny pearl buttons on the tops of expensive skirts.

She drinks me in with her eyes when she finally gets me naked, and I shiver, but she doesn't touch me. Everything feels warm and strange and soft. Inside the wardrobe are different types of lingerie, and she takes her time choosing bottoms for me—red lace—and then hunts for a top while I slip into them.

Have these been worn before? They feel new, but I don't know or really care.

Her hands are soft as she spins me by the hips to face away from her. My breasts and belly are cupped by a corset, but it's too big, and she *tsk*s and removes it, choosing another one that fits better.

I like the way her nails gently scratch my back as she fastens the hooks, closing me inside the lace, making my breasts swell above the cups, making me seem curvier than I am.

She turns me back around and removes her clothes, and she's already perfect. She takes me by the hand again and leads me to the corner, where the other two women have now moved to a leather sling. I swallow, excitement at being near them overtaking me, and my heart beats faster when my guide whispers to me to kneel facing the other women. She teases my hair back over my shoulder before kissing my neck.

"What's your name?" I ask.

"Caroline."

It's now, as the slightest whisper of this woman's skin against mine is making me sigh and shiver, that I'm sure the Swedish model had some kind of drug in the drink she gave me.

But Caroline is pressing her breasts to my back and cupping my breasts from behind and I can't find it in me to be mad or scared that some of my walls have been knocked down by the model's cherry-honey cocktail.

I watch the French girls. One has been suspended in the leather sling; it holds her upper body, and two D-rings attached to chains clip onto the leather ankle cuffs she has on, so she's completely relaxed without having to support her body weight. Her pussy is completely accessible, and covered with hair. I've heard that European women keep a more natural state.

Caroline teases my nipples while the French girl who's on her feet leans in to whisper to the one in the sling as she fingers her pussy. The wetness is visible even from here, and I moan as the girl adds another finger, causing the girl in the sling to moan and say something in rapid French.

Caroline's touch is feather-soft—a perfect contrast to the way the French girls touch.

When the girl employs all four of her fingers, Caroline urges my knees apart and rubs my clit through the crotch of my panties until I'm soaked and gasping. The other two girls murmur and moan together in French, and when the one stuffs her whole hand inside the other's pussy, fisting her deep, my hips twitch and I lean back against Caroline, desperate to feel that same fullness inside me, but she continues teasing me with light, rapid fingertips.

With her other hand, she turns my head, and her impossibly soft mouth finds mine. I've never had a kiss so sensual and sweet. Her tongue strokes mine with equal skill to any lover I've ever had, but seems more nimble and deliciously invasive.

Her touches are firm but her skin is soft, and it's strange to yield to arms that feel so much like my own, but I like how her body feels against mine, the way our lingerie rubs together, catches of lace and satin and silkiness that I've never felt with a man. She knows my body better than any lover I've had.

And yet, I don't want to be teased, I want her to take her fist and do the same to me, make me her fucking puppet of pleasure and fill me up to my throat so I can taste myself on her fingertips.

"Please," I whimper, mesmerized by the hips of the woman in the sling, which are undulating like a snake having a seizure when she looks over at me and tries to smile but gasps instead.

She screams out curses or blessings in French. I shudder as Caroline slides one slender finger inside my pussy, and that's all it takes to slam me over the edge. I come all over her hand to the sound of another woman's moans.

EIGHTEEN

MY SHOULDER PROTESTS A LITTLE when I shrug out of my stiff blouse, but I get the rest of my soiled clothes off, get in the shower, and scrub at my face.

Rivulets of hot soapy water cascade over my body and swirl down the drain.

Standing still, I bring my awareness to my body, deep in my body, and feel the ache on the back of my thigh where I got shot. I swivel and twist to look—there's a bruise half the size of my fist forming to match the one on my chest.

I've been marked by pleasure. It reminds me of the way Anna used to talk about the bruises she wore like temporary tattoos as a signal to others about what she was into.

If I went out in a skirt short enough to bare it, would people think it was caused by an accident, or would there be people who knew it was sexual—a fuck bruise?

I trace the edge of it while my other hand finds my clit, soapy with bubbles, and I go to town working myself up into a lather.

I press the bruise and moan, as much from the pain as from the memory of earlier and from the slip and slide of my fingers on my clit. It sharpens the pleasure, this pain. I thrust two fingers inside my pussy, but it's not enough, I need a fist or more right now like the French girl got, but I don't have the leverage. My hand leaves the bruise, and I abuse my pussy and clit simultaneously with both hands.

I'm walking through the herd of girls, who are now wearing black vinyl. I'm in white vinyl so the guy with the gun can see the marks he leaves on me.

I pinch my chest, feeling the shot when he pulls the trigger.

I twist the skin on my belly when he shoots me there.

I get to his side and take the gun from him, looking at the women begging me with their eyes to shoot them with the gun and make them all mine.

I reach back and savagely press the welt on my leg, knees shaking as I feel someone kneel beside me and wrap their arms around my leg.

I look down at the person hugging my leg, and it's Jack, clad in black leather with guyliner that makes his eyes stand out brilliantly. Staring up at me with so much soft trust and adoration shining from his gaze.

I reach down and caress his jaw, looking him in the eyes as I shoot him in the thigh. His face half crumples in a grimace of pain and pleasure like he can't decide which it is, but he groans as I pull him to his feet and bend to lick the paint-covered welt already forming on his thigh.

The little swell is hot against my tongue. I press against it with one hard lick, and he shivers, his cock springing up and nudging my face. I snap my fingers, ordering the girls to come to me like my subservient little puppies, and they know exactly what I want and begin caressing Jack's body, touching him everywhere except for the parts that belong to me—the parts that only I get to claim—all the while murmuring in sexy, accented voices.

I shoot him in the belly, on the arm, on the chest, on his calf, and each time, he hisses in perfect sips of air that nourish me like manna.

The girls press those bruises as I take his length in my mouth and suck and suck, confusing his senses a little more as to whether he's feeling pain or pleasure, but making damn sure that he doesn't want either to stop. I want him to be ruined for anything but this for the rest of his life, the same way I am.

I tear the showerhead from the wall, aiming it at my clit, twisting the knob as high as it will go so I can twist my fingers into my bruise as I suck Jack dry while the other women jealously watch us both come together, wishing I'd give the same pleasure to them.

I'm wetter than the jets pounding my clit.

I can't fucking breathe.

I spiral higher and higher, feeling like I've come loose from my body, I come so hard. Maybe I do, because when I open my eyes, I'm sitting in the bathtub with the water still aimed at my cunt.

I put everything back the way it was, turn off the water, and towel off.

Pleasantly sore, but relaxed, I smooth lotion over my skin and notice the glow in my cheeks in the reflection of the mirror—making me look beautiful.

What I just did made me radiant. Being with a woman while two more fucked in front of me was sexy as hell, and yet fisting is somehow another one of those taboo things we're never supposed to talk about. It feels good—or it looked like it did.

How can that be wrong or strange?

What is it about society that makes us shrink away from pain as though it's unnatural and unhealthy, even though we're bombarded with it in other areas?

Sports, for example. No pain, no gain. Give one hundred and ten percent. Do it till it hurts. From gym class to the Olympics, we're pressured to find something athletic that we're good at, and to try to exploit that talent in the hopes of making money at it—regardless of the tax on our bodies.

Little girls get ballet, little boys get baseball or football. It's always seemed backward that we try to rub out the violence in girls, make them pretty and docile, and encourage the boys-will-be-boys mentality, then teach women to be afraid of the men society creates.

Maybe if we had little girls in martial arts and boys in dance, the world would be different. But ignoring the archaic gender roles, the expectation of pushing through the pain is there all along. We have to be the best, beat the best, but get along while doing it because Most Congenial is still a thing. But doesn't competition make us stronger?

Not when it comes to pro football players when they hit the latter years of their lives and their brains are curling up and shrinking from the chronic concussions—the brain trying to curdle and protect itself by hardening like an interior helmet.

Hockey players weren't required to wear protective gear for a startlingly long time. And of course, they wore cups long before they put helmets on—showing their true priority when it comes to safety. As long as they can still fuck, who needs headgear?

And now we've got MMA, which is as close to bringing back the old arenas with gladiators as I think we're ever likely to get. People paying money to watch others knock the shit out of each other. The fighters sometimes grapple on top of the blood that the last round's loser left on the octagon floor.

I'm equal parts thrilled and disgusted by it. On the one hand, it's savage, and what's the point of it?

On the other hand, it's fucking savage, and giving manners and propriety the finger once in a while makes me want to purr. Is it wrong to want to be spanked? To revel in controlled chaos like that? Nature is the most violent offender of them all—the world itself is trying to wipe us from its surface with earthquakes, tsunamis, floods, fires.

Certain behaviors are learned, others innate. But all I ever needed to learn about violence, I learned in church.

I slip into my favorite T-shirt and climb into Inana's bed, turning off the lamp. I want everything I've experienced to continue, to be more, bigger, brighter, but I wanted to experience it with Jack. And yet, the times I attempted to broach the subject, he looked at me like I was wrong or crazy for wanting things to be more intense, even though I wanted them with him. Even though I love him more than I've loved anyone and want to share everything with him. I crossed a line tonight, but he's the one who drew the line.

I tried to cross it with him first, but he rejected me completely.

Tears sting my eyes when I check my phone. He hasn't replied to any of my calls or texts. Are we just on a break, or are we well and truly broken?

Maybe I'm the broken one.

There are some things we need to keep only for our partners, but there are also parts of ourselves we need to keep secret, keep for ourselves, things that make us who we are.

The first present I ever remember receiving was a coloring book called *Lives of the Catholic Martyrs*—a horrifying thing to look back on, but these things really exist. I remember my parents parking me at the kitchen table, and I'd flip through the book, deciding which scene I wanted to make more vivid in its grotesqueness—though I never saw it as grotesque until later—happily humming and coloring with my milk and cookies.

There's nothing romantic about Jesus up there on the cross, and yet it's romanticized almost to the point of being a fetish for suffering. I'm no Son of God, but if I died in a horrific way, I would hate for my life to be reduced to the method of my death instead of my message.

Make it a heart, or a symbol of peace. Two hands clasped together, signifying solidarity and equality. Acceptance. But the Church cornered the market on torture porn long before the Internet made it accessible via a mouse click, and you know what sells better than tolerance?

Fear.

A happy Jesus smiling down at you from a comfy chair on a Sunday morning isn't going to fill the collection plate with the people's attempts to assuage guilt and buy their way into a clean conscience and a shiny halo. There's no business in happiness. Guilt, on the other hand, is very lucrative—and it's not like they don't truly believe in the salvation they're selling.

At least, most of them.

The Catholic Church is one of the greatest money-making machines the world has ever known, sacking its neighbors and taking all it could carry and store from the beginning. Their land was annexed over time, but they were paid handsomely for those "sacrifices." They don't even know their own true monetary value— hell, a few years ago, hundreds of millions of Euros were found just tucked away.

Hundreds of millions.

They've got money in every country, including some twenty million in the Federal Reserve, and they're a religion, so, tax-free status.

They get away with murder—sometimes literally, though not openly for some time now, unless we count the way they preach against contraceptives in Africa and to anyone else who will listen.

And don't even get me started on Vatican City.

The Church has been the greatest force holding back progress as well—look at the way the greatest thinkers in the world were persecuted for daring to question things, put to death.

Where do you think the superstition around Friday the thirteenth came from?

Growing up being cinched into a pretty dress and uncomfortable shoes, marched up the aisle, and perched in an uncomfortable pew was bad enough. But then being preached to about hellfire and brimstone, saints and sinners, pain and power?

It's enough to make anyone turn to a life of S&M.

The two aren't that far apart.

I still remember some of those images in the coloring book. My little brother used to draw the Stations of the Cross as a kid and spent a lot of time getting the blood and wounds right, because as they say, the devil is in the details.

We all get introduced to—and fucked up about—these things from childhood, in some way. The idea that movies and video games are the cause of it? Screw that. Religion—particularly Christianity—is a far more powerful and persuasive instigator of ideas about sadism, masochism, sin, and the guilt of pleasure.

Suppress, suppress, suppress.

But the darkness doesn't just swallow our transgressions—it remembers them. Hides them for us until we're ready to remember them, or until we take a drink from a young model in an underground club that knocks our inhibitions down and replaces our "I shouldn't" with "Why the hell not?"

When I was younger, I remember tying my little brother up in a closet and leaving him there, after also attacking him with a pair of scissors and threatening to take his eye out.

Don't get self-righteous—he deserved it for being an unrelenting little shit that day. And I'd never have actually taken his eye out. It was one of those bluffs we make that go too far, but that we'll never actually follow through with.

We all say shit like that when we're younger. Who hasn't told a sibling—or been told by one—that they were adopted? We wield things like weapons when we're kids. And this kind of cruelty, dominance and submission, is also (paradoxically) entirely natural in children, because they have no filter.

Without correction, we gravitate towards this behavior. It's survival—predator and prey. Look at the games we play as kids.

They're about the chase, about war, about domination of the weak.

Kids are the worst bullies there are—and we're all like that before being told we shouldn't be.

It's not just dog-eat-dog, it's *Lord of the Flies.*

Are you Piggy or Ralph?

Ralph or Jack?

These are the questions we never want to ask ourselves, in case the answer is one we don't like to think about.

One of those characters dies. And if it's a choice between being who I want to be, or being perfectly good and dying from a boulder smashing my face in?

I'd still take Jack.

Ironic, no?

NINETEEN

∽ꙮꙮ∾

MY LITTLE BLONDE MODEL FRIEND is sitting alone at a table, and she waves at me with a comically big smile the next night when I walk into the club. I look behind my shoulder to see if she's waving at someone behind me, but no, for some reason she's adopted me as her new bestie.

Call me sentimental, but a part of me warms to the kid. It's got to be lonely here for her if she's searching for friends.

Then again, she did drug me with her drink.

But if she's drinking the same cherry-honey cocktail, maybe her pouty lips will be a little loose with information. I head to her table with a smile.

"Hey, how are you?"

She grins up at me. "I'm awesome! Where did you go last night? I missed you."

"Oh, you know. I was around. There are so many rooms in this place, it's easy to get lost."

She sips her drink. "That's for sure."

This is perfect. I can use this opportunity to ask more about

Gold, try to find out his kinks. "So, you know that time when we met and you had gold on you?"

She narrows her eyes. "Yeah?"

I look around, making sure no one's close enough to overhear before leaning closer to her. "What if I said I wanted to know more about that?"

She slowly and deliberately passes her drink to me. I take a sip. She waits. I take another gulp of the sweet signature drink with who knows what in it. Maybe there's nothing in it today but liquor, but I need to know about Gold.

She takes back her drink and tilts her head, taking a leisurely sip. "I can tell you...or I can show you."

"Show me." My heart pounds inside my chest.

She seizes my hand with surprising strength and pulls me toward the far wall. At the last second, she presses hard, and a door I hadn't noticed was there swings open. There's an ornate number 37 etched faintly onto the door, but there's nothing inside the room but a thick, velvet darkness.

There's nothing but her hand, guiding me along. I reach out with my other hand, but there's nothing but air. She keeps us moving at a quick pace for what feels like longer than it probably is.

"Stop," she whispers, "and don't make a sound. Don't move from this place."

She moves behind me, pinioning my body—using it, and she works her hands up beneath my shirt, tugging at it.

"What are you—?"

Her fingers bite into the flesh of my hips. "I said no talking. You're in or out. Decide."

"In," I breathe, and she strips me of my clothes.

My eyes squeeze shut before I realize a spotlight has come on directly above me. I blink hard, trying to adjust and see what's out there, but I can't see farther than a few feet—or maybe I can, but there's nothing to see.

I'd expected people, or a window maybe, not blank, dark space.

Something warm and fluid drips down my flank, and I turn to look at the model.

She's painting my body with liquid gold—paint, or maybe it's real gold, I don't know, but it's warm and makes my skin tingle slightly. It's pleasant, and I almost ask what it is before biting my tongue.

No questions allowed.

Goosebumps form on my skin at her gentle touch, but the liquid coats me well enough to keep my body heat in. A gleam enters her eyes when she covers my ass and pussy, but she doesn't stop to make things sexual. Up and up the warm gold creeps, changing me from a woman into a gold statue.

An idol to something. Am I to worship or be worshipped? Stand guard or be ignored?

She twists my hair back into a bun and covers it as well. When all that's left is my face, she takes a flat paintbrush and uses that to get the paint everywhere but the inside of my mouth and my eyeballs.

Even my lids are covered, so that when I close them, I'm sure I look like a statue come to life. I shine so bright that I almost hurt my eyes, the light gleaming off every curve. She adds one more thing to my neck—a gold dog collar.

The model fades back into the darkness, and I'm left alone, standing as still as, well, you know what, wondering what to do now.

What would Inana do? What *did* Inana do?

If it's Gold who's watching me from the hungry darkness, then he wants a show. He likes to watch. Statues are pretty but boring, and why? Because they do nothing but stand there. A statue come to life is interesting—depending on what it does.

I make up a story for myself—I'm a statue brought to life, but I don't know how. It doesn't occur to me to see if anyone's watching me. I'm a statue—I'm more captivated by the way my body can suddenly move, limber and fluid. Graceful and willowy.

I stretch and sway, bend and flex, and am not even surprised when another statue comes out of the darkness to join me.

He's not like me. His body is bigger, ruder with muscles, taking up more space than I ever could. The fine hairs on his thighs and the heavier ones on his lower legs stand out, even coated with silver instead of gold like my paint.

I must be worth more than he is.

He must come to me and convince me to be with him.

I cross my arms and raise my head imperiously, archly raising a brow.

He steps closer, head tilting up and down to take all of me in before he lowers himself to his knees and trails his hand from my chest to my belly button.

I startle at his touch and glare at him for what he's done.

A streak of silver is left behind where he touched. I'm offended and push him to his back.

He's easily overpowered, because he's just quicksilver instead of liquid gold. I'm malleable when I'm warm, but he hasn't done that yet.

I step back and look over on the floor—a small container of gold paint is there, along with a syringe without a needle. I step to it and draw it full before easing it inside my pussy and squeezing myself full of the gold.

I squeeze my legs together on the way back to where the silver man lies on his back on the floor. I straddle his face and squat, pushing with my innermost muscles.

A stream of fluid lands on his face, streaking it gold, running back toward his ears.

I stand and walk down his body, still straddling his torso until I reach his cock. Warm gold runs down my inner thighs and I smile and nudge him with a foot, indicating I want him on all fours. He may be bigger than me, but I am in control. This is all about me.

I remove the collar from my neck, fastening it around his to prove a point.

He's my little puppy.

I climb on, hooking my feet around him like a belt and slap his ass, leaving a gold print on the cheek. He crawls and I direct him in a tight circle before growing bored and standing. I leave him on his knees and grab the syringe, loading it up again.

This time he's the one who ends up with liquid gold inside him.

I fuck his ass with that syringe until he comes on the floor with gold paint running from the crack of his ass down to his balls down to his knees.

I spin in a slow circle and go still.

The light turns off, leaving me in the darkness again.

I jump when a robe is laid over my shoulders.

"That was amazing," she whispers in my ear. "He will be so pleased with you."

I don't bother asking who she means. Inana already knew, and so do I, but I'm left with a hollow feeling in the pit of my stomach. I'd forgotten all about Gold in there. I did it for my own experience, for my own thrill, and once again, someone's come and claimed it for himself.

They didn't technically take anything, but it feels like I've been robbed. I wanted the experience for myself, but maybe that's the exchange. Maybe we always end up unknowingly sacrificing something.

How much will I give up? How much is too much for the experience of a lifetime?

TWENTY

"YOU."

The man singles me out of the crowd. "Come with me."

His eyes are dark and I like his hands, so I follow him through a pearly white door with ornate candleholders on either side of it.

Room 328.

The walls are a deep crimson, and it's fairly boxy, but the ceiling is high—almost impossibly high. There's a raised platform in the middle of the room, and it reminds me of an altar. He takes me to it, and I wonder what's going to be sacrificed here tonight.

My clothes are the first to go.

When I'm naked, he coaxes me up onto the platform and maneuvers me until I'm sitting with my legs straight out in front of me.

From a small drawer, he grabs a few lengths of rope, red to match the room.

He gently moves my hands out of the way as he binds my breasts, a strangely constrictive sensation, but I can still breathe comfortably. It seems strange that he'd strip me only to cover me again, but then again, he's covered me the way he wants, so it's not that strange after all.

It's about control.

The ropes aren't rough, but the way they feel against my nipples is a huge contrast in texture. They dig in with a dull pressure, and I hope I end up with marks in my skin afterwards. Anna used to speak of her rope marks as though they were badges of pride. I don't know about that, but I do know that the rope feels good. Solid, tough, like the strongest, longest fingers pressing against me.

Next, he pulls out a shorter length of rope, also red.

There are two tall candles lit nearby, but other than the fragrance of hot wax, they're unscented. The candles are red. I'm noticing a theme.

He uses the rope to tie my hands behind my back, looping it around my neck. It's not tight, but when I try to move my hands, the rope tightens around my neck.

I'm to stay still.

My pulse kicks up in tempo.

One last thing—a long piece of silk. He trails it up my legs, my torso, and covers my eyes. I've had fantasies of being blindfolded like this for ages. What's he going to do to me when I can no longer see him? He leaves my legs free, and I wiggle my toes, noticing other things now that I can't see.

Rope has a scent to it, and this one could almost be made of sweetgrass; it's sweet, natural, earthlike.

The room smells like wax and heat, tinged with my arousal.

Can he smell that sweetness yet?

I hear the hot sizzle of a candle near my head, and jump when I feel a lick of heat on my thigh, unable to stop from crying out, reflexively moving my hands and choking myself with the rope.

His hands stop mine from moving, and I can breathe again. He says, "What do you say?"

Instinctively, I whisper, "Thank you," heart pounding from fear but also arousal at how he's taking care of me, taking his time.

A drip of fire runs down my other thigh, and I jump and tense, waiting for the next one.

"No."

"No?" I ask.

"Relax."

It's difficult to relax knowing he's going to drip more hot wax on my body, but the places he's already done are sore but manageable. The wax has already cooled and hardened against my skin. I take a deep breath.

"Tell me the things you want. Your desires."

"My desires? What I want you to do to me?"

"In general. And don't anticipate the hot wax, or you'll be punished more."

At those words, the sweetness between my legs blossoms, the scent of it filling the air like an exotic flower even though my legs aren't spread.

He changes that, easing them apart. He drips more wax on my inner thigh—higher this time, and I inhale sharply and remember his command.

"I've always wanted to be blindfolded like this." I pause, feeling a slight draft to my right and hearing something scuffle on the floor. Another person, perhaps?

I wince as a river of wax drips onto my lower belly. "I want it rough."

Something hard teases its way between my legs, slicking itself in my juices before easing inside me—rewarding me for my confession, perhaps? I continue. "I want to be taken. I want my"—don't say *Jack*, don't think of him—"partner to fuck me, to make it feel good but to make it hurt too."

With every word, I'm being slowly fucked with mysterious objects, toys, and what I can guess to be a cucumber, or perhaps another phallic vegetable, I don't know, but it feels good.

My hands spring free—someone's released them, and I'm pushed flat on my back, the thrusting inside me never ceasing, but it's impersonal when I'm not being touched anywhere else.

"I wanted to be hit during sex, too. Something, anything to show my partner had gone wild with me, on me, in me." I shiver as someone sucks my fingers one by one, and when the person takes my whole hand into their mouth, fisting it, I tense, about to come.

But the person stops and I whimper. I feel another trickle of burning, slow, hot drips from my hip to my belly.

"I like being in control as well. I like knowing that someone's helpless and that I'm the one making them that way. I want more. I always want more. I want sex to feel like a fantasy."

The thrusting begins again, and hands creep over my body.

"I want it to be surreal, a dream, a nightmare." I shiver with want, with what I'm getting, at the areas of my body that burn beneath the crust of cooled wax. "I want it to be surprising, alluring. Undeniable." The hands stop and start, giving and taking away pleasure, making me crazy with want, with lust as hot as the wax. I'd even take the wax again, anything for them to keep going, keep giving. "It should erase me."

I feel something soft on my arm. Breasts? The hands ram me full of something and I cry out, violently coming in waves of heat and ice, my body turning the orgasm painfully deep, like my pussy is angry it took so long and is punishing me instead of the perpetrator. I feel spurts of warmth on my belly, on my thighs. Come, and something warmer, more liquid. I think it's pee, but I can't be sure. I feel dirty and tattered, and there's nothing better than this moment, now.

More hot wax, but now it's on my arms and dripping into my pubic hair and the heat makes me come again. A woman moans near me, sounding as spent as I feel.

The blindfold is removed, and I'm surrounded by five people, including the man who brought me here. They smile at me, praise me with their words and soft voices and hands, and a man with long blonde hair like a Viking pulls something from between my legs—an enormous purple carrot—and takes a bite with a loud crunch, devouring something that was inside me.

I blink at them. "I want more."

My new friends lead me through a low door we have to crouch to fit through—number 398, which makes no sense, because we were in 328 and that should lead to an odd number—but I don't care, still dripping come down my legs and stinging from the wax.

This room is decorated with zigzags and swirls of black and white. It's disorienting to the eyes, the patterns making me dizzy.

There's a large St. Andrew's cross, and my group presses against me, smothering me with their bodies as they tie me to it spread-eagled with my back exposed using the same sweetgrass-scented rope that was around my hands before. My breasts are still tied, bulging from the rope that binds them. They've never looked so full.

I look over my shoulder when they back away, revealing a masked man with a flogger in his hand.

I take a deep breath and smile.

I turn back to press myself against the hard wood, noting the slight citrusy scent—lemon oil or some kind of cleaner—and a woman on the other side of the cross steps forward, fastening an absurdly large vibrator to my mound before kissing me softly on the forehead. I almost want to laugh, but I want more, so I don't interrupt. The flogging starts before the vibrator does, and it hurts worse than I thought it would, sharp, hot smacks on my thighs and ass.

But soon I'm leaning back, trying to get more of the pain to go with the buzzing on my clit.

I lose track of how many hits I take—slaps to the back as well, with the flogger or something he swaps in that's thinner and bites my skin harder. My friends move to where I can see them, and they watch the masked man hurt me.

They watch him make me tremble and scream.

They come when he moves to stand between my legs and turn the vibrator as high as it will go before fucking me with something long, hard, and cold, adding a new sensation—temperature—to the mix.

He makes me come until I can't breathe, but the cross holds me up; my ropes keep me standing.

I close my eyes and sag against the restraints, smelling the come and sweat, feeling the pleasure and pain mingle in my body and transform into something bigger than I can contain. He holds the dildo still inside me, and that makes me come from being so full, like he's fisting me.

He moves it in and out, and that makes me come.

His chest hair on my back, tickling the places he hurt, makes me writhe, and I can't tell if it's from pleasure or pain.

It's both. It's the sensations Anna wanted me to understand, about what this can do to your body, and now I'm feeling it.

I'm feeling it so deeply I can taste it.

The flavor of letting go. The feeling of what happens when you become sensation and lose yourself completely. Silk and satin are nice on the skin, but I wanted to wear the red of stinging flesh and the rippled edges of rope indentations.

They're the most beautiful thing I've ever worn.

I didn't want to be eased into anything. I wanted it rough—they got the truth from me and gave me my desires.

I beg for more.

My hosts serve me, their submissive.

TWENTY-ONE

I SLEEP FOR TWO DAYS, calling in sick to work, staying at Inana's and living in her bed, relishing the ache in my body. But I wake up no longer as sore, sober, with guilt filling my belly enough that I don't bother with breakfast.

The only thing I'm hungry for is Jack. His cock, his come, his sweetness.

Our connection.

I miss him with a sudden intensity. He's the one who wanted to set a date for the wedding. He picked a number that he thinks is lucky because he wanted us to be together forever, and what the hell am I doing, not fighting harder for that man?

Most women would be jamming themselves into the nearest white dress and cartwheeling down the aisle to be with a man as gorgeous as Jack is, inside and out. He's sweet, honest, caring. He's trying to make the world a better place.

So what the fuck am I still doing here? Okay, he said some shitty things and pressed pause on us, but am I really going to let that be the end? Is that an excuse to throw everything away? Sometimes one person has to suck it up and build that bridge, even if that person wasn't the one who lit the match that burned it down.

I've been sinking into the mire that was Inana's life, and it feels amazing, but to what end? What I'm doing isn't as important as why I'm doing it. Maybe it was just morbid fascination at first, projection and the need to know what could have been.

But what will that gnosis culminate in? If I found out it was The Juliette Society for sure behind Inana's death, what am I willing—or able—to do about that? Sticking my neck out for a story is all well and good, but what is the end result of this investigation? Inana's sister wouldn't be happy to find out that she may be right that Inana's death wasn't a suicide, so I can't pretend it's about comforting her.

My "ghosting" angle was as thin as the wafer that pushed Monty Python's Mr. Creosote over the edge, and we know how big a mess that ended up being. Except instead of being covered with a giant man's vomit and a French waiter's outrage, who knows what will cling to us all if this story comes out.

Is there a point to pursuing this story, beyond selfish gratification?

Am I truly doing more than just using Inana's death as a vehicle for self-exploration? The fact is, if Inana had been into something other than sexual expression as art, I probably never would have taken notice of her. Why would I have? If she was some lady who was into something less provocative, less like my own experiences, I'd have flipped right on past her and never looked back—nor wallowed in it to anesthetize myself against the pain when Jack hurt me.

My boss once said, "The stories will come to you if you're patient enough."

Did this one come to me, or did I go looking for it? If I stop writing it, stop researching it, that means I'd be acknowledging the niggling doubt that I'm doing something I shouldn't be. If I acknowledge that, I have to close the door on this part of myself.

Because if I went in search of it again? That's going past the point of no return, and if Bob's got tabs on me to the point where he knows I'm at the hotel, he damn sure knows what's happening inside it.

I've got to stop this and get my life back. Get my Jack back.

What will I tell Lola?

I'll have to give the diary back.

It's something on my mind as I drive back home, stopping to get a little present for Jack.

Lingerie shopping: one of the most middle-America things you can do to spice things up with your lover without really trying. Modern female armor. Jack and I have a great sex life when we're not both burned out from things in our lives taking over, but that's not why I'm doing it.

It's a giant slice of vanilla that makes me feel both sad and normal, and it's precisely what I need right now. Everything from the fluorescent lights to the snooty salesgirls calms and reassures me that this was the swan dive back into normalcy I needed.

I stroll around taking in and discarding fantasies in the form of costumes, deciding Jack would be more into something simpler, sexier, a little more understated.

Something light pink with black lace to be the wrapping on my grand gesture/apology to my fiancé.

I pause, closing my eyes to imagine the look on his face when he walks in and sees me on our bed. Dressing for sex is sexier than having clothes torn off for sex—as I learned with Caroline. I'm taking a page from her book to thaw the chill between Jack and me.

I find a few bra and panty combinations that may fit the bill and head to the dressing rooms.

In the corner is a huge fake confessional. At first I think it's one of those old photo booths, but it isn't.

What's the purpose of a confessional in a lingerie shop? What's the point of a confession that no one hears?

Unless someone does hear it.

People don't wear lingerie to be heard, they buy it to be seen in.

There's no point to a confessional in here unless someone *sees* all of it. It's taken something normal into provocative territory.

It would be wrong for a lapsed Catholic girl like me not to go to confession, wouldn't it?

What absolution will I find inside?

I step into the booth with my items and undress.

Is someone watching me right now?

It's dark and the air is thick with heat, but it smells vaguely of the pleasant spray they use throughout the store—perfume or air freshener, maybe? I arch my back, move more slowly, more sensuously, imagining a priest on the other side, watching me here, thankful for my sacrifice of modesty on his altar of fantasy.

There's a common understanding people have about confessionals—the oratory booths—that the rest of the congregation can't see who's confessing. That it's a consideration for the privacy of the sinner themselves.

That's true.

But have you ever wondered why you're separated from the priest once you're inside?

Temptation.

Not so much yours, but his.

Naked, I turn my back on the mirror next to me and bend over, sliding my hands up my thighs before slipping the pink panties up my legs and letting the thong slip between my cheeks, giving them a slap for good measure. I let my breasts hang down so when I stand, they have an extra perk in the bra. My mother didn't teach me that trick.

We're not the only lambs who sin, and you're damn right the Church knows that.

So there's a little screen inside that keeps you separated from the priest and his weaknesses, should they present themselves while you're regaling him with a story a little too lascivious for his rosary to handle.

I never understood why it's required for priests to be celibate.

Other faiths allow their clergymen to marry and even have children, and I think that makes them better at their job. How can you counsel someone about the joys of waiting until you're married before consummating a physical relationship if you're not even allowed to masturbate?

The whole thing reeks of hypocrisy and ridiculousness.

They should be allowed to get married, but even if not, they should get to rub one out once in a while at the very least.

I can't see how they don't. Otherwise, how wild does that shit get on a weeknight when no one's there but them?

A confessional would make for a pretty great glory hole.

A *glory, glory, hallelujah* hole, if you will.

If people were allowed to own their sexuality, things would be better all around. When they can't, that's when true perversions come out.

Most are harmless, though still ridiculous.

Have you heard of furries?

In the more extreme cases, people will dress up as stuffed animals and go have orgies as those animals—nothing human visible, except for their crotches, which are exposed for easy access. I'm not saying it's weird to want to fuck a puppet, but...well, to each their own, I guess. You really just wanted the coyote to get that roadrunner? Grab a partner and some costumes, and you can give people a show they'll never, ever forget.

Maybe it all circles back to our childhoods.

You wanted a pony and didn't get one?

Pony play! You can dress up and prance around with a bridle between your teeth, waiting for someone to fuck your rump and smack you with a crop and make you squeal.

Mommy didn't nurture you enough?

There's a recipe for that, too.

People are strange. Some fantasies are absurd.

I smile and touch the glass, remembering how real confessions felt.

"Bless me, Father, for I have sinned. I wandered into something kinky that should have shocked me, but didn't. I've seen things you wouldn't believe, wouldn't suspect." I remember how Anna said my smile was sweet. Is it still? I grin at the glass, wondering if anyone's on the other side, or if it's a ruse, constructed to make the whole thing feel taboo and more scandalous than it really is. Maybe my smile has become as hungry as I feel. Too knowing, like I've been a witness to too much.

But knowing that and feeling it are two different things, and my hand skims down the front of the panties while I talk. "I've done things that would scare other people. Shock other people. I saw a man shoot women with a paintball gun—and they were so into what he was doing that they couldn't wait for him to fuck them. He shot me in the leg and chest with edible paint, and a woman licked it off."

Her tongue was impossibly soft against my chest, against my collarbone. I tip my head back, lifting my leg, gazing at my reflection in the dark glass, the blush on my cheeks and chest visible even in that murky reflection. I rub harder, feeling my juices dampen the panties.

How many other women wore these panties before me, wet them with their cunts?

"I saw two women use a sling." I dip a finger inside, biting my lip, remembering the way she took the other woman's fist all the way inside. I think back to the gun.

Only this time, I remember him differently, picture Jack standing there, legs spread, shooting women, staining them with the paint—funny how the first four letters in that word spell *pain*—and filling my mouth with his thick cock, nudging the back of my throat and laughing as he ignored me to mark the other women as his as well. With my free hand, I scoop a breast out of the demi cups and pinch a nipple, harshly, quietly moaning. "I've seen more, done more, been more than I thought I could."

"Is everything okay in there?" the salesgirl asks.

I grin. "Yes, thank you." I plunge another finger inside myself.

"Do you need another size?"

I add a third finger. "No, this is perfect." I release my breast and grip the seat, holding back a moan, positive I'm going to scream and give it away, like someone with Tourette's frantically trying not to scream obscenities in public.

"Let me know if you need anything," she says.

Can she see? Does she know?

Do I care?

Fuck no.

Jack in leather, me in lace. Him giving exactly what I want without any speech required on my part.

Me taking what I want from him with a hand on his throat so he's not able to talk.

The thought makes me want to scream. But being quiet can be as hot as screaming, and my breath comes in ragged gasps now, hips bucking as I rock them toward my release in panties I haven't purchased, in front of glass that may or may not be a two-way mirror.

But we're all beautiful when we're coming, and even if I didn't think so, it's pretty fucking hard to think about the way I look when my pussy is clamping down on my fingers and light flares behind my eyes as I fall over the edge.

The scent of arousal filters into my consciousness as I come back down to Earth, awareness coming back to my body.

And, like any good Catholic, I expect shame to hit.

It doesn't. But I realize I don't really like these panties.

I should leave them crumpled in a wet, silky ball, walking out before the sales clerks can discover them and what I've done. Then again, I'm not one to flee the scene of the crime. Sure, the thought of the snooty clerk finding them and having to touch them makes me grin. But of course I'll buy them. I'm not just purchasing underwear—now I'm taking home a memory with me.

I could tell Jack about it to see whether shock and feigned outrage or lust fills his eyes, but this is a secret I'd rather keep pressed close to my skin, for me alone.

I sit with my eyes closed for a moment, letting the air cool around me, cool me down, and then I change out of the panties and bra and put my own back on, legs rubbery from my release. In fairness, it's been a crazy twenty-four hours and I didn't sleep well.

I should get something to eat.

I stride to the counter, not bothering to look at anything else.

I got what I came for.

Now I'll buy what I came in.

The salesgirl smiles but is quiet as she rings up my purchase. Can she smell the come in them, feel how heavy they are with me?

I look her in the eyes as she tucks them into a pretty pink and black bag after delicately wrapping them in matching tissue paper, and I smile, feeling like someone else.

Feeling like the unapologetically sexy seductress I could have been.

That Anna was.

That Inana was.

And I like it.

Even though I'm going back home to give this to Jack, to figure out what the hell I've been doing at La Notte, knowing I have something like this inside myself is heady. It dazzles me, reminds me that maybe I'm not as completely wild and uninhibited as Anna and Inana, but I've got something beneath my skin that people wouldn't suspect to look at me.

I'm more than what I am. Maybe just knowing that is enough to be okay with the status quo from now on. I can be Jack's Catherine.

Maybe I was filmed, maybe I wasn't.

Maybe someone saw, maybe they didn't.

It's not about what it is. It's about what it makes us feel.

It's art.

They knew what they were doing, and so did I.

TWENTY-TWO

∿ဏ်္ဎ∿

I'M LYING IN BED WEARING the new lingerie I bought, waiting for Jack to get home, reading the diary, when a particular entry jumps out at me.

A little blonde bombshell with a name hidden inside my own.

She likes to be marked.

I like to mark.

Who is Mark?

Anna? Does she mean Anna? If Inana was in the club a lot, she may have known Anna. Maybe they knew each other well. At least I hope. I turn over, getting more comfortable on top of the blankets, while still in a flattering position in case Jack comes in without me hearing him.

It's strange to think about Inana and Anna hanging out together, doing the things Anna and I did together—or more.

Anna would have loved the things Inana was doing, and I can see her slipping inside of Inana's journey, going along with it as though it were her own. I imagine Inana would have been inordinately pleased to have found a friend, a peer, someone who understood exactly what she felt, what it was like, what she was trying to say.

But it makes me feel jealous, like two worlds that were supposed to be mine alone have collided and there are parts I've been excluded from.

The worst part is that I may not ever know what happened to either of them. Nothing I've read in the diary so far suggests Inana was suicidal. But the more I read the more I worry.

Is the diary real, or something edited like Anaïs Nin's, and more like fiction or the wish of a disillusioned actress? Can it even be trusted as the truth? It's more likely similar to a camera angle—you can only use it to see *one* aspect of the picture. But words in diaries are written by the star and the director—we're shown what they want us to see, and the rest is blacked out by not being mentioned.

What else am I missing? What am I not being shown?

I devoured Anaïs Nin's diaries before I even knew erotica was a genre unto itself, when I was seventeen years old, during a long, hot summer that stuck to my skin like her words. Like the sheets that clung to my body, damp with the exertion of getting myself off to the things she'd done and penned words about. It was the things she'd done, but also the things she said—and how she said them— that mattered.

The woman was a genius, a true literary giant who, like most geniuses, wasn't appreciated until after her death. I still think she is taken for granted and not properly appreciated in a world where people don't care about anything but the money shot. She was a wordsmith and a feminist revolutionary, freely going about her world from tryst to tryst, even being sneaky about love until she died and her two husbands found out about each other from the obituaries. I guess she had a lie box that allowed her to keep her stories straight—which lies she'd told to whom.

Most septuagenarians just collect recipes or arthritis medicines.

I read Anaïs Nin's novels and was disappointed by them, not

because they weren't great, but because they weren't as great as her diaries were. Then again, what could be? She was a mystery, really, saving her truth for herself, only writing her true thoughts in her diary. That's why they shine.

That's why they stand up to the best erotica ever written, even today. Maybe especially today. Have you seen pictures of Henry Miller? In reading the diary, you get this crystalline vision of a rugged male, someone more along the lines of an alpha-male movie star who came along and swept Anaïs off her feet. She was obsessive over him.

I can't express the wrongness I felt when I searched for him online and saw what all the fuss was about—or rather, failed to see what the fuss was about. To each their own, but I was underwhelmed, to say the least. The point was that she made him seem appealing—and that's talent.

Henry Miller allegedly lifted the more salacious bits from her diary to put in his novels, which I find flattering, but also arrogant and mocking. To use her words as his own and be celebrated for them is the cruelest thing a lover can do.

How much of her genius is attributed to him? A foundation built on lies...but she didn't seem to mind. Was he trying to push her, provoke her into being better, into putting herself out there the way he knew she could so she'd shine and everyone else could finally see the brave, luxurious woman he saw when he was inside her, spreading her legs?

And yet, the thing that I wonder the most is, if they were all lies— if every word of the diaries was fiction instead of fact skewed slightly to protect anonymity—would they be as beautiful? Is their import innately tied to the fact that these events happened?

If an artist can reproduce a great artist's painting so accurately that it's indistinguishable from the original, does that make the painting less valuable? Does that make the second artist less talented than the first?

Some would say yes, because it's the inception of the art in the first place, not necessarily the execution, that makes it what it is.

That would mean Anaïs's diaries, if they were completely made up, are even more important.

Because they were still beautiful and heartbreaking.

Real. Fake. Fiction. Fact. Does that matter? Maybe it was all fiction. Maybe Inana's diary is fiction as well. How would I know? How would I know how much is real, the things she's saying, the places she's been?

And even if everything happened, it's all still skewed through her perception of events. They say there are three sides to every story— yours, mine, and the truth. No one can be one hundred percent impartial, even with the best intentions, because our egos get in the way and show us things that are pertinent to our interests.

It makes her words and the truth inside them relative.

And that's even if they're accurate representations of her journey. Maybe she was aware that her words would someday be read, and wrote with a filter in place, lying to her diary as she wrote instead of changing things after the fact. I notice she uses codes and nicknames, but was that because the events weren't real, or because she didn't want to get in trouble if her diary got into the wrong hands?

Can I trust the words when I didn't know the woman who spoke them, wrote them? I can only verify so much through the videos she made, cross-reference people and events and check that the timing adds up, but there are so many things I just can't verify.

The diary of Anaïs Nin.

The diary of Inana Luna.

It's like I'm being spun into Zulawski's *Possession*, only I don't know who I'm supposed to be in love with, where my lover has gone, or how to get her back. I laugh, realizing it's another Anna.

A plague of Annas.

I turn back to the diary, hoping to find more about Anna, even just confirmation that it's her Inana is referencing.

If love is a battlefield, why are people so afraid of the scars? They hide inside soft worlds of protection and hard shells, denying what's right to stay hidden inside loneliness.

We run from ourselves trying to find someone else. We embrace the darkness, hoping for the light to shine on us and illuminate the truth when it's not that simple. It's not one or the other, it's one AND the other.

Dualities.

Dynamic duos.

Superheroes need a villain. They need the shadows to see the light. What is music without silence? Pain without pleasure. Black without white, water without wine, movies without movement.

Stasis is death.

Static is death.

Let go of intention and just be.

If you love someone, let them go.

Fuck that.

There's a door inside the Night where you can find anything you seek. Inside that door is another door. If you enter it, you can find a place behind yourself framed in white, because white is pure...allegedly. Find that place. Find it and you'll know what it means to burn inhibitions. Find it and you'll know what it is to be free.

It's his place, but it's all his place. His reach is pervasive but gentle. Everywhere but nowhere. We were all brought in for a reason.

I was told the reason. I get it, but am not sure it's aligning with my visions of the future. Maybe it's too much for one body to bear. Maybe it's not enough for one giant life lived in the shadows.

Am I a shadow or a light? Which do I want to be?

Which is more important for the world and the people in it who I want to reach?

I can't even fathom the beginnings of the answer yet. There's no rush. Evolution waits for no one and punishes us all.

I can handle that, at least. What wouldn't we all do for the right person, lover, friend?

Is she talking about the VIP door? No, it goes past that. I found that door.

It's obviously a metaphor—find a place behind yourself framed in white?

It's got to be that dark, secret room used by Max. His personal playground where he likes people to become statues for him.

We're taught all about how much we need another person to be complete in our lives, how we're never going to be happy unless we find the One. Why would we fight so hard to find someone only to let that person go at the first sign of trouble? Someone's got to fight to stay together, to keep reaching out, or you're going to inevitably drift apart from each other.

Is that what will happen to Jack and me?

No. I refuse to let that happen—hence the lingerie and coming back to surprise him like this. Sure, this was precipitated by a mistake, but it's the result that matters: realizing we're meant to be together. If I've got to be the one who fixes things, then I'll do it. From now on, I'm renewing myself to us, the way he's invested in us as well. How far will I go for love?

Maybe I never accepted the loss of Anna, and I recognize I'm caught up in pursuing Inana, transferring my energy to her, still focused on her, like in De Palma's *Sisters*. Danielle never accepted the death of her twin Dominique. Sexual experiences awakened "Dominique"—the dark and dangerous side of Danielle's mind—and were the only way she could cope with the survivor's guilt she lived with every day.

Of course, this metaphor works better for Lola and Inana. What would you do if you truly lost someone? What would that do to your mind and heart?

When it comes to Anna, this doesn't fit, except for the fact that no, I never got over losing Anna, and that's probably the sole reason I've been so caught up in Inana and her life to the point where I almost lost Jack.

It's like I've been somehow trying to save Anna…

No, she doesn't need saving. To do that I'd need to *find* Anna.

That's what I really want, I realize, but I'm scared of finding out at the end of all this that there's no resolution at the end of the rainbow. Claudia never finds Anna.

Spoiler alert.

The twists in the plot aren't what are important in that film.

Anyway, it doesn't matter. Jack does. We need to engage the heat again, reforging that connection between us, as well as the emotional one that's solid—no thanks to me. But love isn't about being perfect. Perfection is a construct that inevitably leads to failure. I'm not perfect, but from now on I'm going to try harder—regardless of what happens with the diary.

I'm checking out the light glinting off the facets of my engagement ring when he walks in the bedroom and says, "Shit."

I raise an eyebrow. "That's not quite the reaction a lady wants when she splurges on new lingerie to surprise her sexy fiancé with."

He shakes his head, giving me a quick head-to-toe sweep. "You did this for me?"

Slowly, I turn onto my stomach to give him the rear view. "Yes."

"You really came all the way back here to surprise me with that?" He smiles. "I'm going to rain check the hell out of this."

"Why a rain check?"

He sends a text, then runs his hands through his hair. "There's this charity dinner with Bob that I have to go to. He needs me there."

"Can't he do without you for one day? I've missed you. I want you." I undulate my hips a little. "Skip the meeting. Stay with me."

"I really wish I could."

"There's nothing stopping you. What does he need you for? He'll be busy schmoozing. Does he really need you there to jerk his ego off? Can't he find someone else to fill in for you for one fucking night?" The words come out harshly, pushed out by sexual frustration and guilt, making me lash out because he's spoiling the reconciliation. All because of Bob, which makes me so resentful I can barely see straight.

Trying to take it from resentful back to sexy, I trail my hands down my ribs, toying with the hem of my panties. "Wouldn't you rather hang out with me instead of him? Blow him off."

He loosens his tie. "I can't. And I really think you should come with me, think how awesome it will be for both of us to be there together." His eyes light up, but I feel the scowl overtake my face.

None of this is going the way I'd planned, and now I have to deal with Bob on top of it all? "Who cares about some lame fundraiser?"

Jack frowns. "Babe."

I go from feeling sexy to ridiculous in that one syllable. "Fine."

"Catherine."

What the hell am I doing? I'm here to fix things, and I'm acting like a child. I sigh and smile, a real one this time. "No, it's fine. I'll go put something on." I slide off the bed and head to the closet, hating every inch of exposed flesh for making me feel vulnerable and rejected even though I shouldn't. "How formal is it?"

"Pretty formal, but it's a big group of people. Bob's trying to swing some bigwigs and I'm there to help sway votes. I know you'd be able to help me with that."

I can hear the flattery in his voice, but it's not enough to smooth my ruffled feathers. It's not shocking—women are taught that men are always DTF, and on the rare occasions that we're rejected in any way, it stings like hell. When someone gives you an invitation to possess her, don't turn it down. Then again, it feels like we're okay, so I should count my blessings. "Okay. Where are we going?"

"La Notte."

All the air gets sucked from my lungs.

TWENTY-THREE

‍ ‍

THE RIDE OVER WAS EXHAUSTING, questions burning a hole in my mind from the constant rotation at too high an RPM to measure.

Why is Bob doing this here?

What does Jack know?

What should I tell him? Everything?

Can I fake a realistic seizure and get out of this?

Instead of being led through the lobby, Jack takes us through a private entrance and down the hallway to Ballroom B, and I relax a little.

My new colleagues won't wonder why I'm at a party with Bob DeVille and his friends, since this is the room where events are set up and then, for confidentiality reasons, the waitstaff get out of Dodge.

But twenty minutes in, I'm tired of the posturing.

Everything is calculated with DeVille, from the music to the wine selections, gambits he runs to lull everyone into feeling safe and relaxed, never realizing that just overhead is a spider with perfect teeth, fangs gleaming with poison, legs spread out in every direction, making deals with your potential allies—or other enemies.

It's not a sit-down dinner like I'd assumed it would be. It's a silent auction—yawn—filled with items of cultural import, which makes me wonder why the hell they're here at all, but then I realize they were donated by the guests here and the bidding itself is a metaphor to Bob for world trade or some other concept he's trying to promote at the moment.

Maybe it's me, but I'm not egotistical enough to think all this effort is about me.

The whole situation is surreal. This is my new workplace, and it's also strange because I'm trying to keep my cover, but interested in watching my lives as Inana and as Catherine bleed together like this. Did Bob know Inana?

I have a feeling Bob knows way more than I ever thought he did.

Is Max watching this whole evening take place? All of the guests are actors and musicians, or wealthy artists and politicians.

I wander around the perimeter looking at the items, pausing as though intently studying a tiny gold dolphin pendant, riddled with gemstones like it's got a vicious case of herpes, when really I can't believe someone's bid sixty thousand dollars for it.

And the night's not over yet.

Something brushes my ass—the hand of an older guy, maybe forty-five-ish? "Interesting piece," he says, lurching toward my breast in the most obvious accidental grope ever, but I catch his hand and turn it into a handshake, gripping slightly too hard, putting too much iciness in my eyes.

He has the good sense to look away and speak to me like I'm a human being when I release his hand. "Are you into dolphins?" But there's still a weird glint in his eyes that makes his words feel like a double entendre.

The supercreeps come out at night, drawn by wealth and boredom. I've been immersed in the club so deeply I've almost forgotten the weird situations that occur when sex is implied rather than open. Clumsy attempts at seduction. Lecherous winks over glasses as people try to ascertain your interest level based on the way you respond to their seemingly innocuous questions about the book you're currently reading.

I grit my teeth, raise my eyebrows, and say, "Not really."

An arm snakes around my shoulders. "Catherine, there you are! I'm sorry, sir, I need to steal her away for a while."

From this angle, his doughnut tattoo is especially vivid. I let him pull me to the next piece, never so thankful to see Bundy in my life.

Unfortunately for me, it's a tribal statue of a Pan-like god with a huge, erect penis.

Eighty-four thousand, if you're wondering.

"Sorry to be handsy, but that guy's bad news."

I smile. "I must be giving off some fabulous 'don't touch me' vibes. I've developed a sense for these situations since the first time Jack had me come along to one of these events. I was so worried about saying the wrong thing and making him look bad. Now I try my best not to smash something over the head of the nearest lecherous cretin."

Bundy grins. "Maybe I should have waited a few minutes, then."

"I couldn't afford what all these breakables would cost."

"I did price them a little high." He shrugs. "Fuck 'em."

"What? You're the one who decided to make it a silent auction?" The benefits of which are all going to a foundation that helps combat malaria.

He nods. "I figured that they'd all be trying to impress and outdo each other. Might as well have some good come of it."

"I'm impressed."

"Thank you." He bows. "But you'll have to excuse me. I think I see Senator Crawford's daughter, and I'd very much like to introduce myself to her tits." He wanders off, and I roll my eyes.

Some things never change.

Soon enough, it's been long enough to politely make our excuses and leave. I search the room for Jack and find him seated at a small table. But instead of just my fiancé, I see DeVille settled there, too, halfway through a whiskey, grinning like a proud father at Jack, who's animatedly telling a story.

DeVille's presence makes my heart pound. What's he been saying to Jack? I force myself to relax. If it was bad, Jack wouldn't be smiling like that. Why did Bob choose this place of all places to showboat?

I can't look at him without thinking about our last encounter.

"The Janus Chamber."

I don't want to think about that right now, but I can feel it below, rippling and pulsating through by body, imagining what's happening downstairs, right now. Is Bob going to go down and enjoy the facilities later? What will he get up to in a playground like the one in the basement, endless rooms with endless possibilities and endless willing partners?

I blink hard and take a seat.

Jack leans over and kisses my cheek. "Hey, babe."

Bob smiles at me. "Good evening, Catherine. How are you?"

"Lust," he says, drawing the word out like a hiss. "And power. We couldn't let them take that away from us, so the cult went underground and hid itself in plain view."

"How can you hide in plain view? That doesn't make any sense."

But it had made sense, just like the Purloined Letter. The best place to hide is in the spotlight. POTUS.

Is this my final destination?

Bob smiles. "I'm not staying long. I'll let Jack tell you the good news." He grins and claps Jack on the shoulder as they both stand.

I stay sitting, because screw him.

DeVille leaves and Jack sits, eager to tell me.

DeVille's offered an opportunity for me—exclusive coverage of his campaign for POTUS. It could make my career, but unable to escape the feeling that I'm being bought, or that my silence is a free gift with purchase, I say I'll think about it.

Jack's face falls. "People would kill for this opportunity."

"You know my dream is to be a writer for film, not political journalism." Though I know they're not, I feel like everyone in the room is listening in on me with malicious intent, like violence is about to be unleashed upon me.

Someone's going to smash a glass into my face, try to kill me to remove me because I don't belong here.

The muscles in Jack's jaw are working overtime. "Some opportunities are stupid to pass up."

Yeah, it's a great opportunity, but it's the wrong one for me. We don't talk to each other for the next hour before leaving.

But later, in the room, after my shower, when I'm still wrapped in a fluffy towel, he comes to me and kisses me sweetly, taking the sting of earlier away.

This is all we need. The rest is background noise.

I lean into him and he pulls back. "If you were a part of Bob's team, we'd get to spend way more time together."

"My story isn't finished yet." And I also have less than zero desire to spend more time around Bob and his campaign machine of lies and illusions.

The softness melts from Jack's face and he takes a step back. "I can't believe you didn't snap up the opportunity with Bob if you're serious about journalism."

His words hit like a slap to the face. "The things I want to cover are more substantial than political posturing. Excuse me for wanting to cover things I'm actually interested in."

"Human interest," he sneers, and for the first time I really get it.

He doesn't take my journalism seriously, and having me work with Bob is the only way he'd respect what I do. "Is that how you see my work, Jack?" I cross my arms to feel less vulnerable, but if I have to have this fight in nothing but a goddamn towel, so be it. "Pretty little op-ed pieces that are designed to make people feel good?"

He huffs. "That's not what I said."

I don't fall for the change in tactics. "You didn't answer my question."

"You're not doing anything earth-shattering. I don't understand why you keep doing this when it's coming between us."

"How is it coming between us? Because I'm not doing what you think I should be doing?"

"You don't need to do it. I'll take care of you."

He says it so matter-of-factly I want to slap him. "I'm not your child—this isn't the fifties, Jack. I don't work as some kind of rebellion. I love what I do, and by the way? Art is the most important thing we have. I can't believe you think I should give up something I care about so much."

He puffs out a mirthless laugh. "I thought you cared about us more. You came back to our apartment, put on some sexy lingerie. I thought that was your way of saying you'd finished whatever the hell this was."

"What, I have to choose between who I want to be and you? Why? There's no reason for that choice."

"I think there is. And if our paths go in different directions, take us different places because of your choice?"

My heart stops. "Are you giving me an ultimatum?"

"I shouldn't have to. But you're putting me in an uncomfortable position."

"How?"

He crosses his arms. "I've heard some things about Mr. Gold that make my skin crawl."

"Things like what?"

"Kinky shit. He puts people's lives in danger."

"I don't think he does. Besides, it's not like Bob's an innocent little thing either. I could tell you things about Bob that—"

"I'm so fucking tired of your jealousy of Bob. He's done more for me and my career than you ever have, so don't you dare say another word about him. I won't hear it. You're trying to deflect."

"Deflect what?"

"Come on, Catherine. I'm not an idiot. Max Gold has built a goddamn empire on perversions and you're here at his hotel chasing an alleged story. What have you done for research? How close have you and Max gotten?"

"That's ridiculous." The thing is, Jack is becoming more and more rigid and controlling of me but we are simultaneously changing. Like the opening of *L'Avventura,* we are drifting apart from each other, and it's not fair that he wants me to change after all the time we've been together. "You should know me by now and accept who I am. But all you've done lately is make me feel bad about myself and set insecurity breeding beneath the surface of my skin like mold."

"You're being melodramatic," he scoffs.

But I'm not. We're already bombarded by all the things we're told we should be.

Body image shapes our dreams and perverts our reality. We're all aware of unrealistic expectations, not just about how we look but how we perform. I've started thinking about all the buxom, blonde, terribly white models that are held up as the beauty standard these days. How limited that is in terms of body shape. I wanted to address the way we're not only surrounded by images and narratives concerning sexual violence and sexual titillation, but that they are promoted side by side.

But only one of these is supposedly wrong.

It's like the Ludovico Technique in *A Clockwork Orange,* but instead of aversion therapy, it conflates sex and violence in our heads and stimulates desire. Society is trying to instill this in us while also telling us it's unnatural.

It's keeping us off balance and on the treadmill, not sure what we're supposed to be aiming for, but damned if any of us are getting off.

I sit on the edge of the bed, feeling weak and hating it. "You've been trying to mold me into this unrealistic idea of perfection. Is this what happens when you settle down? If it's just boyfriend/girlfriend then it's okay if your partner has flaws because someone better could always come along and replace them, but when forever comes up, people panic and look to 'fix' their partner's perceived flaws."

He doesn't answer.

Maybe things would be better if all we did was have sex.

I don't understand why people complain about having meaningless sex. As if that's a bad thing. Isn't sex meant to be meaningless? Isn't that the whole point? To lose yourself. When you're fucking and you're really in the zone, your mind is blank, your body is working on autopilot. You're changing gears, shifting up, switching positions, and hitting different rhythms. Total submission to pleasure. You are one with the person inside you and outside of yourself at the same time. When you're fucking and you're really in the zone, that's all there is. The zone. A place without limits, restrictions, or rules. No ego, no agenda, no philosophy, no meaning. Just sweat and electricity. Nothing else.

After a moment, Jack sighs. "You don't fuck your wife, you make love to her. You can fuck your girlfriend's brains out, but that's not appropriate to do to the mother of your children. You're supposed to respect her and—"

"And obviously women are demoralized and devalued by the act of sex itself. We're a commodity with a value that decreases with every strange cock's thrust inside our cunts," I interrupt. "Is that how you see me? Am I some fixer-upper project, someone whose edgy indie views seemed interesting when we were dating, but they're not suitable for your wife?"

He shakes his head. "I just want you to be proud of yourself."

Translation: He's the one who's not proud of me. Somehow, I reflect poorly on him.

This infuriates me, and I get up and push against his chest. "Do you even realize how political you're becoming? What the hell are we doing? I bet you only wanted to set a date to get married because of image, not because of an inner need to be with me."

"You don't understand," he practically shouts, pushing me aside. "This is bigger than you and me and your need to be spanked or whatever. I got a call in DeVille's office from a woman—a very frightened and desperate woman in fear of her life—who made allegations of sexual assault against one of Bob's aides. It occurred in Maximilian Gold's hotel, and she threatened to make it public."

We're in Gold's hotel, where eyes could be everywhere. "Are you sure she wasn't sent by a political opponent or someone trying to scam money from him?" The words are bitter on my tongue, but Jack shakes his head and flops onto the bed.

"She wants justice, not money. I wanted to make sure it was false before telling Bob anything. Before I told him, I decided to do my own quiet investigation into the validity of the woman's claims. I happened to stumble onto something else entirely: there's a criminal conspiracy to hand valuable state gaming contracts over to Gold, who in turn will finance the orchestration of a dirty-tricks campaign to smear the image of one of DeVille's political rivals in the election."

I should be doing backflips about the fact that the blinders are now off where DeVille is concerned, and yet seeing Jack so destroyed by the fact that his idol has fallen only makes me feel sad and protective. How can a man who's been neck-deep in politics for years not understand how that world works—how the world works? He honestly thinks politics is a clean game where no one lies or gets their hands dirty?

It's so innocent and naïve I want to laugh, but you don't laugh at the broken-hearted child who just learned Santa isn't real.

"Some people are good at hiding their true colors." I step closer, taking his head in my arms and pulling him close so his ear is pressed against my chest.

His face is trusting and sad when he looks up at me. "Why would someone want to do this?"

"At least you know. Now we can put this all behind us. You'll get another job easily and never have to speak to DeVille again."

He jerks back. "Are you kidding? I spend hours with the man every day. Bob isn't involved in this—it's all Gold. Bob fired the aide immediately when I told him last night. Someone's done this to try to frame DeVille—to smear him and make it look like he's doing something wrong. We need to gather enough evidence to turn whistleblowers and expose Gold's malfeasance to the media. We owe it to the voters—to the people." He paces around the room before stopping in front of me again. "This will be the biggest story of your career." He laughs. "And DeVille had thought that you covering his campaign was the biggest favor he could help you with."

"Jack, whatever action we take will have serious ramifications for our future." He doesn't even know half the story, and I'm unable to tell him why without revealing my own secret life. I know full well that by going public, effectively revealing the existence of The Juliette Society, Jack would put us both in mortal danger.

This earnest expression on his face proves he doesn't care.

He'd burn both our lives to the ground to expose Gold and save DeVille—and why would DeVille let Jack do that?

"What proof did this woman have?"

"There's a photograph. She's being choked."

"Are you sure he was choking her and it wasn't just a weird angle?"

He glares at me. "He was on top of her. There's no other possible explanation."

"Well, maybe—"

"And she's in her underwear and he's undressed, so it was definitely a sexual thing."

"Where were they?" Chills coat me like a wet suit.

"I don't know. Some hotel room, he's got her on a bed. You know, she's become a real ally to Bob in all of this."

"Jack," I say as I stroke his shoulders and upper arms. "Did you ever think that maybe it was consensual? That they were having sex and doing other things together?" He's already shaking his head, but I push forward. "Then why was it filmed? Who filmed it? You said it was the woman in the picture herself who called you and e-mailed the pictures? What's she got to gain from this?"

He nods. "I believe her. If you'd heard her voice…no one's that good a liar. And she's got nothing to gain. No way she's lying. No one's that good."

"Yes, they are. You know, some women like darker things."

He grimaces. "This isn't like about that time when you and I—"

"It might be exactly like that, Jack. Just because you don't want to believe that there are people out there who like it doesn't make it not true. You judge me for liking things I do and we've been together for years. You want to marry me, but you refuse to even entertain the thought of my tastes being more extreme."

"We're not talking about us right now." He stands and paces the room. "I hand you the biggest story of your career and you're talking about sex."

"I'm talking about us—because lately I'm the only one who gives a damn about this relationship. Since when did you only care about angles and politics? Out there you can be as rigid and fake as Bob, but behind closed doors, you don't get to dictate my pleasure like a crowd's watching. Has that been your hangup the whole time?" I tear the front of his shirt open and rake my nails down his chest. I need to know he's still mine and not just morphing into Bob Junior. "Well, guess what? No one's watching now. It's just you and me, Jack, and I like it rough."

"This isn't normal," he shouts in my face. He grabs my wrists and throws my hands away from his body. "Keep your hands off me. I don't want you anymore."

He storms out and I let him go, stunned.

Does he really think I'm sick? Am I?

I don't think so. I can't believe that the things I want are wrong. It feels more like an excuse for his beloved political aspirations.

He's ashamed of my work and said as much. Is that what this is really about? Appearances? What does he want for me? Is it that he wants to take care of me, or that he wants someone docile and pretty who does nothing with her time but clap for his accomplishments and shower him with accolades on the road to Washington?

I don't ever want that same blank stare Mrs. DeVille has, and that's exactly who he's trying to change me into. He's trying to become Bob. I'm not Gena and never will be. How can he think that's what I would want for my life—to be someone's wife rather than having my own accomplishments and dreams? I love him, love us, but I'm still an individual. What he wants is…archaic. Stifling.

When I first started at the paper, people would do everything to put me down and tell me in a thousand ways how I wasn't going to make it, but then they turned around and acted like they were my friends when I started getting a little notoriety and my articles got more attention.

People told me that the only reason I made it so far was because of Jack's political connections, even though I'd never once used them because my pride wouldn't let me.

It's not like being any kind of artist or creator is easy. Don't fool yourself. The hours suck; it's a lot of eighteen-hour days and sleepless nights when inspiration strikes and you have to act right then at 3:00 a.m. because it might disappear if you sleep on an idea.

Days where nothing comes to you, until you haven't written anything in weeks and you wonder if you were deluding yourself that you ever had any talent at all.

Constant pressure on you from family and friends wondering when you're going to get a real job, or at least stop talking about all the things they think are unrealistic for you to still believe in, as though you're a teenager who still believes in Santa.

Resentment from other people, because they don't have a passion burning them from within, because you don't have to do their job.

Resenting you for wanting to be more. For wanting to make something beautiful, something powerful. They think they understand you, but they don't. Not if they could give it up. Not if they never had a passion to begin with. Not if they think I can give it up. They're like a different species to begin with.

I have no idea how to communicate any of this to Jack without it sounding like a self-indulgent rant about how no one understands me. If you feel like this and others don't, you can't explain it, any more than they can explain how they were able to give up their dream. No amount of spa days with the girls or shoe shopping trips would make me the smallest bit happier if I still weren't being true to my vision.

And now Jack, the one person in the world I love and trust the most, is suddenly telling me to cut out a part of myself, for no real reason other than to do what he thinks I should be doing. I can't believe Jack would second-guess my ambitions this way. My foundations have been shaken—has he truly felt this way all along?

Whenever he bought me a film he knew I didn't have and wanted, was he patronizing me? Was it something he found cute at the start, and then as time went on, he got more and more tired of the things I'd talk about, the plans I'd make? Was he faking it this whole time, faking his confidence in my abilities?

Or did he believe, but now he's sensed me becoming more confident, becoming stronger in myself and my identity, and he hates it, feels threatened by it and is trying to control and lock me down? I always thought he believed in me and was impressed with my independent attitude. I wondered why he wanted to set a date all of a sudden. We're not even married and he's trying to boss me around like I'm no longer his partner but a possession.

Possessions.

Was D'Annunzio right? Can we possess, but not be possessed? Is freedom from possession what one really needs for true independent success? It makes me sad because I want both. I want everything with Jack, but I want to be myself, not become an idealized version of myself that he thinks I should be. Could I even have both if I stayed with Jack?

How can I even stay with someone who thinks I'm sick, wrong, that the things I need in one area of my life make me somehow embarrassing or less than?

How dare he say that to me?

And how dare I let these tears scald my cheeks.

But even knowing that he's the one with the immature hangup, I still cry myself to sleep, alone and feeling like I've done something wrong.

TWENTY-FOUR

∽oʍ𝄙ʍ∽

I'M NOTHING IF NOT RESILIENT, and the next day there's still no apology text or call from Jack.

So, fuck him.

If he wants to punish me with his silence for having dreams and a mind of my own, that's too bad, because I refuse to sit around rending the hem of my apron because my man chastised me. Maybe I'm just too much woman for him and he feels threatened by it.

You know where I go.

Only this time, something is different.

When I get to the bottom of the stairs, there's a line of light that catches my eye.

A door I never noticed before is partway open, and I push inside.

The walls are a meaty red, and it smells earthy to match, tinged with copper like blood. It brings to mind volcanoes and human sacrifices. The hallway is long with no doors—unless they, too, are hidden. I drag my hands along the sides as I go, feeling for a crack, a telltale notch, but there's nothing.

At the end of the hallway are two doors.

I take the one on the left.

It smells sickly sweet, like BBQ pork roasting on a spit. A-frames are set up with women and men tied to them. Lashes fly through the air, smacking flesh. A particularly lovely woman has a bit of a crowd. She writhes, and I catch sight of a tattoo of a man on the inside of her wrist. I can't tell because it's upside-down, but it looks like one of the Hindu gods—I don't know which one. But I recognize one of the men watching her.

Kubrick. He's still the short, fat, Jewish, camp, and bald man I remember, though the beard is shorter now, just reaching his Adam's apple. He's in something strappy and black that shows off the curtain of downy white hair all over his body. He still looks like a sadistic Santa Claus, with the jagged label carved into his chest to prove it: SADIST.

Kubrick was the one who created the Fuck Factory.

"Are you telling me that's how the Fuck Factory started? As an after-hours sex club in the Pentagon?"

"I guess," said Anna. She doesn't say anything after that for a few seconds, as if she's deep in thought. Then she says, "You know, the strangest people work in government."

Kubrick still has pretty good connections, Anna tells me.

"You wouldn't believe the kind of people that come here," she says.

I wait for her to tell me who but she doesn't, and I don't ask because I'm not sure I want to know. It's not just the combination of those two statements that unnerves me, but the totality of everything she's just revealed to me about the executive branch and what really goes on behind the closed doors of the government.

Now I wish I'd asked. Because Kubrick being here at the same time as Bob and the rest of his political cronies is waving red flags at me like a matador on speedballs. How could I suppress something like this, let it go like it meant nothing?

Kubrick's big meaty arms are wrapped around Anna's waist and he's pulling her into him so her breasts smoosh against his chest. He has upper arms like ham bones and forearms like Popeye. On one arm, I can see a faded blue sailor tattoo; on the other, some strange-looking sigil or pictogram that, try as I might, I can't work out what it is.

I look now, but the same sigil is covered by a black leather cuff.

He gives Anna a squeeze and says, "This one, she doesn't know when to stop."

Did she push too far—herself or someone else?

"Just look within yourself," he says, "follow what your heart desires and your body craves. And you will find it."

I let the idea of danger go before because my desire to explore was more important than anything else in that moment. But what about Inana? What did she find? What am I going to find here, tonight, where the past and my present are bleeding together? What do I want to find?

I duck away before he sees me or recognizes me and calls me *sweetheart* like he did before. Would he even remember me?

This room is made for Kubrick and men like him—sadists.

Whips and chains are the least of it.

The scent of pork I thought I smelled?

A man's branding a woman in the corner with something I can't see, but her screams are swallowed behind her gag while her flesh steams and smokes.

I walk faster.

There's suspension in this corner, big frames with lines of thin cord hanging from them with hooks attached to the ends...only the hooks are sunk into the flesh of men's and women's backs, and they sway serenely back and forth, dripping blood to the floor with their eyes closed.

It's a bit too close to the Pain Olympics for me, and I duck inside the first opening I see—a darkened doorway, which isn't always the best idea, but what's worse than burning and needles?

This room is silent, a stark contrast to the loudness outside, and I breathe easier when the door swings shut behind me.

I just need a minute to think, to breathe, to be.

I follow the hall and head into another room—this time on the right.

A line of women stand with their hands against the wall like they're perps being busted by a cop—but instead of a policeman, there's a man in a suit, a little nondescript. He could be a banker or a luxury car salesman, about to approve your loan or sell you a Ferrari, except for the fact he's burying his face in the women's asses one by one.

And waiting as they strain and fart.

There really is a fetish for everyone. You'd be surprised by how popular of a fetish pretty girls farting is—not necessarily in people's faces, but that's big, too. I don't understand it. Is it scat porn lite, for dabblers? Same great scent with none of the calories? They find something fascinating about ladies letting it rip through cotton panties, lacy ones, nothing at all—watching that asshole flex and thrust out as she tries to let loose.

Now in HD on Blu-ray.

I wonder if they eat a special diet in preparation for scenes like this. Lots of cruciferous vegetables.

It reminds me of the cake fart video that went viral a while back.

Didn't see it?

Pretty girl. Naked from the waist down. A chocolate cake. Flatulence.

Apparently it doesn't count as a cake fart unless your asshole touches the frosting, but there you have it. The ultimate in decadent irresponsibility when it comes to Western culture and our wastefulness.

Also, the chocolate cake and frosting seemed like a mistake to me—it ended up looking like she'd shit herself, but maybe that was part of the appeal, that taboo nature of our fetishes. If you're going to go there, you want it to feel all the way wrong, not just dip a toe inside the hole. You want your face buried as deeply as it can go.

In for a penny, in for a pound-cake fart.

Why do the most powerful men like the weirdest things?

The man waits on his knees in front of one woman until her tiny trumpet blast hits his face. He shudders and after a moment moves onto the next woman. An *assembly* line.

Yeah, that was bad, but I'm holding hard to the humor of the situation after seeing the pain outside.

And after being not totally turned off by it.

I continue through another door and am struck by the utter sinuousness that an orgy comprises. It goes back to Strauss-Kahn and the *orgies sans frontières*—I cackle at the thought. I would imagine most orgies are "without boundaries." Anything goes in the battle for pleasure and the perfect decadence. Where do the clothes go when an orgy happens? I look around for hooks or a closet and find none. Did these people come through secret passages where they didn't need clothes, showing up fully naked and ready to fuck?

Will they leave the same way? Will robes appear as though by magic, and other guests of the hotel notice a lot of people returning to their rooms cloaked in them, perhaps assuming they're returning from the swimming pool? Would they see these people's faces and envy the relaxation on them?

I feel myself swell and ripen as I watch, and I wish I had a cock so I could sink it into somewhere wet and warm and soft. How would it feel to do that?

To spear someone upon a part of myself and have her beg for more.

Hands snake around my body and palm my heavy breasts, rub my nipples through the thin tank top I wear.

I arch into the touch and press back against the stranger, grinding my ass into his crotch, but then I feel us switch places. Suddenly I'm him pressing against me, nudging my legs apart to pull my skirt up with big hands and cupping the heat of my pussy through my panties.

Rubbing the wetness over my pussy and clit, and then back to slick my asshole.

It feels good. I feel good. Swells of curves, and soft skin that smells like mandarins and roses.

I want to fuck me. I turn to look at the man pressed behind me.

He's attractive, short, stocky, and his pale skin is completely covered with tattoos, like he's wearing an ink suit. I don't know if his body is pretty near hairless naturally or if he grooms, but the slivers of his pale skin contrast well with his black hair, styled in a neat fade. He's exactly the type of guy Jack hates based on a single glance. My normally logical mate judges guys like this as troglodytes based on nothing more than shallow perception—an attitude that's fairly recent. Jack's all about what other people think as of late.

Which makes this guy perfect.

The perfect contrast to my perfectly suited up Jack.

I launch myself at the stranger, attacking him with a kiss that makes him grip my biceps and growl into my mouth as though to say he's the dominant and I am the submissive.

He's the predator and I'm the prey.

He pushes me against the wall and I hold my panties to the side, and he thrusts up inside me in short, sharp jabs that make me pant.

But it wasn't because he wanted me that way, but because I couldn't wait to do it anywhere else.

In for a penny.

Now that he's slicked with my juices, I pull back and turn around, sticking my ass out in invitation. A bee without its stinger. *Stick it in me, honey, make it sting a little bit.*

He's not gentle, but I don't want him to be. He's taking something no one else but Jack has had. I want to punish Jack the way he's punished me, and this is the only connection to him I've got—the last frontier, and it's time for someone else to claim it and sever the tie to Jack.

The pain flares, enveloping me, making a cocoon that separates us from everything else in the room as he thrusts in and out of my tight little hole.

I breathe and bear down, rubbing my clit in quick little circles to mitigate the pain, transform it into pleasure again, and it works. Soon I'm grunting and crying out while he pushes deep inside in a way that men new to anal do.

You can't fuck an asshole like it's a pussy. Not unless your partner is experienced at it. Even then, it's different. It feels different, reacts differently. Tastes and smells different.

But it feels good as well, and I grind my hips harder when he reaches down and hooks his middle finger into my pussy, palpating the G-spot with a skill that makes me shatter around his digits inside and outside of me.

We collapse to the floor in a heap alongside the other bodies playing with one another.

When awareness returns, there's nothing but hands and mouths all over my body, and we're surrounded, enveloped by the rest of the borderless people. It's the most primal dance we've ever done, and unlike what happens on the dance floor, we're all professionals at this type of dancing. The movements are innate, carved into our DNA when we were still evolving thousands of years ago.

I'm where I was meant to be. It's not wrong. It's good. It's natural. It's home.

I know this place. I reach out for anything hard, stroking it enthusiastically, pausing to slick my hands with saliva, with come, with anything that can be used as natural lubricant. People do the same to me, rubbing and teasing, touching and stroking, prodding any open orifice I've got until I'm full everywhere again, full and aching.

Aching and throbbing.

I want to touch everyone and make them feel the release I felt a moment ago. I wish I could morph into Kali, not to smite any enemies or bring anyone to justice, but so that I would have more arms I could use to get people off. I feel like I was created to bring pleasure and take it. To be a conduit of sensuality.

Hands and mouths and cocks and I come and come and come in flashes of red and black and gold.

TWENTY-FIVE

WHEN JACK WALKS IN THE next morning to pack, I'm showered and ready for him. For the Hail Mary pass.

"Are we going to talk about this?"

He looks at me. "Are we really going to go here again?"

I lie on the bed and spread my legs. Naked beneath my towel. "I am, Jack. Why does it bother you when I tell you I want something more intense—maybe just like the woman in the photos?"

"Because it's not right. I don't want to hurt you. That's sick."

I smirk and lick my fingers, rubbing them over myself. "Is it? It sounds a lot more like you're trying to apply your idea of what's wrong to a situation where it doesn't apply. You're fine with sex before marriage. Maybe she was into the thing being done to her—it's called autoerotic asphyxiation, by the way—but then later thought, 'Maybe this is a way to get some money from a man who would be desperate to avoid a scandal.'"

"Don't you say that about her! She'd never do something like that. She's the victim in all this."

I shake my head, weary that it took me so long to put the pieces together.

His distance.

His worry about appearances.

The way he wasn't that worried when I told him I was coming here and would be away from him.

"How long have you been fucking the witness, Jack?"

He has the good grace to turn red and look uncomfortable, at least. "I never planned it, okay? It just happened."

"I'm sure."

"She's different. You were always preoccupied with your stories, and she was there. She needed me."

"Wow, I'm impressed by your high standards. 'She needed me.'"

"She's more compatible; she isn't into the kinky things you keep trying to get me to do despite my telling you it makes me uncomfortable."

"Some people like the darker side of sex, Jack. And that's okay—it's completely natural. Why can't you do things I tell you it's perfectly fine to do to me in bed?" I start masturbating right in front of him, because now the truth is out and I no longer care to hide. I want to drag him to my base level. "Is it because you won't respect me in the morning, Jack, or are you more afraid you're the one who will like it?"

His entire body ripples from a tremor, like he's a mirage, but I keep talking, provoking, goading, because his judgment is the thing making me feel dirty and wrong—not my desires.

"Who the fuck are you to get in the way of what I want? I'm reclaiming my power as a woman. I'm not becoming less, I'm becoming stronger. Does that threaten you? Maybe that woman wasn't a victim at all. Maybe you're the one who insists on seeing us that way. Do you have issues with strong women who know what they want, Jack?"

He reaches me in two large strides and crashes into my body, making us tumble across the mattress and fall off onto the floor.

"Don't you talk about her." He lands on top and pulls my hair, biting the skin of my neck, and I moan beneath him and tear at his pants, freeing his cock.

"All I ever wanted was you." I open my legs, spreading them as wide as I can, like Anaïs opening hers for Henry Miller, but there's not enough room between the bed and the wall, and I bend my knees, spreading like butterfly wings.

He shoves his cock inside me and my butterfly wings flap for him.

It's so much, it's everything, like getting fucked by a rockslide or a wildfire: dangerous and overwhelming and a lover unleashed.

"Is this what you want?" he grunts, rutting into me in time to his hot breaths.

"Yes."

Every movement of his hips jerks me up higher, giving neat little friction burns all up my ass and back.

"You want me to just use you like you're nothing?"

Yes. I claw at his back, at his biceps, at his thighs and ass—anywhere I can reach in an attempt to get him to give me more, to go deeper and harder and faster.

"Use you like a toy made to get me off?"

Yes. I imagine lying in bed at night, him coming in and fucking me awake. All I wanted was for him to lose control just once, because then I'd know he wanted me as much as I wanted him. There's always been an imbalance of power in our relationship, because I've never truly believed this man could actually be in love with someone like me. He's so conventionally perfect. And yet he's been fucking someone else behind my back—someone who acted like a fucking victim. My perfect dream guy has finally caved in.

Well, I'll be his victim all night long if that's what it takes.

He grips my thigh hard enough that I know it's going to bruise, and I moan at how it sharpens everything, honing the moment to a point of stillness where I can feel everything—even the stubble on my legs.

He thrusts harder and up until we're against the wall and my head hits it over and over in tempo to the jabs of his cock slamming against my womb. I like that, too, the way it hurts, and I know I should stop for a minute and readjust, but everything else feels too good and all I can do is feel him stretching me, pounding me, battering my pussy hard enough to bruise it.

I want to shave off my pubic hair tomorrow to see if he's left marks with his cock.

He pinches my nipples hard enough to make me yelp. "Do you like this?"

Yes, yes, yes, I'm going to come so hard on your cock and you'll feel exactly how much I like this and how could you not like something your lover likes this much? How can you not like something that makes my pussy milk your cock for every last drop of come?

"You want me to treat you like a slut?" He moves my arms above my head, fucking harder, and I watch the way he watches my tits bounce.

He loves this, too. I smile up at him.

He tosses my hands out to the sides and pushes up away from me, staring down with a snarl. "You like it when I fuck you without love?"

Wait, what? No, that's not it, and I open my mouth to tell him, but he slides his hips to the side and I come violently, like I'm *possessed*, and I can't talk it's so deep and complete, and I'm lost to the roaring of my pulse, the way my pussy clamps down on him like it never wants him to be separated from my body.

I come to when he pulls out of me and his come dribbles to the floor in a sad little puddle.

Fuck without love? Is that what he thinks was happening?

"Jack, wait. That's not what happened."

"That, Catherine, it was."

"You're leaving me for her, aren't you?"

"Yeah. Because I just can't look at you the same way anymore."

He stands and tucks himself into his pants on the way to the door, not looking back at me once.

I sit up and slide back, wishing for a cigarette, because this is one of those moments in life where you need smoke to swirl, mirroring your thoughts.

Until the last bit, it was everything I wanted it to be. Until he ruined it. Afterward, though satisfied, I'm left with a feeling of sickness and disgust. Why do I need to be the one to make up?

Women don't need to be soft and yielding.

I feel no shame for wanting what Jack just gave me.

What he almost gave me and tried to take away.

I refuse to let him make this feel wrong or dirty. It's goodbye.

If anything, I feel disgusted that I'm supposed to feel ashamed for wanting the things I want. He's judging me for something that makes me feel good, when I've asked him for it repeatedly, and he treats me like I've asked him to commit a crime against me. Any guilt I might have felt for doing anything in the clubs below us dissolves, because he's the one who cheated on me this time.

There was no exploration, only abandonment.

I don't know if he's going to try to bring Gold down, but I do know he needs time to cool down. His anger is sullen and feeds upon itself like a human centipede. I'll wait for him to remove his head from his own ass, and then we'll talk.

I'm tired of being made to feel like what I want is wrong. Like I'm a silly little girl who doesn't know her own mind, when Jack doesn't even realize that the world isn't black and white—that morality isn't absolute.

Can we ever have just the good without the bad? Can I have the rush without the crash? Is this the rush before Jack brings things toppling down?

It reminds me of D'Annunzio: "Wherever were all his vanities and his cruelties and his expedients and his lies? Where were the loves and the betrayals and the disillusionments and the disgust and the incurable repugnance after pleasure? Where were those impure and rapid love affairs that left in his mouth the strange sourness of fruit cut with a steel knife? He could no longer remember anything."

TWENTY-SIX

~oooOooo~

I LISTEN TO THE MESSAGE on my phone, unable to place the voice at first, but eventually I realize that it's Lola, asking for an update and wondering if I've seen the news. I go online, wondering what she's referencing, when I realize that Maxxy the missing pop star has been found. She'd sneaked off to rehab to kick an undisclosed substance abuse problem, but hadn't wanted anyone to know about her addiction because it's so taboo these days to admit that you can't handle a life most people think they'd kill for.

People on Twitter are already tearing her apart, talking about #FirstWorldProblems and #PoorLittleRichGirl and #CheckYour-Privilege. I'm so over the language of the social justice warriors. Who cares if she's famous—she's trying to get better, and all they're doing is trying to tear her down.

Ironic, since they're all about calling out microaggressions and building women up.

I turn the TV on to listen to the soundbite they've been playing on all the stations, from the looks of it.

Maxxy smiles beatifically from behind a podium at the press

conference. "Being honest is more important than my ego—and potentially helping my fans with similar addictions was more important. I care about each and every one of you. We all need to get better and do better." She reaches up to tuck a lock of glossy hair behind her ear, and I see it: the tattoo on her wrist. It's the same one I saw the other night on the woman being flogged.

Maxxy was at the hotel when I was.

Maxxy isn't the squeaky-clean pop princess everyone thinks she is. I wonder if she even has an addiction, or if that's just a story she's decided to roll with to tarnish her image a little to help her transition from bubblegum to something a little stronger in time for her next album. Street cred can be bought after all.

Is she another woman getting sucked into something that's biding its time waiting to chew her apart, suck the marrow from her bones and spit her out like she's not even worth swallowing? Is she another victim in the making, like the girls who brought Bundy's businesses crashing down?

Or is she a new breed of player, someone with steel inside her? Someone The Juliette Society doesn't see coming, but grab onto and try to keep hold of any chance they get? Is she someone strong enough to come and go whenever she pleases, never once realizing that that is the greatest privilege of all when it comes to that club?

Is she like Anna?

Is she like Inana?

Is she like me?

Where do I fit into it? Am I the tale, or the person telling it? The paper, the pen, or the writing?

Maybe I'm none of those things.

I wake up with a gasp, cramped from sleeping on the couch with the blanket bunched up around my throat. Annoyed, I toss it to the ground and check my phone.

My fiancé left me for a damsel in distress, so I do what every woman my age would do:

Get drunk and make poor choices to celebrate my freedom.

I'm in a room deep inside the bowels of the Janus Chamber, on all fours in the same cage Anna was in—or one that's exactly like it.

The slightest movement, and my skin touches the cage. When that happens, I get a jolt of electricity through my body—and inside it. When I got here, a man asked for volunteers, and because he had eyes like the sea after a thunderstorm, I said yes.

Now my labia are clipped apart, and there's a silver butt plug inside me—and it's hooked up, too, only they vibrate instead of shock, and they don't stop.

Not after the fourth orgasm. Not after the fifth.

I'm sweating, and my even my fingernails are painfully sensitive as wave after wave of sensation courses through my system, confusing my senses. For a while I think I black out, and I come to leaning heavily against the bars of the cage, rivers of electricity arcing through me, but at this point I can't tell if it's pain or pleasure because they've become the same thing.

I'm hot and cold all over, inside as well, shivering with release and need all at once. Experiencing the same things Anna did.

I realize there are people around the cage, watching, drinking, never taking their eyes off me, as though I'm the best program they've ever seen.

I feel better than I've ever felt, and when they finally release me from the cage, I've lost all concept of time and am sure I will shock anyone who touches me, I'm buzzing that much.

But I don't, and the crowd moves on as another girl is placed inside the cage.

I go back to the club and drink until the world spins, but it spins me in the right direction, because somehow I wind up in a room with a young man whose lips are a little too red, as though someone tried to suck them from his face and gave up partway through.

He's beautiful in a vulnerable way.

I've been the ultimate submissive tonight. It's time to flip the coin.

He's vulnerable because I've tied his ankles and wrists to the bedposts and am marking him with a rod. Arms, thighs, belly. I'd do his back, but his erection wasn't comfortable and I didn't want to make him keep lying on it.

What I'm doing is meant to hurt him, but I'm not cruel. Not like some people.

Line after line, I enjoy seeing the redness spring up against the white. He's like a tiger or a zebra I'm creating one slap at a time.

He smiles, and tears of joy and relief leak from his eyes, but I know he won't say a word, because I ordered him not to. It feels strange to be the one giving orders, and yet I've taken to it. Something about it is strangely comforting.

I want to discover what his limits are.

The lines I make on his skin are warm on my tongue.

I go further, lose myself in the surrealism of the scene, in the sadistic person this man wants me to be, taking joy in causing him pain. I turn into claws and hurt and teeth and sharpness, and I'm a razor's edge away from flaying the meat of us both from our bones just to see if we're the same inside when Max steps into the room and pulls me off the man.

I can tell from the look in his eyes that he'd underestimated me, but that I've not only redeemed myself—I've impressed the shit out of him.

Look what we made me into, Jackie boy.

And yet I still feel a little…untethered from reality as I walk outside and get in my car, turning down Gold's offer to let me stay in one of the suites instead of driving back to Inana's.

What happens now? Am I to end up unhappy and alone, like Claudia? I thought I was leading-lady material, but Jack's given up on me as though we haven't spent years together. If he wasn't it, who was my Tommaso? Anna? Inana? How long have Jack and I been going through the motions, trapped together by what we thought was love, was right, was a fit? I used to believe in it with no room for doubt. But cracks formed in the brittleness of who I thought I could be, should be, and now there's air and light and freedom leaking into me and I want more and more. The good and the bad of it on my terms—it won't all be good, but how will I know if I cut that part of myself off completely, suppressing it forever and living a life where I'll always look back and wonder what I might have been if I'd known more about myself?

I was doing this to get it out of my system. Is it wrong that I discovered that this is who I am and don't want to give it up? Shouldn't your partner accept who you are deep down? Isn't that what love is?

TWENTY-SEVEN

I GET ONE OF THOSE "just checking in" e-mails from my editor, which isn't as innocuous as it seems. Normally I'm around the office a lot more than I have been—even when doing other in-depth pieces, I've at least made an appearance.

Funny how I don't seem to give a shit if I get fired, but that seems like textbook unhealthy behavior and I refuse to spiral. That feels like validating Jack's judgmental pearl-clutching.

I know damn well he enjoyed the other night as much as I did until he left, going back to whomever the fuck he left me for. Maybe he was right to leave—he doesn't know me anyway.

I feel like I'm just getting to know the real me, so how can I be mad about Jack breaking up with me? Already it feels like months ago instead of days.

I reply with a canned "I'm on it, hot lead, sensational story" response I know will buy me another week or two.

I send and refresh my inbox, sighing at a new e-mail from an unknown sender. People write in with the most boring shit that they think should be a headline. Tattling on neighbors, ratting out exes, trying to impress new lovers or old friends. I almost don't click it, but my editor's e-mail has shamed me into feeling neglectful, so I open it.

It's a picture of Inana when she was alive, obviously involved in a similar scenario to the one I participated in for Max. I recognize the place, if not the particular room, and wonder if Inana had had a scene with someone like Bob, only they'd squeezed too hard or gone too far and then framed it to look like a suicide.

Had Anna ever been to La Notte? Is that where she met Inana? Was it another place entirely?

How similar are we all at the end of the day? Plucked from our lives and dropped into this maze of The Juliette Society, never to find our way out—or in, unless they want us to. We had to pass the tests to get inside.

But the picture in my hand isn't a picture. It's more than that—it's a key. It's an answer that raises even more questions than before.

I squint and zoom in to the spot just above Inana's left shoulder. It's the view of a two-way mirror looking out, onto the VIP club below La Notte—I recognize the bar from this angle, even though the people there are faded like ghosts and insubstantial.

I feel like if they were in the room beside Inana they'd still appear washed out next to her.

But the picture. The window. The mirror. It's a doorway, and now I know exactly where to go now to find what comes next for myself.

Thanks to Inana. Her slim body is bent into a pose that showcases her flexibility. Her skin is radiant. She was radiant. No matter how she went out of the world, while she was in it, she blazed exactly the way she wanted to.

I almost miss the words on the wall behind Inana, I'm so focused on the contortions of her body in the picture and the bliss on her face and the fact that I can get inside now because of this photograph.

Audācissimē Pēdite.

I know I've seen that before.

Vertigo slams into me full force and I stumble.

It's been beneath my feet the whole time.

And yet, I'd assumed it was only a similarity, not the same thing.

How could it have found me again?

An inscription is carved around its upper lip, and stained in red like a tattoo:

AUDĀCISSIMĒ PĒDITE

The ogre's mouth is open wide, as if it's laughing or screaming, I can't tell which. Or maybe just screaming with laughter at some private joke. The ogre is looking at me, laughing at me, as if it's recognized someone who doesn't belong. Part of me feels like I just want to run inside its mouth and hide, no matter what I might find in there, in the pitch black, just so I don't have to meet its gaze anymore. Because that's where the path leads, into the mouth of the ogre. That's where it ends.

This place isn't like The Juliette Society.

It *is* The Juliette Society. The Janus Chamber is their safe club where there's no threat of discovery.

It's for them. It's full of them.

It's their elite playground, and I've been dancing through it, thinking it was something like it, something safe, as if I were the one in control because I found my way to it instead of it finding me and coercing me into doing things I didn't want.

Whether I'm the prey or the hunter doesn't matter when it's their world I'm moving in. Their lines I'm coloring inside.

How many places like this are there in the world?

Why didn't they tell me from the start if we're somehow the same? I lived it, gloried in it, and they accepted me. Why didn't they just open the door instead of sending this picture now?

Why would someone send this to me? It's more than a photograph, it's a map to where I wanted to go—but it's somewhere that somebody else obviously thinks I should be as well, or they wouldn't have given this to me. Maybe this is the invitation that will take me to the depths I've never imagined.

But was it sent by friend or foe?

Someone trying to show me the truth, or bury me in another lie? I'd be an idiot to go. It's a trap, there's no way it can be safe.

And yet…

Who would have sent this to me? And what are his or her intentions for me? Illumination or harm? Was it Lola? If so, why didn't she send it to my phone or personal e-mail address?

I grab my phone and scroll through the contacts, selecting Lola's number.

It doesn't ring before telling me the number is no longer in service.

That can't be right. I received the message from her today. I look through my recent calls and select Lola's number.

Again, the electronic voice tells me that that number doesn't exist.

Was the witness ready to expose something darker than Bob's involvement in TJS? Is there something darker? I search for Lola online, trying to find contact information.

It's like she never existed. Nothing, not even the original interviews I read, are to be found. Why would someone scrub her from the Internet, even removing her from website caches? There's one place I have some evidence—other than the voicemail she left earlier. I listen to it again, finding solace in the warm tones of her voice, as though they somehow prove I'm not losing it.

I go back to my other tab, but it's timed out and booted me. I'd copied everything—sources must be cited so we can't get sued—and kept it in its own file with the rest of my sources. I log in.

Password Invalid.

The red letters appear, and I check to see if caps lock is on.

I try three more times, unsuccessfully, to log in to my account. What the hell is going on?

Why would someone want to sever my connection to Inana and Lola? There's nothing I would….*Jack,* I realize. Instead of cooling down and getting back in touch with me, what if Jack made good on his threat to take Gold down by going public with the information—

or worse, went directly to him first and told him about his plan to go public?

Jack's exactly the type of young idealist who would give a corrupt asshole one chance to do the right thing himself, believing it would actually happen. My stomach swoops and my palms sweat.

I pull out my phone to text Jack, but I don't want any of this written down anywhere.

Feeling sick, I punch in his number, half expecting it, too, to be out of service, but it rings three times before going to voicemail. I try again and again, but he doesn't answer.

There's that saying, "thrown for a loop"? Now I get it.

I don't know who else to call about this, so I contact the one person I shouldn't.

"Bob DeVille speaking."

"Where's Jack?"

"Catherine, what a pleasant surprise. Excuse me for a moment." I hear him breathe in and out a few times, and noise fades away as he takes his half of the conversation to a more private place. "What can I do for you?"

I wonder if he told Jack about the hotel—everything about it, my reasons for being there—and the things I've done there while telling myself it was all in the name of getting a story, in an attempt to sabotage our relationship. "You've probably been waiting for this moment for four years," I say. "How does it feel to have finally taken something from me, gotten your revenge?"

"You're really not making any sense. I haven't said anything to Jack—what would I say to him? He's been so preoccupied with his new...friend."

"You're a bastard."

"He's like the son I never had, and I'm doing my best to help Jack follow along in my footsteps."

"You son of a bitch."

"Careful," he says with a laugh. "Do you remember what I said about hiding in the open? How no one truly believes rumors? No matter what you think you could do trying to take me down, I can't be hurt by a scandal no one would believe. For what it's worth, I think they're a match made in heaven."

"Real comforting." I have to wonder if tearing us apart was the only way DeVille could distract Jack from discovering his dark secrets, feeding him half-truths.

"I did try to tell you when you came to dinner."

DeVille had hinted that I may not be Jack's priority. Funny how I'd assumed DeVille was talking about himself.

"With friends like these…" I hang up.

What the hell do I do now? What would Inana do now?

A calmness spreads through my belly like a shot of whiskey taken straight with no chaser.

Is there something that needs to be done or exposed, or should I continue feeding my own journey? I can explore my sexual desires and just…be Inana for a while, at least until I figure out my next move. Why not? Win-win.

Certain things only gain life through the people inside them at any given time.

Airports. Shopping malls. Theaters. That's why directors use them for post-apocalyptic shots in worlds taken over by flesh-eaters or emptied out after a large portion of the population has died from some unnamed disease—because they feel innately wrong and more than a little creepy when you take away the bustle of humanity.

Certain places get too quiet, and you wonder when the aliens came and took everyone away.

What's looming behind you?

I can feel the emptiness as soon as I get through the first door—before I use my black key in the second door and walk down the stairs.

Silence, except for my own footfalls echoing in front of me. I want to take my shoes off and tiptoe so as not to betray my presence, but I sense time slipping by like grains of sand sliding through an hourglass, so instead of stopping, I rush ahead.

The emptiness has a presence to it, like it's waiting for me to make noise, make movement, help it hide in the shadows I create for it.

The bar is empty, too, and without people in it, it feels cavernous, like a gaping maw of nothingness.

If I screamed, would it echo? Or would it be swallowed up like I never made a sound?

Where is everyone?

I expect Bundy to pop up behind the bar with a rag and a *gotcha* smile, maybe a few other people from my past—Marcus, even, with his young face and hair gone white from the who-knows-what he's gotten up to. How would he relieve his sexual tensions now that Anna's no longer fulfilling his Oedipus complex?

Something shiny catches my eye from across the room, in front of one of the mirrors.

Just like that, I know I'm being watched. That this moment was always going to happen. That I've been led here by some unseen hand the whole time, like I'm nothing more than a pawn in a game of chess someone else is playing—and I never saw the black and white of the board beneath my feet.

Only a queen I was trying to find.

Or maybe a couple of them, in a quest for more power, more knowledge, self-knowledge.

Gnosis.

I crack my neck and walk to the mirror, my poise returning like a soft cloak of velvet. I am no pawn.

Maybe that's something that the rest of the players forgot.

But I'll be damned if I turn and run and miss out on whatever lies behind the mirror.

I bend and pick up the coin. How old it is, I have no idea, but I know before flipping it over that there are two faces on it.

I saw the same coin—or one identical to it—on a page in Inana's diary. This one now belongs to me. There's no heads or tails, no this or that. The Janus Chamber isn't about *or*.

It's about *and*. This side *and* that. I am this *and* that. Dark *and* light. Strong *and* vulnerable.

Cat *and* mouse.

The people who find themselves granted access to the Janus Chamber are both sides of the coin.

Is this the new key that will unlock more information? What test have I passed that I'm being granted even more access to something this big?

How did they know I was going to be here right now?

The mirror swings open.

I step behind it.

TWENTY-EIGHT

SOMETIMES YOU KNOW EXACTLY WHAT fate has in store for you.

And sometimes you walk into a room behind a mirror, take one look, and recognize the place.

SODOM.

SODALITY OF DOMINANTS.

I don't know if I could consider this coming full circle, or even where that nascent point is. A movie theater. A classroom.

A dream inside a tired mind.

Through the door to the right is a huge warehouse where everything on SODOM, the website Anna was on, was shot. How could I not have seen that this place was The Juliette Society's?

As I walk through a door into a hallway, there are more rooms that splinter off, devoid of people, but with equipment inside, doors left open.

I recognize the equipment, the toilet with the drilldo, the machine where Inana lay in a puddle of her own come, shuddering and trying to see who would win in a battle of pleasure in woman versus dildo.

Electrified cages shaped like people on all fours—like the one I was in the other night.

Clawfoot tubs because they're deep enough to be immersed in.

Platforms with frames built to suspend.

Platforms with frames built to restrain.

Slings sitting around waiting for asses to climb into them.

It's a stadium where gladiators could come to fuck and watch each other take part in the wildest things their minds could dream up, but it's all strange with no one using the equipment. It's where the objects of pleasure and torture are stored before use. It's the world's kinkiest storage locker, but also a set—this is where things get filmed.

Each one smells like stale come and sweat. And more than a little blood.

Where are the people?

I step inside the third room down. It's empty as well, but somehow it feels warmer, and calm. It's not waiting to be filled—or maybe it's that it's had enough.

I'm sure you've already asked the question that occurred to me as well: Wouldn't a smart girl, a reporter, especially after noting the practices and the sex club, wonder if she's being played by being offered admittance? Yes. But then, perhaps that's just the nature of the game—new flesh, new intrigue, welcoming the players willing to pay the ultimate price. And I was willing to pay the price for my own journey, for Inana.

I walk back out the door and go the other way instead, because blood on the floor isn't the way I want my journey to end. Through another door and up a hallway, I come to a red door.

And I want to paint it…

It's closed, but I take a deep breath and twist the knob.

And what do you know, I walk right into Bob DeVille's office—or a room that's set up to look exactly like it, right down to the lemony scent of the wood polish and the picture of Gena on the desk.

He turns in his chair, wearing the mask he wore that night at the private mansion we fucked at, and part of me wonders irrationally if this place is connected to others via deep underground passageways. Whether it's all connected, and all we would have had to do to find it was dig. That place had no name, either. But I'm not here for the logistics of it all. The *hows*. I'm here for the *whys*.

I take a deep breath and squint at the wilder, bad, older version of my now-ex-fiancé. "Bob."

"What took you so long?" He smiles. "You're late."

"I came as fast as I could," I say wryly. "It might have been quicker if someone had just told me the truth."

"Where's the fun in that?"

I walk forward. "You think this has been fun for me? I've lost things, people."

"You lost things that were dragging you down, holding you back." He scoffs. "I'd have thought you would understand that, at least."

And I guess I do. "What about Jack?"

DeVille shrugs. "He's not a part of this."

"Thank you."

He raises his head in acknowledgment. "You were informed before about the mythos of The Juliette Society. Do you remember it?"

"Yes. Like the Illuminati for fucking," I downplay it, suddenly cavalier, because I don't want him thinking this is easy because of who he is. I want him to work for it, to know that this is all my choice. What's about to happen is only going to occur because I want it to.

He holds his hands out to the sides. "If you know the name of a secret society, it's a pretty ineffective secret society, isn't it?"

Indeed. "Sort of like how if you see a chameleon, that means it's a pretty awful chameleon. Tell me something I don't know. Where's Max? Where does he fit into all of this?" I'd thought it was Max who was the more powerful man of the two, and yet Bob is here in Max's empty club, not Max.

I impressed Max and leveled up to Bob. But who's the final boss?

Bob continues as if I hadn't spoken. "There are protectors of our society that have taken notice of you."

"Is that a good thing?" My heart pounds in my chest with a strange validation. We all like to hear that we're unique and noteworthy, even if it's to a secret society built around kink and wealth.

"It can be." Bob's voice comes from behind me, and I turn, disbelief at what I'm seeing morphing into a scared laughter and utter confusion, turning back , my mouth agape at the Bob sitting behind the desk, pulling the mask off.

Are they twins or is one a double? Who have I been dealing with this whole time?

I face the one who came in behind me. "Which one are you?"

He shrugs, undoing the buttons of his shirt. "Does it matter? Who are you?"

Inana. I smile. "Limitless." I raise my hands above my head, letting him strip off my shirt. Maybe it seems like a strange thing to do, but I've already fucked one of them and almost killed the other— what's the harm in doing both at once?

Maybe I'd done both to one of them and never before met the other.

If you could have sex with yourself, would you? In a way, I am DeVille and always have been.

Either way, a balance needs to be made.

Limits have to be broken.

They cage me between them with their muscular bodies, closing their arms around me until I am held against them, locked in an embrace for a moment like puzzle pieces snapping into place. It feels violently right. So good it hurts my mind.

One article at a time, clothes are lost. Even before, when I thought he was anonymous, that first time, I was attracted to him.

Like attracts like. We smell the depths of depraved imagination and come up licking our fingers with the juices dripping down our chins.

Where one body stops, another begins.

They go at me, one from the front and the other from behind, and I just know that the way they're lavishing attention on me, making me the star of the show, means I'm going to have to pay them back in a big way.

The steady licks become my world, and I look from one to the other, marveling at the identical faces.

Is there a good one and a bad one?

Which one do I know better?

I urge them both to stand, and I kneel and go back and forth, tugging, licking, sucking, in a frenzy to make them lose control with pleasure.

One lies on the floor. The other pushes me on top.

I slide down onto his cock, bracing myself for the other Bob to ram himself home inside my ass at the same time.

Double penetration.

It was always going to come down to this. Him and him and me. I brace my hands on his chest, but the one fucking my asshole from behind takes my wrists, stretching them above my head until my tits jut out and he's holding my weight.

Bob's stronger than he looks.

I grind down harder onto their cocks, more swiveling my hips than anything, letting the one behind drive the rhythm for us all. No point fighting gravity when it feels this good to give in to it.

We rut and gyrate and grind, an unholy trinity of grunts and moans.

I lose track of time. I lose track of myself.

I've never been impaled like this before, both holes at once, so deeply it feels like I'm going to be permanently damaged, but if anyone quit I'd kill them for stopping.

I see stars. I see atoms. I'm infinitely small and pantagruelian huge all at once, wrapped in thick strands of semen that bind us all together.

And that's when the one below me moves his hands from my breasts to my collarbone to my neck. The one behind me holds me in place. I don't try to remove his hands. Instead, I lock mine around the neck of the one in front of me as well.

This time, as his hands close, his eyes stay kind and gentle. He smiles as I tighten my grip involuntarily when the orgasm flickers at first deep within me, then turns to a raging inferno of molten heat as we fuck and fuck and fuck. My hips nearly dislocate with the power of their thrusts, and still I wish for more, urge them harder with shakes and shimmies of my ass, desperate to come, but the edges of my vision are going darker and darker.

I need to come before I disappear.

If you could be anyone, why be a pale imitation of the person you want to be? Why should I be Catherine when I can be Inana? Inana wouldn't care as much about my troubles—like worrying about my job or errant fiancé. They're petty and not as interesting as her exploration; at least, they are since I realized everything I thought Jack was is a lie. And yet, there's something tugging at me, my ego, maybe, that wants to remain myself while experiencing the things, the growth Inana did.

I want to be the best Catherine I can be, not a pale imitation of Inana. One already existed. It's time for another to rise up.

I went because I *wanted* to, not because I was trying to save my relationship with Jack, but because I crave the lust and the desire and the exploration of who I can be with these people. Maybe it's dragging me deeper in and closer to more danger, but I've got nothing to lose.

No one to lose but myself. In a way, I've already sacrificed Jack, and he sacrificed me...we just have different motives. But I realize that I'm more like Bob than I am like Jack.

And that brings a smile to my face. Miles to go before I sleep, and all that jazz.

It's like discovering a whole new color palette. I'm going to embrace that side of myself and see how far I can go, see how limit-less I can be.

Inana's diary is all about her trying to discover her own limits. I don't know if she ever found a limit. If she's the one who killed herself, that was a limit. She found something she couldn't take, or unsee.

If someone killed her, that was a limit, too. But maybe she wasn't strong enough. Maybe Anna wasn't, either. This isn't going to end with a neat little bow and a happy reunion over tea and cookies. Like in *L'Avventura*, I haven't found the woman I'm searching for.

But maybe that's only because I've been looking for someone else the whole time instead of trying to find myself.

Maybe Inana wasn't strong enough. Maybe she had the innova-tion, the imagination, but without the tenacity and stability as a solid base for the things she'd eventually learn about the world. Some people can take knowledge like that and integrate it. Others can't live with the things they've seen and done.

Can I take it further than Inana? Let's find out.

TWENTY-NINE

∽༄༄∾

THE DESERT BREEZE BLOWS IN through the window of my car, warm and clean. The grit exfoliates my skin as I go, sloughing off parts of me like I'm a snake shedding its skin, but my eyes aren't clouded any longer. I can finally see myself, see the world and the way it's connected through people and places.

I imagine that if I tried hard enough right now I could turn into some serpentine creature and bare my fangs, daring the world to fuck with me.

I turn on the seat warmer, letting it gently burn my ass even though it's near eighty degrees even this late at night.

Where did the sun go?

Truths whispered in my ear are harder to hold onto right now with the way the night tastes.

I pull into Inana's driveway, tumble from the car for a moment, forgetting how to walk. When I get up I buck and sway and undulate to the door, feeling the new movements of a dance I never learned suddenly taking me over like a fugue state.

I stop at the threshold, nose high in the air, breathing deeply. *Something's off,* sings the night.

I feel it in my bones, the emptiness calling to me and echoing through my heart.

I head for the bedroom and feel beneath the pillow.

The diary's gone.

Was it ever really there?

I sit down and hold the pillow to my chest, considering. Without the diary, where would I be right now? Without searching for the woman who left those words, where would I be? Inana's words brought me to where I needed to be, but living another person's words can only ever get you so far. Sometimes you need to stop searching for who you think you should be and just be the person you are.

Both sides—the dark and the light. Flaws and all.

There are limits to how far another person's shoes will take you. I've got to forge my own path from here on out, and that's okay.

I toss the pillow back onto the bed, and something falls to the floor with a gentle slap.

The diary's gone.

But in its place is a USB drive with a note folded around it in heavy, creamy vellum.

The note is handwritten in ink so red it's almost black.

You've come this far. Can you go a little further?

I turn the USB drive over and over in my hand, the temptation burning a hole in my palm as I weigh my options.

SASHA GREY

∽⟬⟬⟭⟭∼

SASHA GREY first made her debut as one of the most popular adult film stars of the early 2000s; but in 2009 at age 21 she moved on from her former career without any regrets. She went on to star in HBO's *Entourage*, published *NEÜ SEX*, a book of photographs, and even works as an international DJ. In 2013 she published her first novel, the wildly successful *The Juliette Society*, in 25 countries. She regularly tours around the world as an artist, author, actress, and DJ.

Sasha's career kicked off in 2006 when, at the age of 18, Sasha made a name for herself in the adult film world. With a great propensity for sex positivity and self-exploration, Sasha used the adult film industry as a platform for experimentation and performance art, and as a means to encourage individuals to take pride in their sexuality. Frustrated by societal perceptions of female sexuality and preferences, she embodied an independent and sexually confident spirit both on and off screen.

Her fierce performance and determination to challenge the norm garnered attention both inside and outside of the adult industry, making Sasha a national sex icon. *The New York Times* described her pornographic career as, "distinguished both by the extremity of what she is willing to do and an unusual degree of intellectual seriousness about doing it." She was profiled in *Los Angeles Magazine* the same year, which led to appearances on several entertainment news shows and collaborations with several artists and musicians. In 2008, she landed a leading role in Steven Soderbergh's experimental film *The Girlfriend Experience*.

It became increasingly difficult to balance her role as an adult film producer and performer, with her passion for photography, music, and traditional acting; as a result, Grey left the industry in 2009.

After this move, she kept busy hosting TV specials for G4 TV in Australia, USA, and Thailand, and started touring as a DJ in 2010. Her filmography also includes: *Open Windows* (Nacho Vigalondo), *Smash Cut* (Lee Demarbre), *I Melt With You* (Mark Pellington), and *Would You Rather* (David Guy Levy).

As a musician, she has both written and produced her own original songs and remixes. She's also lent her voice to tracks by artists Infected Mushroom, Current 93, and X-TG (Throbbing Gristle). United over their shared love for the bands Throbbing Gristle and Chris and Cosey, Richard Fearless, of the electronic music group Death in Vegas, recently partnered with Grey as writer and vocalist for a new album, *Transmission*. Her lyrics resonate across the soundscape of visceral techno and unsettling, discordant drones weaving into a state of dreamlike euphoria. *Transmission* was released by a London-based Record Label called Drone in 2016.

Sasha's second novel, *The Juliette Society, Book II: The Janus Chamber*, will be released by Cleis Press in 2016.

Exhibitions & Selected Works:

Forum du Futuro (Oct. 2015)
Teatro Municipal do Porto Porto, Portugal

White Nights (2012)

Juliao Sarmento's I Want you: Text (2012)

Leporello (2011)

Bodies Of Babel (Sept. 2011)
Mousonturm Frankfurt, Germany

Neü Sex (May 2011)
Martha Otero Gallery Los Angeles, CA

Case (Nov 2009)
New Museum New York, NY